P9-DHI-644

Great Lessons in

VIRTUE *and* CHARACTER

Great Lessons in
VIRTUE *and* CHARACTER

A Treasury of
Classic Animal Stories

Edited with Commentary by
William K. Kilpatrick

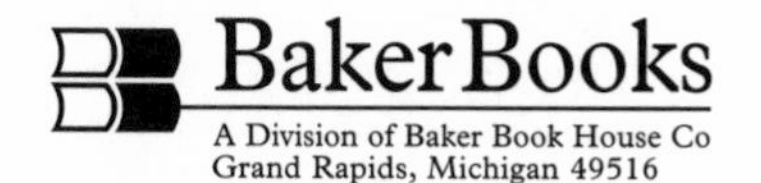

BakerBooks
A Division of Baker Book House Co
Grand Rapids, Michigan 49516

Published by Baker Books
a division of Baker Book House Company
P.O. Box 6287, Grand Rapids, MI 49516-6287

Printed in the United States of America

Permission acknowledgments appear on pages 277–80.

Library of Congress Cataloging-in-Publication Data

Great lessons in virtue and character : a treasury of classic animal stories / edited with commentary by William K. Kilpatrick.
p. cm.
ISBN 0-8010-1243-0 (cloth)
1. Animals—Fiction 2. Didactic fiction, American. 3. Didactic fiction, English. I. Kilpatrick, William, 1940–
PS648.A5 G74 2002
813.008′0362—dc21 2002007799

For current information about all releases from Baker Book House, visit our web site:
http://www.bakerbooks.com

To Colleen

In the hope that you will grow in
courage, kindness, and responsibility,
and still remain as mirthful and merry as you are now.

Contents

Acknowledgments

My deepest thanks to Rebecca Feil, Anna Higgins, and Kathleen Rice for their help in recommending selections. Thanks also to the Wilberforce Forum, the Fieldstead Institute, and Sir John Templeton for their support. Particular thanks are due to my wife, Gemma, for her tireless work on this project.

Introduction

The stories in this collection can be read on two levels. First, they can be read for pleasure. Between the covers of this book, you'll find the thrilling story of a horse and his boy racing against time and fear; you'll meet an old man and a faithful horse and share their special secret; and you'll find an unforgettable story of a noble dog who shepherds a hunted boy to freedom.

On the second level, they tell us about good and bad, right and wrong. One of the best-known animal stories is *Black Beauty*. The author, Anna Sewell, tells us that she wrote it with the intent of inducing "kindness, sympathy and an understanding treatment of horses." But *Black Beauty* is as much about people as it is about horses—good people and bad people and people in-between. More than simply an animal story, it is truly a book of virtues and vices.

In short, we can learn a lot about people from stories about animals. For example, in the story of *Beautiful Joe* we can see that people who treat animals badly will probably treat people badly too. Likewise, those who show friendship and responsibility toward animals tend to be trustworthy in general. And in a story such as *The Dog on Barkham Street,* we see that we can't always rely on our initial impressions of people. Through reading we can become better judges of character. More important, we can become better judges of our own character—better able to see our strengths and weaknesses and better able to work on improving ourselves.

Of course, reading stories about courage and honesty is no guarantee that we will become brave and honest. For that to happen, we need to practice the virtues. Aristotle, one of history's wisest thinkers, said, "We become brave by doing brave acts, just by performing just acts." We get better at basketball or gymnastics or ballet through practice, and so it is with honesty, responsibility, and self-discipline. A short but useful definition of character is this: character is moral strength—the strength to do the right thing. A person with strength of character might not be physically strong, but still there *is* a similarity between character strength and physical strength. Physical strength and skill give us control over our bodies, allowing us to do difficult things such as a handstand on the parallel bars or a triple axle on the skating rink; strength and skill of character give us control over ourselves, allowing us to act in unselfish and even heroic ways.

Just as we master a sport by practicing it, we master the virtues by practicing them. You don't learn to play tennis just by reading about it. You have to practice until your responses become "second nature." Virtue, too, must be practiced until it becomes second nature. It has to be in the "muscles" as well as in the mind.

So reading stories about virtue won't automatically make us good people, but reading does help in several ways. How? First, by giving us examples of good behavior. A young tennis player or skater needs to practice, but in addition, he or she needs heroes. Just as we imitate sports stars to improve our skills, so we need to pattern our moral actions after the example of virtuous people. Sometimes we find the examples we need among family and friends, but we can also find them between the pages of a book. Hopefully, you'll find some in this book. Of course, one of the nice things about reading stories is that you'll get to know the characters much more intimately than you will ever know your favorite sports star. Stories give us a chance to live along with the characters, feel what they feel, struggle their struggles, and taste their victories.

A second benefit we receive from reading is inspiration, or as one writer calls it, "moral energy." Why do we need it? Simply because it's not enough to *know* what's right; you also have to *want* what's right. It's hard to practice the virtues unless we love virtue, and reading stories of courage and perseverance is a way of strengthening our desire to do right. Another way of putting it is this: there is a link between "moral" and "morale"; in other words, the best way to meet moral challenges is with spirit, confidence, and cheerfulness. Good stories strengthen our morale and spirit—they give us "heart." A good example of a morale-boosting story is *Mrs. Miniver,* a book that was made into a movie during World War II. Winston Churchill, the prime minister of England, said it was worth six army divisions in the war against Hitler. He meant that the movie lifted the spirits of soldiers and citizens alike, giving them new courage and new resolve to perform their duties. By reading stories that challenge, thrill, and excite, we also can find some of the morale we need to do our best and be our best.

Although this book is divided into sections—each one dealing with a different virtue—you will see that there is much overlap. For example, the chapter from *Lassie Come-Home* is about perseverance, but it's about loyalty, honesty, and justice too. The virtues really depend on one another, and they work best when they work together. Loyalty, honesty, and perseverance often require courage, but courage works best when it is combined with compassion and good judgment.

Don't be discouraged if you find that the virtues aren't all working together in your life. It takes time to build strength of character, and you can expect setbacks and failures along the way. Acquiring good character is like setting out on a long journey. In fact, many stories of courage and perseverance take the form of a quest or a journey. *Lassie Come-Home* is a perfect example. In order to reach her destination, Lassie has to cross over four hundred miles of difficult and dangerous terrain. Her desire and determination eventually see her through. Winning through to the goal of good character is one of life's most important journeys. Think of it as a long, difficult, but rewarding quest. What makes it worthwhile is that along the way we become better people and—just as important—better able to be of service to others.

Courage

"Courage," said C. S. Lewis, "is all the other virtues at the sticking point." Without courage we would have difficulty practicing the other virtues because there always comes a point when it takes courage to be loyal, courage to be honest, and courage to persevere. When we see someone treated unfairly, our sense of justice may tell us to intervene, but it usually takes courage for us to act. For this reason, Winston Churchill described courage as "the quality which guarantees all others."

Courage is not the same as fearlessness. It's possible to act bravely while feeling very afraid. Even at the moment of doing brave deeds, soldiers in war report feeling sick with fear. It's possible to overcome some of this natural fear by trying to make a habit of acting courageously. Acting bravely, even in little things, helps us to become more courageous people. We can see how this works with firefighters and law enforcement officers. In a sense, they have been trained to be brave, and this training helps them to do things they might otherwise be afraid to do. In a similar way, we can train ourselves to become more courageous persons. This is exactly what Mafatu does in *Call It Courage*. He is not a courageous boy at first, but little by little, by facing his fears, he forces himself to become one.

In what other ways can we build courage? As with the other virtues, it helps to find inspiring examples. In other words, there is a link between courage and encouragement. Courage demands that we rise above our ordinary selves—not an easy thing unless we have encouragement from others. One of the best places to find it is in reading stories about bravery or in studying the lives of great men and women. Not surprisingly, when we look at the lives of courageous leaders, we usually find that they drew inspiration from the lives of others. For example, Abraham Lincoln read biographies of George Washington, and Martin Luther King, Jr. looked to Frederick Douglass and Mahatma Gandhi as models.

There are different kinds of courage. Physical courage is the willingness to face bodily danger as does Shasta in *The Horse and His Boy*. Moral courage is the courage to stand up for the right thing even though it may earn us mockery or contempt. Intellectual courage is the strength to pursue an idea or an ideal despite opposition or ridicule. There is such a thing as false courage too: showing off, acting recklessly, taking unnecessary risks, and heedlessly putting others in danger. Our courage needs to be guided by reason and good judgment. We need to decide what action is appropriate in a particular situation, what is worth fighting for, when to advance, and when to retreat. "Choosing your battles" is another way to describe this kind of judgment. George Washington, for example, often retreated rather than put his men at risk of fighting battles they would certainly lose. Like Washington, we should be less concerned with our "reputation" and more concerned with doing right.

1

The Black Stallion

Walter Farley

After spending two months with his uncle in India, Alec is homeward bound on the steamship *Drake* when a mysterious Arab brings a wild stallion on board.

The *Drake* stopped at Alexandria, Bengasi, Tripoli, Tunis and Algiers, passed the Rock of Gibraltar and turned north up the coast of Portugal. Now they were off Cape Finisterre on the coast of Spain, and in a few days, Captain Watson told Alec, they would be in England.

Alec wondered why the Black was being shipped to England—perhaps for stud, perhaps to race. The slanting shoulders, the deep broad chest, the powerful legs, the knees not too high nor too low—these, his uncle had taught him, were marks of speed and endurance.

That night Alec made his customary trip to the stall, his pockets filled with lumps of sugar. The night was hot and still; heavy clouds blacked out the stars; in the distance long streaks of lightning raced through the sky. The Black had his head out the window. Again he was looking out to sea, his nostrils quivering more than ever. He turned, whistled as he saw the boy, then again faced the water.

Alec felt elated—it was the first time that the stallion hadn't drawn back into the stall at sight of him. He moved closer. He put the sugar in the palm of his hand and hesitantly held it out to the stallion. The Black turned and once again whistled—softer this time. Alec stood his ground. Neither he nor anyone else had been this close to the stallion since he came on board. But he did not care to take the chance of extending his arm any nearer the bared teeth, the curled nostrils. Instead he placed the sugar on the sill. The Black looked at it, then back at the boy. Slowly he moved over and began to eat the sugar. Alec watched him for a moment, satisfied; then as the rain began to fall, he went back to his cabin.

He was awakened with amazing suddenness in the middle of the night. The *Drake* lurched crazily and he was thrown onto the floor. Outside there were loud rolls of thunder, and streaks of lightning made his cabin as light as day.

His first storm at sea! He pushed the light switch—it was dead. Then a flash of lightning again illuminated the cabin. The top of his bureau had been swept clear and the floor was covered with broken glass. Hurriedly he pulled on his pants and shirt and started for the door; then he stopped. Back he went to the bed, fell on his knees and reached under. He withdrew a life jacket and strapped it around him. He hoped that he wouldn't need it.

He opened the door and made his way, staggering, to the deck. The fury of the storm drove him back into the passageway; he hung on to the stair rail and peered into the black void. He heard the shouts of Captain Watson and the crew faintly above the roar of the winds. Huge waves swept from one end of the *Drake* to the other. Hysterical passengers crowded into the corridor. Alec was genuinely scared now; never had he seen a storm like this!

For what seemed hours, the *Drake* plowed through wave after wave, trembling, careening on its side, yet somehow managing to stay afloat. The long streaks of lightning never diminished;

zigzagging through the sky, their sharp cracks resounded on the water.

From the passageway, Alec saw one of the crew make his way along the deck in his direction, desperately fighting to hold on to the rail. The *Drake* rolled sideways and a huge wave swept over the boat. When it had passed, the sailor was gone. The boy closed his eyes and prayed.

The storm began to subside a little and Alec felt new hope. Then suddenly a bolt of fire seemed to fall from the heavens above them. A sharp crack and the boat shook. Alec was thrown flat on his face, stunned. Slowly he regained consciousness. He was lying on his stomach; his face felt hot and sticky. He raised his hand, and withdrew it covered with blood. Then he became conscious of feet stepping on him. The passengers, yelling and screaming, were climbing, crawling over him! The *Drake* was still—its engines dead.

Struggling, Alec pushed himself to his feet. Slowly he made his way along the deck. His startled eyes took in the scene about him. The *Drake,* struck by lightning, seemed almost cut in half! They were sinking! Strange, with what seemed the end so near, he should feel so calm. They were manning the lifeboats, and Captain Watson was there shouting directions. One boat was being lowered into the water. A large wave caught it broadside and turned it over—its occupants disappeared in the sea.

The second lifeboat was being filled and Alec waited his turn. But when it came, the boat had reached its quota.

"Wait for the next one, Alec," Captain Watson said sternly. He put his arm on the boy's shoulder, softening the harshness of his words.

As they watched the second lifeboat being lowered, the dark-skinned man appeared and rushed up to the captain, waving his arms and babbling hysterically.

"It's under the bed, under the bed!" Captain Watson shouted at him.

Then Alec saw the man had no life jacket. Terror in his eyes, he turned away from the captain toward Alec. Frantically he rushed at the boy and tried to tear the life jacket from his back. Alec struggled, but he was no match for the half-crazed man.

Then Captain Watson had his hands on the man and threw him against the rail.

Alec saw the man's eyes turn to the lifeboat that was being lowered. Before the captain could stop him, he was climbing over the rail. He was going to jump into the boat! Suddenly the *Drake* lurched. The man lost his balance and, screaming, fell into the water. He never rose to the surface.

The dark-skinned man had drowned. Immediately Alec thought of the Black. What was happening to him? Was he still in his stall? Alec fought his way out of line and toward the stern of the boat. If the stallion was alive, he was going to set him free and give him his chance to fight for life.

The stall was still standing. Alec heard a shrill whistle rise above the storm. He rushed to the door, lifted the heavy bar and swung it open. For a second the mighty hoofs stopped pounding and there was silence. Alec backed slowly away.

Then he saw the Black, his head held high, his nostrils blown out with excitement. Suddenly he snorted and plunged straight for the rail and Alec. Alec was paralyzed; he couldn't move. One hand was on the rail, which was broken at this point, leaving nothing between him and the open water. The Black swerved as he came near him, and the boy realized that the stallion was making for the hole. The horse's shoulder grazed him as he swerved and Alec went flying into space. He felt the water close over his head.

When he came up, his first thought was of the ship; then he heard an explosion, and he saw the *Drake* settling deep into the water. Frantically he looked around for a lifeboat, but there was none in sight. Then he saw the Black swimming not more than ten yards away. Something swished by him—a rope, and it was attached to the Black's halter! The same rope that they had used to bring the stallion aboard the boat, and which they had never been able to get close enough to the horse to untie. Without stopping to think, Alec grabbed hold of it. Then he was pulled through the water, into the oncoming seas.

The waves were still large, but with the aid of his life jacket, Alec was able to stay on top. He was too tired now to give much thought to what he had done. He only knew that he had had his choice of remaining in the water alone or being pulled by the Black. If he was to die, he would rather die with the mighty stallion than alone. He took one last look behind and saw the *Drake* sink into the depths.

For hours Alec battled the waves. He had tied the rope securely around his waist. He could hardly hold his head up. Suddenly he felt the rope slacken. The Black had stopped swimming! Alec anxiously waited; peering into the darkness he could just make out the head of the stallion. The Black's whistle pierced the air! After a few minutes, the rope became taut again. The horse had changed his direction. Another hour passed, then the storm diminished to high, rolling swells. The first streaks of dawn appeared on the horizon.

The Black had stopped four times during the night, and each time he had altered his course. Alec wondered whether the stallion's wild instinct was leading him to land. The sun rose and shone down brightly on the boy's head; the salt water he had swallowed during the night made him sick to his stomach. But when Alec felt that he could hold out no longer, he looked at the struggling, fighting animal in front of him, and new courage came to him.

Suddenly he realized that they were going with the waves, instead of against them. He shook his head, trying to clear his mind. Yes, they were riding in; they must be approaching land! Eagerly he strained his salt-filled eyes and looked into the distance. And then he saw it—about a quarter of a mile away was a small island, not much more than a sandy reef in the sea. But he might find food and water there, and have a chance to survive. Faster and faster they approached the white sand. They were in the breakers. The Black's scream shattered the stillness. He was able to walk; he staggered a little and shook his black head. Then his action shifted marvelously, and he went faster through the shallow water.

Alec's head whirled as he was pulled toward the beach with ever-increasing speed. Suddenly he realized the danger of his position. He must untie this rope from around his waist, or else he would be dragged to death over the sand! Desperately his fingers flew to the knot; it was tight, he had made sure of that. Frantically he worked on it as the shore drew closer and closer.

The Black was now on the beach. Thunder began to roll from beneath his hoofs as he broke out of the water. Hours in the water had swelled the knot—Alec couldn't untie it! Then he remembered his pocketknife. Could it still be there? Alec's hand darted to his rear pants pocket. His fingers reached inside and came out with the knife.

He was now on the beach being dragged by the stallion; the sand flew in his face. Quickly he opened the knife and began to cut the rope. His body burned from the sand, his clothes were being torn off of him! His speed was increasing every second! Madly he sawed away at the rope. With one final thrust he was through! His outflung hands caressed the sand. As he closed his eyes, his parched lips murmured, "Yes—Uncle Ralph—it did—come in handy."

2

The Horse and His Boy

C. S. Lewis

The Horse and His Boy is one of seven books that make up *The Chronicles of Narnia*. This fascinating series recounts the history of a land inhabited by talking animals, fauns, centaurs, and giants. It is ruled over from afar by an extraordinary, but seldom seen, lion, who occasionally takes an active role in the lives of his subjects. This part of the story tells of the attempt by Aravis and Shasta and their talking horses to outrun the invading army of the Calormenes and to warn Narnia and Archenland of the coming attack.

At the first ridge Shasta turned in the saddle and looked back. There was no sign of Tashbaan; the desert, unbroken except by the narrow green crack which they had traveled down, spread to the horizon.

"Hullo!" he said suddenly. "What's that?"

"What's what?" said Bree, turning round. Hwin and Aravis did the same.

"That," said Shasta, pointing. "It looks like smoke. Is it a fire?"

"Sand-storm, I should say," said Bree.

"Not much wind to raise it," said Aravis.

"Oh!" exclaimed Hwin. "Look! There are things flashing in it. Look! They're helmets—and armour. And it's moving: moving this way."

"By Tash!" said Aravis. "It's the army. It's Rabadash."

"Of course it is," said Hwin. "Just what I was afraid of. Quick! We must get to Anvard before it does." And without another word she whisked round and began galloping north. Bree tossed his head and did the same.

"Come on, Bree, come on," yelled Aravis over her shoulder. This race was very gruelling for the Horses. As they topped each ridge they found another valley and another ridge beyond it; and though they knew they were going in more or less the right direction, no one knew how far it was to Anvard. From the top of the second ridge Shasta looked back again. Instead of a dust-cloud well out in the desert he now saw a black, moving mass, rather like ants, on the far bank of the Winding Arrow. They were doubtless looking for a ford.

"They're on the river!" he yelled wildly.

"Quick! Quick!" shouted Aravis. "We might as well not have come at all if we don't reach Anvard in time. Gallop, Bree, gallop. Remember you're a war horse."

It was all Shasta could do to prevent himself from shouting out similar instructions; but he thought, "The poor chap's doing all he can already," and held his tongue. And certainly both Horses were doing, if not all they could, all they thought they could; which is not quite the same thing. Bree had caught up with Hwin and they thundered side by side over the turf. It didn't look as if Hwin could possibly keep it up much longer.

At that moment everyone's feelings were completely altered by a sound from behind. It was not the sound they had been expecting to hear—the noise of hoofs and jingling armour, mixed, perhaps, with Calormene battle-cries. Yet Shasta knew it at once. It was the same snarling roar he had heard that moonlit night when they first met Aravis and Hwin. Bree knew it too. His eyes gleamed red and his ears lay flat back on his skull. And Bree now discovered that he had not really been going as fast—not quite as fast—as he could. Shasta felt the change at once.

Now they were really going all out. In a few seconds they were well ahead of Hwin.

"It's not fair," thought Shasta. "I *did* think we'd be safe from lions here!"

He looked over his shoulder. Everything was only too clear. A huge tawny creature, its body low to the ground, like a cat streaking across the lawn to a tree when a strange dog has got into the garden, was behind them. And it was nearer every second and half second.

He looked forward again and saw something which he did not take in, or even think about. Their way was barred by a smooth green wall about ten feet high. In the middle of that wall there was a gate, open. In the middle of the gateway stood a tall man, dressed, down to his bare feet, in a robe coloured like autumn leaves, leaning on a straight staff. His beard fell almost to his knees.

Shasta saw all this in a glance and looked back again. The lion had almost got Hwin now. It was making snaps at her hind legs, and there was no hope now in her foam-flecked, wide-eyed face.

"Stop," bellowed Shasta in Bree's ear. "Must go back. Must help!"

Bree always said afterwards that he never heard, or never understood this; and as he was in general a very truthful horse we must accept his word.

Shasta slipped his feet out of the stirrups, slid both his legs over on the left side, hesitated for one hideous hundredth of a second, and jumped. It hurt horribly and nearly winded him; but before he knew how it hurt him he was staggering back to help Aravis. He had never done anything like this in his life before and hardly knew why he was doing it now.

One of the most terrible noises in the world, a horse's scream, broke from Hwin's lips. Aravis was stooping low over Hwin's neck and seemed to be trying to draw her sword. And now all three—Aravis, Hwin, and the lion—were almost on top of Shasta. Before they reached him the lion rose on its hind legs, larger than you would have believed a lion could be, and jabbed at Aravis with its right paw. Shasta could see all the terrible claws extended. Aravis screamed and reeled in the saddle. The lion was tearing her shoulders. Shasta, half mad with horror, managed to lurch towards the brute. He had no weapon, not even a stick or a stone. He shouted out, idiotically, at the lion as one would at a dog. "Go home! Go home!" For a fraction of a second he was staring right into its wide-opened, raging mouth. Then, to his utter astonishment, the lion, still on its hind legs, checked itself suddenly, turned head over heels, picked itself up, and rushed away.

Shasta did not for a moment suppose it had gone for good. He turned and raced for the gate in the green wall which, now for the first time, he remembered seeing. Hwin, stumbling and nearly fainting, was just entering the gate; Aravis still kept her seat but her back was covered with blood.

"Come in, my daughter, come in," the robed and bearded man was saying, and then, "Come in, my son" as Shasta panted up to him. He heard the gate closed behind him; and the bearded stranger was already helping Aravis off her horse.

They were in a wide and perfectly circular enclosure, protected by a high wall of green turf. A pool of perfectly still water, so full that the water was almost exactly level with the ground, lay before him. At one end of the pool, completely overshadowing it with its branches, there grew the hugest and most beautiful tree that Shasta had ever seen. Beyond the pool was a little low house of stone roofed with deep and ancient thatch. There was a sound of bleating and over at the far side of the enclosure there were some goats. The level ground was completely covered with the finest grass.

"Are—are—are you," panted Shasta. "Are you King Lune of Archenland?"

The old man shook his head. "No," he replied in a quiet voice, "I am the Hermit of the Southern March. And now, my son, waste no time on questions, but obey. This damsel is wounded. Your horses are spent. Rabadash is at this moment finding a ford over the Winding Arrow. If you run now, without a moment's rest, you will still be in time to warn King Lune."

Shasta's heart fainted at these words for he felt he had no strength left. And he writhed inside at what seemed the cruelty and unfairness of the demand. He had not yet learned that if you do one good deed your reward usually is to be set to do another and harder and better one. But all he said out loud was:

"Where is the King?"

The Hermit turned and pointed with his staff. "Look," he said. "There is another gate, right opposite to the one you entered by. Open it and go straight ahead: always straight ahead, over level or steep, over smooth or rough, over dry or wet. I know by my art that you will find King Lune straight ahead. But run, run: always run."

Shasta nodded his head, ran to the northern gate and disappeared beyond it. Then the Hermit took Aravis, whom he had all this time been supporting with his left arm, and half led, half carried her into the house. After a long time he came out again.

"Now, cousins," he said to the Horses. "It is your turn."

Without waiting for an answer—and indeed they were too exhausted to speak—he took the bridles and saddles off both of them. Then he rubbed them both down, so well that a groom in a king's stable could not have done it better.

"There, cousins," he said, "Dismiss it all from your minds and be comforted. Here is water and there is grass. You shall have a hot mash when I have milked my other cousins, the goats."

"Sir," said Hwin, finding her voice at last, "will the Tarkheena live? Has the lion killed her?"

"I who know many present things by my art," replied the Hermit with a smile, "have yet little knowledge of things future. Therefore I do not know whether any man or woman or beast in the whole world will be alive when the sun sets tonight. But be of good hope. The damsel is likely to live as long as any of her age."

When Aravis came to herself she found that she was lying on her face on a low bed of extraordinary softness in a cool, bare room with walls of undressed stone. She couldn't understand why she had been laid on her face; but when she tried to turn and felt the hot, burning pains all over her back, she remembered, and realised why. She couldn't understand what delightfully springy stuff the bed was made of, because it was made of heather (which is the best bedding) and heather was a thing she had never seen or heard of.

The door opened and the Hermit entered, carrying a large wooden bowl in his hand. After carefully setting this down, he came to the bedside, and asked:

"How do you find yourself, my daughter?"

"My back is very sore, father," said Aravis, "but there is nothing else wrong with me."

He knelt beside her, laid his hand on her forehead, and felt her pulse.

"There is no fever," he said. "You will do well. Indeed there is no reason why you should not get up tomorrow. But now, drink this."

He fetched the wooden bowl and held it to her lips. Aravis couldn't help making a face when she tasted it, for goats' milk is rather a shock when you are not used to it. But she was very thirsty and managed to drink it all and felt better when she had finished.

"Now, my daughter, you may sleep when you wish," said the Hermit. "For your wounds are washed and dressed and though they smart they are no more serious than if they had been the cuts of a whip. It must have been a very strange lion, for instead of catching you out of the saddle and getting his teeth into you, he has only drawn his claws across your back. Ten scratches: sore, but not deep or dangerous."

"I say!" said Aravis. "I *have* had luck."

"Daughter," said the Hermit, "I have now lived a hundred and nine winters in this world and have never yet met any such thing as Luck. There is something about all this that I do not understand: but if ever we need to know it, you may be sure that we shall."

"And what about Rabadash and his two hundred horse?" asked Aravis.

"They will not pass this way, I think," said the Hermit. "They must have found a ford by now well to the east of us. From there they will try to ride straight to Anvard."

"Poor Shasta!" said Aravis. "Has he far to go? Will he get there first?"

"There is good hope of it," said the old man.

Aravis lay down again (on her side this time) and said, "Have I been asleep for a long time? It seems to be getting dark."

The Hermit was looking out of the only window, which faced north. "This is not the darkness of night," he said presently. "The clouds are rolling down from Stormness Head. Our foul weather always comes from there in these parts. There will be thick fog to-night."

Next day, except for her sore back, Aravis felt so well that after breakfast (which was porridge and cream) the Hermit said she could get up. And of course she at once went out to speak to the Horses. The weather had changed and the whole of that green enclosure was filled, like a great green cup, with sunlight. It was a very peaceful place, lonely and quiet.

Hwin at once trotted across to Aravis and gave her a horse-kiss.

"But where's Bree?" said Aravis when each had asked after the other's health and sleep.

"Over there," said Hwin, pointing with her nose to the far side of the circle. "And I wish you'd come and talk to him. There's something wrong; I can't get a word out of him."

They strolled across and found Bree lying with his face towards the wall, and though he must have heard them coming, he never turned his head or spoke a word.

"Good morning, Bree," said Aravis. "How are you this morning?"

Bree muttered something that no one could hear.

"The Hermit says that Shasta probably got to King Lune in time," continued Aravis, "so it looks as if all our troubles are over. Narnia, at last, Bree!"

"I shall never see Narnia," said Bree in a low voice.

"Aren't you well, Bree dear?" said Aravis.

Bree turned round at last, his face mournful as only a horse's can be.

"I shall go back to Calormen," he said.

"What?" said Aravis. "Back to slavery!"

"Yes," said Bree. "Slavery is all I'm fit for. How can I ever show my face among the free Horses of Narnia?—I, who left a mare and a girl and a boy to be eaten by lions while I galloped all I could to save my own wretched skin!"

"We all ran as hard as we could," said Hwin.

"Shasta didn't!" snorted Bree. "At least he ran in the right direction: ran *back*. And that is what shames me most of all. I, who called myself a war horse and boasted of a hundred fights, to be beaten by a little human boy—a child, a mere foal, who had never held a sword nor had any good nurture or example in his life!"

"I know," said Aravis. "I felt just the same. Shasta was marvellous. I'm just as bad as you, Bree. I've been snubbing him and looking down on him ever since you met us and now he turns out to be the best of us all. But I think it would be better to stay and say we're sorry than to go back to Calormen."

"It's all very well for you," said Bree. "You haven't disgraced yourself. But I've lost everything."

"My good Horse," said the Hermit, who had approached them unnoticed because his bare feet made so little noise on that sweet, dewy grass. "My good Horse, you've lost nothing but your self-conceit. No, no, cousin. Don't put back your ears and shake your mane at me. If you are really so humbled as you sounded a minute ago, you must learn to listen to sense. You're not quite the great horse you had come to think, from living among poor dumb horses. Of course you were braver and cleverer than *them*. You could hardly help being that. It doesn't follow that you'll be anyone very special in Narnia. But as long as you know you're nobody very special, you'll be a very decent sort of Horse, on the whole, and taking one thing with another. And now, if you and my other four-footed cousin will come round to the kitchen door we'll see about the other half of that mash."

3

Call It Courage

Armstrong Sperry

Mafatu is scorned by his tribe because he fears the sea that claimed his mother's life and nearly took his own. Determined to prove himself, he sets off on an outrigger with his dog, Uri. Here is one of the adventures he encounters.

One morning, wandering far down the beach, Mafatu came upon a sheltered cove. His heart gave a leap of joy; for there, white-gleaming in the sun, was all that remained of the skeleton of a whale. It might not have meant very much to you or to me; but to Mafatu it meant knives and fishhooks galore, splintered bone for darts and spears, a shoulder blade for an ax. It was a veritable treasure trove. The boy leaped up and down in his excitement. "Uri!" he shouted. "We're rich! Come—help me drag these bones home!"

His hands seemed all thumbs in his eagerness; he tied as many bones as he could manage into two bundles. One bundle he shouldered himself. The other Uri dragged behind him. And thus they returned to the camp site, weary, but filled with elation. Even the dog seemed to have some understanding of what this discovery meant; or if not, he was at least infected with his master's high spirits. He leaped about like a sportive puppy, yapping until he was hoarse.

Now began the long process of grinding the knife and the ax. Hour after long hour, squatting before a slab of basalt, Mafatu worked and worked, until his hands were raw and blistered and the sweat ran down into his eyes. The knife emerged first, since that was the most imperative. Its blade was ten inches long, its handle a knob of joint. It was sharp enough to cut the fronds of coconut trees, to slice off the end of a green nut. *Ai*, but it was a splendid knife! All Mafatu's skill went into it. It would be a fine weapon as well, the boy thought grimly, as he ground it down to a sharp point. Some sea robber had been breaking into his bamboo trap and he was going to find out who the culprit was! Probably that old hammerhead shark who was always cruising around. . . . Just as if he owned the lagoon!

Fishing with a line took too long when you were working against time. Mafatu could not afford to have his trap robbed. Twice it had been broken into, the stout bamboos crushed and the contents eaten. It was the work either of a shark or of an octopus. That was certain. No other fish was strong enough to snap the tough bamboo.

Mafatu's mouth was set in a grim line as he worked away on his knife. That old hammerhead—undoubtedly *he* was the thief! Mafatu had come to recognize him; for every day when the boy went out with his trap, that shark, larger than all the others, was circling around, wary and watchful. The other sharks seemed to treat the hammerhead with deference.

Hunger alone drove Mafatu out to the reef to set his trap. He knew that if he was to maintain strength to accomplish all that lay ahead he must have fish to add to his diet of fruit. But often as he set his trap far out by the barrier-reef, the hammerhead would approach, roll over slightly in passing, and the cold gleam of its eye filled Mafatu with dread and anger.

"Wait, you!" the boy threatened darkly, shaking his fist at the *ma'o*. "Wait until I have my knife! You will not be so brave then, Ma'o. You will run away when you see it flash."

But the morning that the knife was finished, Mafatu did not feel so brave as he would have liked. He hoped he would never see the hammerhead again. Paddling out to the distant reef, he glanced down from time to time at the long-bladed knife where it hung about his neck by a cord of sennit. It wasn't, after all, such a formidable weapon. It was only a knife made by a boy from a whale's rib.

Uri sat on the edge of the raft, sniffing at the wind. Mafatu always took his dog along, for Uri howled unmercifully if he were left behind. And Mafatu had come to rely upon the companionship of the little yellow dog. The boy talked with the animal as if he were another person, consulting with him, arguing, playing when there was time for play. They were very close, these two.

This morning as they approached the spot where the fish trap was anchored, Mafatu saw the polished dorsal of the hated hammerhead circling slowly in the water. It was like a triangle of black basalt, making a little furrow in the water as it passed.

"*Aiá*, Ma'o!" the boy shouted roughly, trying to bolster up his courage. "I have my knife today, see! Coward who robs traps—catch your own fish!"

The hammerhead approached the raft in leisurely fashion; it rolled over slightly, and its gaping jaws seemed to curve in a yawning grin. Uri ran to the edge of the raft, barking furiously; the hair on the dog's neck stood up in a bristling ridge. The shark, unconcerned, moved away. Then with a whip of its powerful tail it rushed at the bamboo fish trap and seized it in its jaws. Mafatu was struck dumb. The hammerhead shook the trap as a terrier might shake a rat. The boy watched, fascinated, unable to make a move. He saw the muscles work in the fish's neck as the great tail thrashed the water to fury. The trap splintered into bits, while the fish within escaped only to vanish into the shark's mouth. Mafatu was filled with impotent rage. The hours he had spent making that trap—But all he could do was shout threats at his enemy.

Uri was running from one side of the raft to the other, furious with excitement. A large wave sheeted across the reef. At that second the dog's shift in weight tipped the raft at a perilous angle. With a helpless yelp, Uri slid off into the water. Mafatu sprang to catch him but he was too late.

Instantly the hammerhead whipped about. The wave slewed the raft away. Uri, swimming frantically, tried to regain it. There was desperation in the brown eyes—the puzzled eyes so faithful and true. Mafatu strained forward. His dog. His companion. . . . The hammerhead was moving in slowly. A mighty rage stormed through the boy. He gripped his knife. Then he was over the side in a clean-curving dive.

Mafatu came up under his enemy. The shark spun about. Its rough hide scraped the flesh from the boy's shoulder. In that instant Mafatu stabbed. Deep, deep into the white belly. There was a terrific impact. Water lashed to foam. Stunned, gasping, the boy fought for life and air.

It seemed that he would never reach the surface. *Aué*, his lungs would burst! . . . At last his head broke water. Putting his face to the surface, he saw the great shark turn over, fathoms deep. Blood flowed from the wound in its belly. Instantly gray shapes rushed in—other sharks, tearing the wounded hammerhead to pieces.

Uri—where was he? Mafatu saw his dog then. Uri was trying to pull himself up on the raft. Mafatu seized him by the scruff and dragged him up to safety. Then he caught his dog to him and hugged him close, talking to him foolishly. Uri yelped for joy and licked his master's cheek.

It wasn't until Mafatu reached shore that he realized what he had done. He had killed the *ma'o* with his own hand, with naught but a bone knife. He could never have done it for himself. Fear would have robbed his arm of all strength. He had done it for Uri, his dog. And he felt suddenly humble, with gratitude.

Compassion

The word "compassion" comes from a Latin word which means "to suffer with" another person. In practice it means that we ask ourselves how we would feel if we were in another person's place. Psychologists, who have studied moral development, say that compassion is one of the most important building blocks of character. Compassion is the virtue by which we realize that others experience the same hopes, fears, and pain that we feel; it's the realization that they have as much right to respect and fair treatment as we want for ourselves.

Criminals often show a lack of feeling for their victim's distress. When a teenage boy who had severely beaten an elderly blind woman was asked by a reporter why he felt no guilt, he replied, "What do I care? I'm not her." Studies of killers, torturers, and mass murderers show that either they failed to develop this virtue or they deliberately tried to erase it in themselves by dehumanizing their victims. Those who hurt or kill others often do so after they have convinced themselves that their victims are unimportant or even subhuman.

Many thoughtful people in our society worry that too much exposure to violent movies, video games, and song lyrics can damage a young person's ability to empathize, both by making violence seem exciting and by turning victims into targets for whom little sympathy is felt. The more that people are presented as objects, the easier it is to forget that they have thoughts, feelings, and families of their own. If we live too much in these violent fantasy worlds, we risk losing our sense of connection with others.

Compassion for animals is a good indication of compassion toward people. As we see in the story of *Black Beauty*, the way we treat animals reveals what kind of person we are. In fact, studies show that children who are cruel to animals are more likely to grow up to be cruel to other people. In *Beautiful Joe*, Laura declares of the man who maimed Joe, "If he is bad enough to ill-treat his dog, he will ill-treat his wife and children." And indeed, it turns out that he has been abusing them.

Is there such a thing as too much compassion? No, not if it's genuine compassion that seeks to do what's best for the other. But sometimes you will meet people who are more interested in showing off their compassion than in really thinking about moral issues. Just as loyalty to a friend does not mean doing whatever your friend asks you to, so true compassion does not mean we have to approve of behavior that violates our moral principles. For example, if someone we know is hurting themselves by drinking or gambling or taking drugs, it is not compassionate to turn a blind eye to their behavior. Sometimes compassion may mean trying to persuade another to change his or her self-destructive habits. As we see in *Beautiful Joe*, Laura, who wants to see Jenkins "checked and punished" in the hope he may reform, is actually more concerned about the man's future than Harry, who wants to ignore the painful incident.

One of the great rewards of reading is that it enlarges our sympathies by letting us inside the lives of others. But it's important to understand that feelings of sympathy are just the starting point for compassion. Some people weep over characters they read about in books but are unmoved by actual suffering. Dreaming is not the same as doing, and we need to remind ourselves that compassion is more than a feeling. When we have true compassion for someone in need, we try to do something to help.

4

Beautiful Joe

Marshall Saunders
Retold by Anna Higgins

Beautiful Joe is a true story that happened in Maine over one hundred years ago. Like *Black Beauty*, the story is told from the animal's point of view.

My name is Beautiful Joe. Anyone looking at me would find this an odd name, and the story of how I came by it is worth knowing.

I was one of seven pups born in a stable on the outskirts of a small town in Maine called Fairport. The first thing I remember is lying close to my mother and being very snug and warm. The next thing I remember is being always hungry. My mother never had enough milk for us. She was always half starved herself, so she could not feed us properly. But my mother was blessed with a kind and loyal nature in spite of the rough treatment she received from her owner, a milkman named Jenkins.

Each morning Jenkins stumbled into his dirty barn, hung the lantern on the peg and kicked at anyone or anything in his way. My mother sent us scurrying out the barn door as soon as he entered, in order to dodge his heavy boots.

He was equally rough in his treatment of his cows, keeping them in the dirty stable, where chinks in the wall were so big that in winter the snow swept through in drifts. His horse, old Toby, was also ill fed and poorly groomed, but he bore the beatings and rough language without making a sound, never biting or kicking his cruel owner.

Each day my mother followed him on his rounds. When I asked her why, she hung her head and said she was sometimes given bones or scraps at the houses along the route. She also liked Jenkins, in spite of his meanness, and wanted to be with him.

One rainy day when we were eight weeks old, Jenkins, followed by two or three of his ragged, dirty children, came into the stable and looked at us. Then he began to swear because we were so ugly, and said if we had been good looking he might have sold some of us. Mother watched him anxiously, and, fearing some danger to her puppies, she ran and jumped in the middle of us and looked pleadingly up at him.

It only made him swear the more. He took one pup after another, and right there put an end to their lives. I was the only one spared, though I never knew why.

His children cried, and he sent them out of the stable and went out himself. Mother picked up all the puppies, brought them to our nest in the straw and licked them, and tried to bring them back to life. But it was no use; they were quite dead.

My mother was never quite the same after that. She became even more weak and miserable. One day she licked me gently, wagged her tail, and died.

When Jenkins returned I was lying on the straw next to my mother, miserable with grief. I could not bear to look at the man who killed my mother. I was filled with hate for him but kept still, even when he turned her over with his foot to see if she was really dead. He seemed a little sorry, for he looked at me with scorn and said, “She was worth two of you. Why didn’t you die instead?”

I remained still until he came over to kick me. I was so broken-hearted I could stand no more. I flew at him in a rage and gave him a savage bite on the ankle.

He yelled out in his rage and grabbed the back of my neck, dragging me out to the tree stump. "So you want to be a fighter? I'll fix that," he spat out between gritted teeth. His face was red and furious. "Bill," he called to one of his children, "bring me the hatchet."

He quickly forced my head to the stump and swiftly cut off one ear, then the other, close to my head. There was sharp awful pain as he turned my struggling body and furiously cut off my tail close to my body.

He let me go and watched as I rolled bleeding on the ground, yelping in agony. He was so angry that he did not take heed that people passing by on the road might hear me.

A young man riding by on the road heard my screams. Leaping off his bicycle, he came running along the path yelling, "What have you been doing to that dog?"

"I'm fixing him for bitin', no law against that," said Jenkins.

"And there's no law to keep me from giving you a beating," shouted the young man. He grabbed Jenkins by the throat and began to hit him with his full strength. Mrs. Jenkins stood in the doorway weeping, but made no attempt to help her husband.

After knocking Jenkins to the ground the young man called to her, "Bring me a towel." She ran to him and quickly gave him her apron, which he used to wrap me up. He carried me gently out of the yard and asked one of the boys in the crowd that had gathered to follow him with his bicycle.

Though I was miserable and whimpering in pain, I took the occasional look out of the apron to see where we were going. We went near the center of town to a big yellow house with a wide porch. The young man gave the boy who helped a few coins and we followed the lane leading to the back of the house.

We entered into a small clean stable. He gently put me on the floor and uncovered my body. Some boys were playing about the stable and I heard them say in horrified tones, "Oh, Cousin Harry! What is the matter with that dog?"

"Hush," he said. "Don't make a fuss. You, Jack, go down to the kitchen and ask Mary for a basin of warm water and a sponge, and don't let your mother or Laura hear you."

A few minutes later my rescuer had bathed my bleeding ears and tail and had applied some cooling, soothing ointment. He then used cotton strips to bandage them firmly. I felt better and could take a look around.

I was in a small stable that seemed like a playroom, with a swinging bar suspended from the ceiling, and toys scattered about. Most remarkable were the other animals present. A guinea pig in a box watched with bright eyes. A longhaired rabbit was hopping about freely, and a tame rat sat on the shoulder of one of the youngsters. As he stared at me with his little red eyes he took no notice of the gray cat who was also watching me from her perch on a beam. A pretty spaniel lay asleep in the corner of the yard as pigeons pecked grain only a few feet away. My wonder over the harmony between the animals nearly took the pain away.

"Here comes Laura," called one of the boys.

A young woman was coming up the walk to the stable. She was tall and slender, and had lovely brown eyes and brown hair, and a sweet smile. Just to look at her was enough to make one love her. I stood shakily at the door, eager to please.

"Why, what a funny dog," she said as she stopped next to me. I realized I was a sorry sight and crept into a corner to hide.

"Poor doggie, have I hurt your feelings?" she said, and came up to the guinea pig's box, behind which I had gone.

"What is the matter with your head, good dog?" she said curiously, as she stooped over me.

Harry walked up and put his hand on her shoulder. "Laura, he was hurt and I had to bandage him."

"Who hurt him?"

"I had rather not tell you."

"But I wish to know." Her voice was gentle as ever, but she spoke so decidedly that the young man was obliged to tell her everything.

While he told her the story of rescuing me from Jenkins, her touch was gentle on my sore body. When the story ended her voice was firm. "You will have the man punished?"

"How will that help? It won't stop him from being cruel."

"It will put a check on his cruelty."

"I don't think it will do any good," said Harry.

The young girl stood up very straight and tall, her brown eyes flashing, and one hand pointed at me. "Will you let that pass? That animal has been wronged, and it looks to you to right the wrong. The coward who maimed it for life should be punished. A child has a voice to tell its wrong—a poor, dumb creature must suffer in silence; in bitter, bitter silence." She went on quickly as the young man tried to interrupt her. "And you are doing the man himself an injustice. If he is bad enough to ill-treat his dog, he will ill-treat his wife and children. If he is checked and punished now for his cruelty, he may reform. And even if his wicked heart is not changed, he will be obliged to treat them with outward kindness, through fear of punishment."

The young man's face reddened and he looked almost as ashamed as if he had been the one to crop my ears.

"What do you want me to do?" he said.

"I want you to report that man immediately. I will go down to the police station with you, if you like."

"Very well," he said, his face brightening, and together they went off to the house.

5

Black Beauty

Anna Sewell

Black Beauty tells the story of his life from his days as a carefree colt with loving masters through his later mistreatment by foolish, drunken, or greedy humans. As Black Beauty passes from owner to owner, each one is implicitly judged by the way he treats the horse.

Hard Times

I shall never forget my new master; he had black eyes and a hooked nose, his mouth was as full of teeth as a bulldog's, and his voice was as harsh as the grinding of cart wheels over gravel stones. His name was Nicholas Skinner, and I believe he was the same man that poor Seedy Sam drove for.

I have heard men say that seeing is believing; but I should say that feeling is believing; for much as I had seen before, I never knew till now the utter misery of a cab horse's life.

Skinner had a low set of cabs and a low set of drivers; he was hard on the men, and the men were hard on the horses. In this place we had no Sunday rest, and it was in the heat of summer.

Sometimes on a Sunday morning, a party of fast men would hire the cab for the day; four of them inside and another with the driver, and I had to take them ten or fifteen miles out into the country, and back again. Never would any of them get down to walk up a hill, let it be ever so steep, or the day ever so hot—unless, indeed, when the driver was afraid I should not manage it, and sometimes I was so fevered and worn that I could hardly touch my food. How I used to long for the nice bran mash with niter in it that Jerry used to give us on Saturday nights in hot weather that used to cool us down and make us so comfortable. Then we had two nights and a whole day for unbroken rest, and on Monday morning we were as fresh as young horses again; but here, there was no rest, and my driver was just as hard as his master. He had a cruel whip with something so sharp at the end that it sometimes drew blood, and he would even whip me under the belly and flip the lash out at my head. Indignities like these took the heart out of me terribly, but still I did my best and never hung back; for, as poor Ginger said, it was no use; men are the strongest.

My life was now so utterly wretched that I wished I might, like Ginger, drop down dead at my work, and be out of my misery; and one day my wish very nearly came to pass.

I went on the stand at eight in the morning, and had done a good share of work, when we had to take a fare to the railway. A long train was just expected in, so my driver pulled up at the back of some of the outside cabs to take the chance of a return fare. It was a very heavy train, and as all the cabs were soon engaged ours was called for. There was a party of four—a noisy, blustering man with a lady, a little boy, and a young girl, and a great deal of luggage. The lady and the boy got into the cab, and while the man ordered about the luggage, the young girl came and looked at me.

"Papa," she said, "I am sure this poor horse cannot take us and all our luggage so far; he is so very weak and worn out. Do look at him."

"Oh! he's all right, miss," said my driver, "he's strong enough."

The porter, who was pulling about some heavy boxes, suggested to the gentleman, as there was so much luggage, whether he would not take a second cab.

"Can your horse do it, or can't he?" said the blustering man.

"Oh! he can do it all right, sir. Send up the boxes, porter. He could take more than that," and he helped to haul up a box so heavy that I could feel the springs go down.

"Papa, papa, do take a second cab," said the young girl in a beseeching tone. "I am sure we are wrong; I am sure it is very cruel."

"Nonsense, Grace, get in at once, and don't make all this fuss; a pretty thing it would be if a man of business had to examine every cab-horse before he hired it—the man knows his own business of course. There, get in and hold your tongue!"

My gentle friend had to obey; and box after box was dragged up and lodged on the top of the cab, or settled by the side of the driver. At last all was ready, and with his usual jerk at the rein, and slash of the whip, he drove out of the station.

The load was very heavy, and I had had neither food nor rest since the morning; but I did my best, as I always had done, in spite of cruelty and injustice.

I got along fairly till we came to Ludgate Hill, but there the heavy load and my own exhaustion were too much. I was struggling to keep on, goaded by constant chucks of the rein and use of the whip, when, in a single moment—I cannot tell how—my feet slipped from under me, and I fell heavily to the ground on my side. The suddenness and the force with which I fell seemed to beat all the breath out of my body. I lay perfectly still; indeed, I had no power to move, and I thought now I was going to die. I heard a sort of confusion round me, loud angry voices, and the getting down of the luggage, but it was all like a dream. I thought I heard that sweet, pitiful voice saying, "Oh! that poor horse! It is all our fault." Someone came and loosened the throat strap of my bridle, and undid the traces which kept the collar so tight upon me. Someone said, "He's dead, he'll never get up again." Then I could hear the policeman giving orders, but I did not even open my eyes. I could only draw a gasping breath now and then. Some cold water was thrown over my head, and some cordial was poured into my mouth, and something was covered over me. I cannot tell how long I lay there, but I found my life coming back, and a kind-voiced man was patting me and encouraging me to rise. After some more cordial had been given me, and after one or two attempts, I staggered to my feet, and was gently led to some stables which were close by. Here I was put into a well-littered stall, and some warm gruel was brought to me, which I drank thankfully.

In the evening I was sufficiently recovered to be led back to Skinner's stables, where I think they did the best for me they could. In the morning Skinner came with a farrier to look at me. He examined me very closely, and said:

"This is a case of overwork more than disease, and if you could give him a run-off for six months he would be able to work again; but now there is not an ounce of strength in him."

"Then he must just go to the dogs," said Skinner. "I have no meadows to nurse sick horses in—he might get well or he might not. That sort of thing don't suit my business; my plan is to work 'em as long as they'll go, and then sell 'em for what they'll fetch, at the knacker's or elsewhere."

"If he was broken-winded," said the farrier, "you had better have him killed out of hand, but he is not. There is a sale of horses coming off in about ten days. If you rest him and feed him up, he may pick up, and you may get more than his skin is worth, at any rate."

Upon this advice, Skinner, rather unwillingly, I think, gave orders that I should be well fed and cared for, and the stable man, happily for me, carried out the orders with a much better will than his master had in giving them. Ten days of perfect rest, plenty of good oats, hay, bran mashes, with boiled linseed mixed in them, did more to get up my condition than anything else could have done; those linseed mashes were delicious, and I began to think, after all, it might be better to live than go to the dogs. When the twelfth day after the accident came, I was taken to the sale, a few miles out of London. I felt that any change from my present place must be an improvement, so I held up my head, and hoped for the best.

Farmer Thoroughgood and His Grandson Willie

At this sale, of course, I found myself in company with the old, broken-down horses—some lame, some broken-winded, some old, and some that I am sure it would have been merciful to shoot.

The buyers and sellers, too, many of them, looked not much better off than the poor beasts they were bargaining about. There were poor old men, trying to get a horse or a pony for a few pounds that might drag about some little wood or coal cart. There were poor men trying to sell a worn-out beast for two or three pounds, rather than have the greater loss of killing him. Some of them looked as if poverty and hard times had hardened them all over; but there were others that I would have willingly used the last of my strength in serving; poor and shabby, but kind and human, with voices that I could trust. There was one tottering old man that took a great fancy to me, and I to him, but I was not strong enough—it was an anxious time! Coming from the better part of the fair, I noticed a man who looked like a gentleman farmer, with a young boy by his side; he had a broad back and round shoulders, a kind, ruddy face, and he wore a broad-brimmed hat. When he came up to me and my companions, he gave a pitiful look round upon us. I saw his eye rest on me; I had still a good mane and tail, which did something for my appearance. I pricked my ears and looked at him.

"There's a horse, Willie, that has known better days."

"Poor old fellow!" said the boy, "do you think, grandpapa, he was ever a carriage horse?"

"Oh yes! my boy," said the farmer, coming closer, "he might have been anything when he was young; look at his nostrils and his ears, the shape of his neck and shoulders. There's a deal of breeding about that horse." He put out his hand and gave me a kind pat on the neck. I put out my nose in answer to his kindness; the boy stroked my face.

"Poor old fellow! see, grandpapa, how well he understands kindness. Could not you buy him and make him young again, as you did with Ladybird?"

"My dear boy, I can't make all old horses young. Besides, Ladybird was not so very old, as she was run down and badly used."

"Well, grandpapa, I don't believe that this one is old; look at his mane and tail. I wish you would look into his mouth, and then you could tell; though he is so very thin, his eyes are not sunk like some old horses'."

The old gentleman laughed. "Bless the boy! he is as horsey as his old grandfather."

"But do look at his mouth and ask the price; I am sure he would grow young in our meadows."

The man who had brought me for sale now put in his word.

"The young gentleman's a real knowing one, sir. Now the fact is, this 'ere hoss is just pulled down with overwork in the cabs; he's not an old one, and I heerd as how the vetenary should say that a six months' run-off would set him right up, being as how his wind was not broken. I've had the tending of him these ten days past, and a gratefuller, pleasanter animal I never met with, and 'twould be worth a gentleman's while to give a five-pound note for him, and let him have a chance. I'll be bound he'd be worth twenty pounds next spring."

The old gentleman laughed, and the little boy looked up eagerly.

"Oh! grandpapa, did you not say the colt sold for five pounds more than you expected? You would not be poorer if you did buy this one."

The farmer slowly felt my legs, which were much swelled and strained; then he looked at my mouth. "Thirteen or fourteen, I should say; just trot him out, will you?"

I arched my poor thin neck, raised my tail a little, and threw out my legs as well as I could, for they were very stiff.

"What is the lowest you will take for him?" said the farmer as I came back.

"Five pounds, sir; the lowest price my master set."

"'Tis a speculation," said the old gentleman, shaking his head, but at the same time slowly drawing out his purse, "quite a speculation! Have you any more business here?" he said, counting the sovereigns into his hand.

"No, sir, I can take him to the inn, if you please."

"Do so, I am now going there."

They walked forward, and I was led behind. The boy could hardly control his delight, and the old gentleman seemed to enjoy his pleasure. I had a good feed at the inn, and was then gently ridden home by a servant of my new master's and turned into a large meadow with a shed in one corner of it.

Mr. Thoroughgood, for that was the name of my benefactor, gave orders that I should have hay and oats every night and morning, and the run of the meadow during the day, and "You, Willie," said he, "must take the oversight of him. I give him in charge to you."

The boy was proud of his charge, and undertook it in all seriousness. There was not a day when he did not pay me a visit, sometimes picking me out among the other horses, and giving me a bit of carrot, or something good, or sometimes standing by me while I ate my oats. He always came with kind words and caresses, and of course I grew very fond of him. He called me Old Crony, as I used to come to him in the field and follow him about. Sometimes he brought his grandfather, who always looked closely at my legs.

"This is our point, Willie," he would say. "But he is improving so steadily that I think we shall see a change for the better in the spring."

The perfect rest, the good food, the soft turf, and exercise soon began to tell on my condition and my spirits. I had a good constitution from my mother, and I was never strained when I was young, so that I had a better chance than many horses who have been worked before they came to their full strength.

During the winter my legs improved so much that I began to feel quite young again. The spring came round, and one day in March Mr. Thoroughgood determined that he would try me in the phaeton. I was well pleased, and he and Willie drove me a few miles. My legs were not stiff now, and I did the work with perfect ease.

"He's growing young, Willie. We must give him a little gentle work now, and by midsummer he will be as good as Ladybird. He has a beautiful mouth, and good paces; they can't be better."

"Oh! grandpapa, how glad I am you bought him!"

"So am I, my boy, but he has to thank you more than me; we must now be looking out for a quiet, genteel place for him, where he will be valued."

My Last Home

One day during this summer the groom cleaned and dressed me with such extraordinary care that I thought some new change must be at hand; he trimmed my fetlocks and legs, passed the tarbrush over my hoofs, and even parted my forelock. I think the harness had an extra polish. Willie seemed half anxious, half merry, as he got into the chaise with his grandfather.

"If the ladies take to him," said the old gentleman, "they'll be suited, and he'll be suited. We can but try."

At the distance of a mile or two from the village we came to a pretty, low house, with a lawn and shrubbery at the front and a drive up to the door. Willie rang the bell, and asked if Miss Blomefield or Miss Ellen was at home. Yes, they were. So, while Willie stayed with me, Mr. Thoroughgood went into the house. In about ten minutes he returned, followed by three ladies; one tall, pale lady, wrapped in a white shawl, leaned on a younger lady, with dark eyes and a merry face; the other, a very stately looking person, was Miss Blomefield. They all came and looked at me and asked questions. The younger lady—that was Miss Ellen—took to me very much; she said she was sure she should like me; I had such a good face. The tall, pale lady said that she should always be nervous in riding behind a horse that had once been down, as I might come down again, and if I did, she should never get over the fright.

"You see, ladies," said Mr. Thoroughgood, "many first-rate horses have had their knees broken through the carelessness of their drivers, without any fault of their own, and from what I see of this horse, I should say, that is his case; but of course I do not wish to influence you. If you incline, you can have him on trial, and then your coachman will see what he thinks of him."

"You have always been such a good adviser to us about our horses," said the stately lady, "that your recommendation would go a long way with me, and if my sister Lavinia sees no objection, we will accept your offer of a trial, with thanks."

It was then arranged that I should be sent for the next day.

In the morning a smart-looking young man came for me. At first he looked pleased; but when he saw my knees he said in a disappointed voice:

"I didn't think, sir, you would have recommended my ladies a blemished horse like that."

"Handsome is that handsome does," said my master. "You are only taking him on trial, and I am sure you will do fairly by him, young man, and if he is not as safe as any horse you ever drove, send him back."

I was led home, placed in a comfortable stable, fed, and left to myself. The next day, when my groom was cleaning my face, he said:

"That is just like the star that Black Beauty had; he is much the same height too. I wonder where he is now."

A little further on he came to the place in my neck where I was bled, and where a little knot was left in the skin. He almost started, and began to look me over carefully, talking to himself.

"White star in the forehead, one white foot on the off side, this little knot just in that place"—then looking at the middle of my back—"and as I am alive, there is that little patch of white hair that John used to call 'Beauty's threepenny bit.' It must be Black Beauty! Why, Beauty! Beauty! do you know me? little Joe Green that almost killed you?" And he began patting and patting me as if he was quite overjoyed.

I could not say that I remembered him, for now he was a fine grown young fellow, with black whiskers and a man's voice, but I was sure he knew me, and that he was Joe Green, and I was very glad. I put my nose up to him, and tried to say that we were friends. I never saw a man so pleased.

"Give you a fair trial! I should think so indeed! I wonder who the rascal was that broke your knees, my old Beauty! You must have been badly served out somewhere; well, well, it won't be my fault if you haven't good times of it now. I wish John Manly was here to see you."

In the afternoon I was put into a low park chair and brought to the door. Miss Ellen was going to try me, and Green went with her. I soon found that she was a good driver, and she seemed pleased with my paces. I heard Joe telling her about me, and that he was sure I was Squire Gordon's old Black Beauty.

When we returned, the other sisters came out to hear how I had behaved myself. She told them what she had just heard, and said:

"I shall certainly write to Mrs. Gordon, and tell her that her favorite horse has come to us. How pleased she will be!"

After this I was driven every day for a week or so, and as I appeared to be quite safe, Miss Lavinia at last ventured out in the small close carriage. After this it was quite decided to keep me and call me by my old name of "Black Beauty."

I have now lived in this happy place a whole year. Joe is the best and kindest of grooms. My work is easy and pleasant, and I feel my strength and spirits all coming back again. Mr. Thoroughgood said to Joe the other day:

"In your place he will last till he is twenty years old—perhaps more."

Willie always speaks to me when he can, and treats me as his special friend. My ladies have promised that I shall never be sold, and so I have nothing to fear; and here my story ends. My troubles are all over, and I am at home; and often before I am quite awake, I fancy I am still in the orchard at Birtwick, standing with my old friends under the apple trees.

6

Androcles and the Lion

Retold by Louis Untermeyer

Androcles is a slave sentenced to death for escaping from his master. This is the story of how the kindness he has shown is returned to him in an unexpected way.

Androcles was a slave. His father had been a slave, and so had his grandfather. All his family had come to accept slavery as something which they had to endure. But not Androcles. He hated being overworked and underfed; he loathed the idea that the masters not only compelled the slaves to labor endlessly without payment but that they held the power of life and death over their unhappy serving men who were treated worse than dogs. Dogs and horses were well cared for. Most of all, Androcles hated confinement. He loved the idea of liberty; he did not dare plan for it, but he never stopped dreaming about a day of freedom.

One day the dream became reality. It was a spring morning when Androcles could no longer bear the hardships and cruelties of his condition. Working in the field he somehow managed to break the chain that held him. He knew that there was little chance for an escaping slave; he knew that if one were captured he would be tortured and put to death as an example to other slaves. But, without further thought and against all reason, he ran away.

He ran all day and all night—ran without stopping to eat or drink—ran from the fields into the forest—ran until he could run no more. Exhausted, he sank into lifelessness, but just before losing consciousness, he realized, with the instinct of an animal, that he must find shelter somewhere. Dragging himself along the ground he saw a hole among the rocks, crept in, and fell asleep.

When he woke he could not tell where he was; it was even hard for him to recognize himself. Briars had torn his clothes to rags; there was blood where his body had been scratched by thorns, bruises where he had run against boughs, a swelling where a stone had struck his ankle. He could tell it was nearly dawn, for a thin light trickled through the branches that framed the hole, and the birds were waking each other. Raising himself, he saw he had crawled into a cavern and, from the strong smell which penetrated his nostrils, he knew it was a cave belonging to some animal. "I could scarcely have chosen a worse place," he thought. "I must not stay here another minute." He rose shakily to his feet and stumbled toward the light. Then he was aware that the light had gone. A monstrous form had blacked out the opening.

It was a huge lion returning from his nightly hunt. He stood there roaring. "This is the end," thought Androcles. "Too bad it had to come so soon. But," he added with painful philosophy, "I'd rather be eaten, especially if the creature is as hungry as I am, than be tortured to death."

The lion continued to roar, but he did not spring; he did not even show his teeth. Slowly it occurred to Androcles that it was not a roar of anger but a roar of pain, an almost plaintive roar, more of a moan than a menace.

"Is something hurting you?" inquired Androcles politely.

The lion groaned.

"I thought so," said Androcles in a consoling tone. "Let's see what it is."

The lion lifted a great hairy paw.

"Oh," sympathized Androcles, "that's it—a long, nasty thorn. No wonder you're crying. I'm surprised you can walk."

The lion, full of self-pity, moaned again. He moved a step closer.

"Now, don't be frightened," said Androcles who was still trembling. "We'll see what we can do. It is going to hurt a little, but you must—er—grit your teeth. No biting, remember, and keep your claws to yourself. Now let's have the poor foot."

The lion, whimpering softly, held out the injured paw. Androcles took it in his hand, stroked it for a moment, and then tugged at the thorn. The lion pulled back and let out another roar, this time a roar of unmistakable rage.

"Now, now," said Androcles, "you mustn't talk like that to the doctor. You must be a big, brave lion, not a cowardly little cub. We'll have it all out the next try. Once more, now—ready?" Androcles' fingers tightened around the thorn, the lion held still, his eyes shut, and suddenly the thorn was out.

"There," said Androcles, as the lion shook himself. "It didn't hurt so much, did it? Now let's see how it feels when you walk."

Gingerly the lion put the sore paw upon the ground; then he took a step or two; then he bounded up to Androcles and licked his face.

Life with the lion was a continual pleasure. There was no question as to who was the master and who was the slave; there was not even a distinction between man and beast. They were companions, friends in the forest, safe, secure, and serene in their happiness. They were well nourished with a variety of food. Every morning the lion would bring home his kill—a plump rabbit, a young deer, a wild turkey—and Androcles would catch fish and gather berries, which he taught the lion to like. It was a rare thing, this understanding between a naturally wild creature and the man who had gone back to nature. The two were united by a bond of mutual respect and something close to love. They roamed the woods, swam streams and, after Androcles had cooked the meal, sat about the fire together. Androcles talked, and the lion listened attentively, purring to show he agreed with every word.

Things went on like this for a long while—a year, two years, three years, Androcles could not tell, for he had stopped counting the days. Then the companionship came to a sudden end. One afternoon he was tempted to stray a little beyond the forest toward an orchard where fruit was ripening. It was then he heard a sound that alarmed him more than the roaring of any animal. It was the sound of human voices, and Androcles turned to run to the cave which had become his home and his haven. But it was too late. There were six armed men searching for fugitive slaves. They spread out, cut off his retreat, and without a struggle, captured him.

"A dirty-looking specimen," grumbled the leader. "More like a beast than a man. I've half a mind to let him go. No one would want him around the house, not even the workrooms."

"There can't be too many slaves, and we can't be too particular about them," said one of the other men. "Besides, those who aren't fit for work can be used for sport in the arena."

"That's so," replied the leader. "The Emperor has just declared another big holiday—free bread and circuses for everybody—and," he laughed unpleasantly, "free food for the wild beasts in the Colosseum."

And they snapped the chains on Androcles.

The Colosseum was crowded to the last seat; fifty thousand spectators had come to witness their favorite spectacle. They had been promised a gala Roman holiday, and they cheered lustily when the Emperor, robed in purple, entered the royal platform and seated himself on the imperial couch. All the first-ranking nobles were there: Senators, Pontiffs, Magistrates, and the holy Vestals. The Emperor raised his hand and the performance began.

First there was a parade to dazzle the eye and indicate the excitement to come. At the head of the procession, accompanied by a military band, marched the Praetorian Guard, the Emperor's own soldiers, clad in scarlet embroidered with gold. There followed the captains of the regular army in shining armor, troops from occupied territories, regiments newly arrived from abroad carrying their trophies, embattled veterans and beardless young volunteers. Another band separated the conquerors from the conquered—prisoners of foreign wars, men and women to be put to work, traitors and captured slaves to be put to death. Some shambled past, with their eyes on the dust; others, in spite of the chains, carried their heads high; but all knew that the drums were pronouncing their doom. This was the part of the spectacle that the crowd enjoyed least; although it displayed the power of Rome, people were glad when it was over and the gay part of the pageant was resumed.

There was a new burst of music as the gladiators swept into the amphitheatre. Those on foot flourished their swords and bucklers; those in chariots whipped up the horses, while their brilliantly colored scarves streamed into the wind. Then came the other combatants: fighters carrying daggers or short swords; retiarii with nets to entangle their victims and with tridents to stab them; fire-throwers; spear-hurlers; lancers; archers with bows and arrows.

Last of all came the beasts: elephants who were to be pitted against horned rhinoceri; bears that were trained to attack buffalo; wild horses that were to be matched against savage boars; bulls that were to be goaded and killed by men brandishing pieces of red cloth. The only animals missing were the lions—these were too ferocious to be let loose, for they had been confined in dark pits and starved for days to make them more bloodthirsty.

There was a fanfare of trumpets and the parade stopped. All the combatants faced the Emperor's box and, raising their right hands, cried as with one voice: "Hail, Caesar! We who are ready to die salute thee!"

Then the games began. They began harmlessly enough with a series of chariot races—the deadly gladiatorial combats were always kept for the climax—and the spectators cheered their favorites. Every charioteer had his group of admirers; even the horses had their ardent followers. Exhibitions of skill and danger came next: Egyptians who juggled naked swords, swords that were so sharpened that they would cut to the bone; wrestlers whose bodies were smeared with oil and who fought in a small square lined with knives; boxers wearing brass knuckles studded with nails; bowmen who used small torches instead of arrows, and whose targets were human beings.

An intermission allowed black attendants to mop up the blood, strew fresh sand, carry off the dead and dying, while the onlookers refreshed themselves with wine and sweet drinks. Then, as a diversion before the struggles of beast against beast, a few runaway slaves were to be thrown to the lions. The first of those chosen was Androcles.

Thrust into the middle of the colossal arena, he stood helpless. He had been given a cudgel, but it was so pitiful a defense against a starved and ravening lion that it seemed an added cruelty. He stood up straight—at least he would not die like a slave groveling on the ground. He heard a gate being swung back on its hinges, and he closed his eyes. He heard a tremendous roar, but he did not see the lion that was looking for its prey. He did not see the leaps with which the lion sprang furiously across the sand, nor did he understand why the lion suddenly stopped and the spectators grew quiet. In the hush he was aware of a curious sniffing and he felt something rubbing his ankles. He opened his eyes—and could not believe them. For there was the lion—his lion—brushing a paw against his clothes, fawning on him, standing up to lick his face, purring and rolling over with joy.

The crowd went wild. "Magnificent!" "Marvelous!" "A miracle!" they shouted, holding out their fists with the thumbs pressed back to show that the man's life should be spared. The Emperor stood up. A life, especially the life of a slave, lost or saved, meant nothing to him, but he liked the approval of the crowd.

"Come here," he called to Androcles. "You are either a brave man or a lucky one. Or you are a magician. It does not matter to me. But it seems to matter to my people. They want you to live. You shall be my Chief Keeper of Animals."

"Oh, your majesty, I couldn't do that," said Androcles. "Thank you all the same, but I couldn't. I—I am afraid of animals."

The Emperor smiled. "That is amusing enough to earn you something extra. This great beast here acts as though he were your loyal, long-lost dog. Would you, perhaps, like to be set up in business as a caretaker and doctor of pets? It's a pleasant way of living, I'm told, and profitable, too."

"Thank you again, your majesty, but no. There's only one thing I would like to do."

"And what is that?" asked the Emperor.

"I would like to go back to the forest, and live there—with the lion, of course."

"If that is all—and it is little enough—you are free to go, free in every sense. The gods have been kind to a slave, and I, who do their bidding, can do no less. Go," said the Emperor, "and our protection goes with you."

Not as a master and his creature, but side by side, Androcles and the lion walked out of the Colosseum. Through the streets of Rome they went, across the fields and, quickening their pace, into the forest.

Responsibility

A study conducted by Harvard University researchers followed the lives of a group of boys as they grew from childhood to adulthood. They found that the factor which best predicted success and happiness in adult life was having regular chores to do as a boy. These men could handle life's large responsibilities because they had learned to accept smaller responsibilities when young. Of course, adults aren't the only ones with large responsibilities. Sometimes young people have to shoulder heavy obligations, as in the case of the boy in *Old Yeller* or the even younger boy in *All Alone*.

Chores and other duties often seem irksome when we are young, but as we mature and better understand the reasons for them, we become more likely to voluntarily undertake obligations. One thing we come to realize is that responsibility is really a way of showing our love for others. When we take a burden on our shoulders—for instance, by helping our parents—we are taking a burden off of someone else. This is the meaning of old sayings such as "deeds speak louder than words" and "charity begins at home." In other words, it's easy to feel love and talk about love, but the proof of love is in deeds. And one of the best places to prove our love for humanity is by starting at home to help those in our family who need our help right now. But, of course, charity shouldn't end at home. As the boy, Marcel, understands in *All Alone,* we also have a responsibility to our neighbor when he needs our help.

Responsibility also means a willingness to accept accountability for our actions and not to blame our misdeeds on others. One thing we need to guard against is the fact that our sense of responsibility often gets watered down in crowds. Sometimes we do things we shouldn't do because "everyone else is doing it." In school we might make fun of or exclude another student because others are doing it. In adult life men and women sometimes let peer pressure push them into cowardly behavior, like standing by and doing nothing while others are being persecuted or joining in the persecution themselves.

One other thing worth knowing is that irresponsibility sometimes appears in a charming guise. Irresponsible people often have winning personalities. Particularly at first, they seem appealing and attractive. A good example can be found in *Black Beauty*. One of Beauty's grooms is a man named Alfred Smirk, "a tall, good-looking fellow" who, unfortunately for Beauty, is more interested in grooming himself than the horse. He spends much time fixing his hair, moustache, and tie but neglects to clean Beauty's feet or tend to his shoes or change his hay, with the result that Beauty becomes seriously lame. Yet everyone thought "he was a very nice young man, and that Mr. Barry was very fortunate to meet with him. I should say he was the laziest, most conceited fellow I ever came near." You will find an even more seductive example of attractive irresponsibility in the character of Uncle Josh in *A Dog on Barkham Street*.

7

All Alone

Claire Huchet Bishop

"Each man for himself" is the motto of the village of Monestier. As young Marcel goes off to guard the family cows, his father reminds him: "Now, listen. You keep the cows on the Little Giant pasture, and don't talk to anyone—to anyone, do you hear me? And you have nothing to do with other cows but your own. That brings trouble. . . ." But now Marcel is high up on the mountain pasture and his neighbor needs help.

Marcel had been up on the Little Giant pasture for a whole week already. Every day had been the same—the heat, the watch, the lack of sleep, and, early in the morning, the cold. Only now at least he could make a little fire after dawn, as there was enough cows' dung to burn. During the day Marcel made the rounds, spotted the dung that was crusty on top, carefully turned it inside out to make it dry right straight through. Then, in the morning he could make a fire. He loved to see the flames going up; they were not only warmth but also life and color, even though the smell was foul.

Of Pierre he never caught a glimpse. But every night, just before the heifers made ready to settle down, Pierre began to yodel, and Marcel yodeled back. It meant "Another day is over. I am here. Good night." That's what the two boys said to each other in their call across the mountain solitude. And each time, afterward, Marcel did not feel so lonesome, and fear receded somewhat from his heart.

Papa came up on Sunday. He brought a fresh loaf of bread and cheese. He guessed Marcel would still have enough onions left, which he did.

Papa slapped Marcel on the back. "Doing all right, eh? You lucky bird! Nothing to do all day long but to look at cows and eat like a king. Think of it! To feast on bread, onion, and cheese every day, three times a day, instead of mush. I would not mind being a shepherd boy all over again myself. Well, I can see we still have our three cows. None of them has gone over the ridge so far, or sprained her ankle, or wandered away. And they seem to fare well. They'll be beauties by the end of the summer. Our fortune, my boy, the family's fortune! By the way, you did not have anything to do with that Pierre Pascal, did you? You did not visit with him, I hope," said Papa with a frown.

"No, Papa."

"And, at the torrent, when you take the animals to drink—?"

"I did not see him. Nobody was there. Ever."

"Good. Just as well. The moment you start mingling with anyone something goes wrong. As I told you before, keep to yourself, attend strictly to your own affairs, no matter what happens pay no attention to your neighbor's business—that's his own worry, isn't it? That way, if anything goes wrong, nobody can put the blame on anybody else, can they? Every man for himself, that's the way we have to be in Monestier."

Marcel did not say anything. He was familiar with Monestier's way. How could he explain to Papa that he, Marcel, felt different? Papa would say it was nonsense. Ideas, he would call it. If Papa knew, for instance, about the yodeling at night, he might even get very angry. Besides, it might sound sissy to him, just as if Marcel were afraid.

"You are not afraid, are you, at night, Marcel?" asked Papa suddenly.

"Not a bit," said Marcel, straightening up and puffing his chest. "Not a bit."

"Ah! Ah! Ah!" roared Papa, laughing. "Your father's son all right, eh? And how! Afraid of nothing, by golly, not even of lying! Ah! Ah! Ah!" And he gave Marcel a big shove which sent him sprawling on the ground. He got up, red in the face and confused, but already Papa was after him again, still chuckling, and they both had a good, rough tussle, tumbling over the grass.

When Papa got up he was serious again. "I have been a shepherd boy up here too, understand? I know. The first season is the hardest. But you'll be all right, Marcel. Well, I have to start back now. Remember—the heifers, the family's fortune. Good-by, my boy, good-by. Keep it up, keep it up. Such is life."

Next day, as the sun rose, Marcel noticed clouds gathering far away, behind Mont Blanc, the highest peak of the Alps. Gradually through the morning they worked their way up the sky. The air was heavy and sultry. In the afternoon, when Marcel tucked his head under the rhododendron bush, the heat was unbearable, and for a few minutes, try as hard as he could, he was overcome by sleep.

He dreamed that his cows had split in two—two Virginias, two Geraldines, two Eunices—and that he, Marcel, kept running like mad after this suddenly increased flock to keep it from falling off the ridge. Such terror gripped his heart that he woke up shrieking, and as he did he quickly raised his head to look at his cows. His eyes nearly popped out. There were indeed two Virginias, two Geraldines, and two Eunices. He got up, pinched himself. But no, it was no longer a dream; in his pasture were now six cows. Whom did the extra three belong to? Marcel eyed their bells shining brilliantly in the sun. Copper bells! Only Pascal had such. So here were Pierre's cows gone astray. What was Marcel going to do? What was he supposed to do?

Papa's words rang in his ears. "Pay no attention to your neighbor's business." It's his own worry. So the thing to do, evidently, was to shoo Pierre's animals off the Mabout pasture as quickly as possible. Marcel started toward the first heifer. He would shoo them off in the direction of the torrent and trust that they would find their way back to the Big Giant. Probably Pierre was asleep. Too bad. He, Marcel, was very glad that they were not his own cows which had gone astray while he slept. God only knows where they might have wandered, getting lost, spraining their legs, or falling off a ridge. You never knew what could happen to cows left to themselves. . . . Marcel stopped short in his tracks. What would happen to Pierre's heifers once Marcel had shooed them off his pasture? Would they go back to the Big Giant? How could he be sure of that? He could not. It was impossible for him to accompany them even so far as the torrent. So there was absolutely no telling what they would do, once alone.

Marcel snatched a blade of grass and, biting it, sat down and eyed the cows. What about his keeping the stray heifers until Pierre came to look for them? He was bound to do so, sooner or later. Later? That was it. Suppose Pierre slept for the rest of the afternoon? Well, it would be a little harder on Marcel—but, just the same, no harm would come to the cows, while if he shooed them off—No harm? And what about their getting into trouble right on the Mabout pasture? And what about Marcel's own cows? Suppose one of them slipped while he was busy with Pierre's cows. The family's fortune! Marcel got up again. Better shoo Pierre's cows off. But that amounted to sending them to their doom. He tried to say that it did not, that whatever happened to them, once off his pasture, was not his business—that it would be Pierre's fault, the result of his negligence. Didn't he, Marcel, know well about it himself? Hadn't he been asleep a few minutes ago? Suppose his own cows had wandered off to the Big Giant?

Marcel went on arguing—to keep Pierre's cows, not to keep them? . . . Papa? Well, after all, Papa had not said anything about what to do in this particular case, had he? One thing was clear—if Marcel shooed the cows off there was but one chance in ten of Pierre's finding them safe and sound; whereas if Marcel kept them—But what about the family's fortune? It was going to be awfully hard to look after six cows. "Well"—Marcel braced himself up—"I've got to do it. That's all."

It turned out to be much harder than he had expected. It was always nerve-racking to look after the three Mabout cows, but it was nothing compared to looking after six heifers, three of which he did not know, on the relatively small expanse of the Mabout pasture. All afternoon Marcel had to keep a keen eye on them all, anticipating their moves and whims, calling quietly, "La! La! La!" to make them stop, and "Haro! Haro! Ta! Ta! Ta!" to round them up, over and over again, toward the center of the pasture. The dreaded ridge had never looked so near! More than once he was tempted to give up the job and send Pierre's heifers to their fate, whatever it might be. But he did not. He would stick it out, though he was exhausted by the watch and the constant mortal fear that one of the animals would sneak away by herself and fall off the ledge while he was busy with the others. Besides, they were all nervous and fidgety—probably because of the heavy atmosphere, and also because they were not used to one another. Geraldine especially seemed to consider it an occasion for playful scudding about, and she charged Pierre's cows repeatedly, head down. Marcel, trying to stop her, barely dodged her horns several times, and meanwhile all the other heifers got excited and skipped all over the place, to the terror of Marcel, who nevertheless had to keep his wits about him and firmly but gently call them and quiet them down.

And still Pierre did not come. It was a harrowing afternoon for Marcel. It seemed to him it would never end, that it had been going on forever. It was like a nightmare.

As the day wore on and Pierre did not appear, Marcel's anxiety grew. He would have to take it upon himself to bring the whole herd down to drink, and what a ticklish job that would be! He decided that the best he could do was to give himself plenty of time to go down. He would start much earlier than his usual time. It would make no difference to Pierre's cows, who probably were used to an early drinking time, since Marcel had never met them at the torrent and the way back to the Big Giant was much longer than the stretch back to the Little Giant. And as for his own heifers, with the heat and the excitement of this afternoon they too would welcome the chance to go down sooner. Yes, that was the best arrangement, he thought. If he waited until his usual time, and Pierre had not showed up, he still would have to take the whole herd down to drink—but then it would be too late to do it leisurely, and Marcel did not trust himself to handle the whole herd quickly when going down the steep bank.

He had no difficulty in rounding up the animals. They were indeed all very willing to go down. Carefully, slowly, his heart in his mouth at every step, Marcel took the herd down the two-mile stretch. And all the while his anxiety mounted. Would he meet Pierre? And if he did not—? When the pool came into view he was scared to look at it. And when he did Pierre was not there—but there was a cow drinking; and as Marcel came down he saw she had a copper bell. What a relief! It was Pierre's cow. Pierre must be not far away—probably looking for his other cows upstream and worrying to death. Marcel wanted to shout—but no, he would keep quiet and give Pierre a big surprise when he came back.

Marcel eyed the cows with pride and joy, Here they were, Pierre's cows, safe and sound—and, for that matter, so were the Mabout cows. Nobody seemed the worse for helping. Of course it had been a dreadful afternoon, but Marcel had well nigh forgotten it as he stood there, surrounded by all the cows. There were footsteps across the bank, and Pierre appeared, wild-eyed, an intensely worried expression on his face. All of a sudden he caught sight of his heifers. He shrieked happily, waved his hand, and started to run. Marcel smiled back broadly and extended his arms as if he were taking in the whole herd. And as he did so Pierre seemed to check himself; a dark look spread over Pierre's face, and as he slowly reached the other side of the pool his mouth was set and his eyes hard.

"So," he snarled, "you are the one who took my cows?"

"I did not take them!" retorted Marcel. "They came over to my place."

"Everybody knows that kind of story," sputtered Pierre. "You just managed to lure them away, didn't you?"

"I did not!" protested Marcel, indignant.

"You did!" shouted Pierre.

"I did not!"

"You did! My father told me right—that I should have nothing to do with you."

"*My* father told *me* right—that I should have nothing to do with you!"

"But you did, didn't you? Are my three cows with you or aren't they?"

And with that, both boys bent down quickly, picked up small stones, and started to throw them at each other. They ducked, picked up new stones, threw, ducked again. Pebbles, aimed short, rained into the water. The drinking cows raised their heads, splashed around uneasily, bumped into each other. And suddenly Eunice slipped. "Oh!" shrieked Marcel, stopping abruptly, a stone in his hand. He let it go at once as he rushed to Eunice. Gently he led her away, out of the water, eagerly watching her feet. No, thank God! She was all right. He shuddered—the family's fortune! Anger swelled within him. He turned around and faced Pierre, who had remained motionless, a stone in his hand, on the other side of the pool.

"You silly fool!" shrieked Marcel, shaking his fist. "See what you are doing? I wish I had shooed off your dirty cows when they came to my place. My father was right! It does not pay to lend a hand; you always get the blame. I wish I had let the darned animals wander off by themselves and lose their way—and break their necks, for all I care! But I warn you, don't ever fall asleep again, because there won't be any next time with me for your ill-starred beasts. If I ever set eyes on them again in my pasture you'll never get another chance of finding them with me. I'll shoo them off all right, and no mistake. Take back your precious cows, and go back to sleep, you good-for-nothing soft sissy shepherd!" And Marcel spat into the torrent. Then he called his own heifers, turned his back, and started to climb up the slope toward the Little Giant.

"Wait!" cried Pierre as he gathered his strength, jumped clean over the pool, and landed next to Marcel. "How did you know I was asleep?"

"Leave me alone!" grunted Marcel, walking on.

"Why did you do it?" went on Pierre, stepping on beside him. "Why did you not shoo my heifers off? It was your right to do so! Everybody in Monestier would have done so. In fact, you *should* have done so. Why didn't you?"

"You were asleep," grunted Marcel again, still walking on.

"How did you know I was asleep?" asked Pierre, putting himself squarely in front of Marcel.

"You asked that once already," said Marcel impatiently, trying to bypass Pierre. "You just can't guess, can you?"

He raised his angry face toward Pierre. The boys looked at each other—and they burst out laughing.

"Go back to sleep, you good-for-nothing soft sissy shepherd!" chanted Pierre with a twinkle in his eyes. And they both laughed again and pushed each other away playfully.

"Listen," went on Pierre, "it was mighty good of you. Mighty good. Nobody else would have done it. Nobody." He extended his hand. Marcel took it. "I nearly went crazy when I woke up and found three out of four gone. Never expected to see them again, except maimed or dead. Must have been awfully difficult to look after so many on your small pasture—and how did you manage to bring them all down?"

"That's why I had to start so early," said Marcel.

"Yes," said Pierre, "that was the only safe thing to do. Well, *mon vieux,* thanks, and if you are ever in trouble you can count on me too. Say, you don't yodel badly at all. I've had more practice at it because it's my second year up here. But you are good."

"Really?" asked Marcel, beaming. "About yodeling—and everything else—I won't tell my father—"

"'Course," said Pierre. "I won't tell mine either, cross my heart. It's between us boys. Grownups, they never understand. . . ."

8

A Dog on Barkham Street

M. S. Stolz

Edward Frost desperately wants a dog, but his parents think he is too irresponsible. When his footloose uncle visits, bringing along the perfect dog, Edward is delighted. No one could ask for a better dog or a better uncle. But Edward's initial infatuation with Uncle Josh's wandering lifestyle is soon put to the test.

"What's her name?" said Rod, leaning forward to look in the dog's face. She licked his nose and he smiled with rapture.

"Argess."

"How do you spell it?"

"I don't know."

"She's beautiful."

"She sure is," said Edward.

"How long's she going to be with you?"

"As long as my Uncle Josh is."

"How long's that?"

"He said quite a while."

"Crums," said Rod, and grew silent.

But though the boys were content to sit, each with a hand in her thick fur, and look at her, Argess soon grew restless. She got up and started for the hall, whimpering a little, her nails pattering on the linoleum.

"Looking for my uncle, probably," Edward decided. "She's a loyal type dog."

"Not a one-man dog," Rod said. "One-man dogs are vicious. A collie is never a vicious dog."

"Oh, no," said Edward. "After she gets to know me, she'll like me. And you, too," he added kindly. "You're around so much she'll get to know you, too."

"I'll probably be around plenty, from now on," said Rod. Edward wasn't sure whether this was altogether because of Argess, or partly because of the people who were going to be filling up Rod's house.

Argess by now was in the living room, where Mrs. Frost and her brother were sitting. She trotted to the man, lay down beside him in a composed, possessive way, and was still. The boys stood in the doorway, Rod simply watching the dog with loving eyes, Edward waiting to see what his mother would say to an animal in the living room. What she would say, in fact, to the whole idea of an animal in her house. He didn't see how she could ask Argess to leave without asking her brother to leave, too. On the other hand, the dog question was very big in his family, and so was his mother's insistence that there was not to be one until Edward got more responsible.

He felt in his heart and in his bones responsibility rising by the minute, but how to make his mother recognize it? He began to wish he hadn't announced, over and over in the past, that the sense of duty was now so strong in him that there really wasn't room for anything else. No one believed him, and he had to admit there wasn't much reason why they should. "Your sense of duty," his father had said, "usually lifts its shy head when you want something, and then disappears immediately, whether you get what you want or you don't. Not very reliable, now is it?"

Edward felt a lot of sympathy for that boy in the fable who'd cried, "Wolf, wolf. . . ."

Everyone but Uncle Josh was looking at the dog. He was looking fondly around the room, as a man will who returns to a loved place after a long absence.

"She's a very quiet dog, isn't she?" Mrs. Frost said at last.

"Eh? Oh, Argess," said Uncle Josh. "Yes. She has dignity. Odd, in such a young dog. Does it bother you? That I have her, I mean?"

"The dog doesn't bother me," Mrs. Frost said slowly. She glanced at the two boys, who sidled into the room and sat down, as if in class. "I like dogs. What bothers me is that we—Edward and his father and I—have discussed this matter for . . . oh, for years. And Edward knows that he is not to have a dog yet. He isn't old enough."

"I had a dog when I was six," said Uncle Josh.

Edward and Rod glanced at each other.

"You had the dog, and Mother took care of it," Mrs. Frost said tartly. "I don't want to take care of Edward's dog. I want him to. It has something to do with character."

"Oh well, character," said Uncle Josh with a smile. "I wouldn't know anything about that."

Mrs. Frost just looked at him, not speaking.

"Still," Uncle Josh went on, sounding a little uncomfortable, "Argess here is not Edward's dog. I suppose she's mine."

"Suppose?"

"Let's say we met up and we're traveling together. I don't like to *own* anything, you know that. Especially something living. I don't even like the word 'own.'"

"I know," said Mrs. Frost, and added, "But you will take care of her?"

"Oh, now—" said Uncle Josh. He put a hand down and gently massaged the collie's head. "I'll feed her, if that's what you mean. Have up till now. No reason why I should stop."

"But, Josh, a dog in a suburban house requires more taking care of than merely feeding. For one thing, they have to be walked."

"Walked! I don't have to help Argess *walk*."

"Dogs aren't permitted to run loose in this town."

Uncle Josh looked horrified, and then indignant. "I never heard of such a thing. What sort of community have you got yourself into? Won't let dogs run. Why I—"

"There are very good reasons for it," said Mrs. Frost. She sounded exactly as if she were explaining a rule to Edward. "They destroy people's gardens, they frighten small children, sometimes they bite. And we live in a very *nice* community, Josh, which Ed and I happen to like and want to live in. Peacefully. Without violating rules. Argess can't run loose. You do understand, don't you?"

"All right, all right," said Uncle Josh, his brows drawn down. *"Walked,"* he repeated in a low voice. "Never heard of such a thing."

Edward, unable to keep still another second, burst out, "Mom, lookit, I got a great idea. Let *me* take care of Argess. I mean, walk her and feed her, and you know—take *care* of her. I can practice on her. And then you'll see if I've got some responsibility, huh?"

"I'll help," said Rod. "I'll get up every morning at five o'clock and come over here and help walk her, and my mother can see, too. I mean, about *my* responsibility."

"I never heard so much about responsibility in my whole life before," said Uncle Josh.

"I didn't think you'd heard about it at all," said Mrs. Frost. She looked at the boys, at her brother, and flushed a little. "I'm sorry. I shouldn't have said that."

"Perfectly all right with me," said Uncle Josh. But Rod and Edward, defensive for this wonderful man, were reproachfully silent.

Mrs. Frost sighed and got to her feet. "I have to leave. I hate to, on your first morning, Josh, but this is my morning at the Visiting Nurse Association. I can hardly back out at the last minute."

"Of *course* not," said Uncle Josh warmly. "More of your volunteer stuff?"

"Yes," said Mrs. Frost. She stood uncertainly for a moment, and then smiled at her brother. "You'll find the guest room ready." She paused, changed it to, "Your room. It's good to have you here. Argess, too. She seems to be a lovely animal. Oh, and Rod—please don't get here at five in the morning. You're welcome to help Edward practice on the dog, but not at that hour."

"Okay," said Rod. "What time shall I?"

"Work it out among you. The three of you."

"I resign in favor of the boys," said Uncle Josh. "If they're going to practice responsibility, they won't want me interfering."

Mrs. Frost opened her mouth, closed it again, then gave that half-laugh of hers, and turned to Edward. "Don't forget the errand."

"What errand?"

"If you recall, dear, you offered to ride over to Mrs. Ferris' for me and get those swatches of material. For the slipcovers I'm going to make."

"Oh, yeah. I forgot."

"Well . . . remember."

"Sure thing," said Edward, wishing she'd go, so he and Rod could talk to Uncle Josh and play with Argess. She did, after a few more words with her brother, and when she'd driven off, the two boys turned to the man, their faces alight, and waited for him to say something, anything.

What he said was, "What's all this stuff about responsibility?"

Puzzled, Edward tried to think of an answer, since Rod was clearly leaving it up to him. "I guess," he said at length, "that it's about how Rod and I don't have any. I mean, we *are* sort of careless. Leave stuff around, forget things, lose things. You know. Once I almost burned the house down."

"How?"

"Making cocoa. I forgot to turn off the gas and went away and a potholder caught fire, and then a roll of towels, and then the cabinets were starting, only Mom got here in time."

"When your mother and I were children, I once burned the roof off our house. She ever tell you about that?"

Edward shook his head. "How did you do it?"

"Oh . . . it was pretty simple. Sort of simpleminded, too, I'll have to admit. I put a magnifying glass in the rain gutter. It was full of dry leaves, and it hadn't rained for weeks, so there wasn't a bit of moisture anywhere. The sun burned right through that glass and set the leaves on fire, which was what I was trying to see if it would do, and it did all right. Only I'd forgotten it was there and had gone off somewhere or other. Like you. Burned the whole darned roof. Funny thing, it was your mother came home that time, too, and caught it and called the fire department before the whole place went. You sure she never told you about it?"

Privately, Edward thought that this was the last sort of thing his mother would be apt to tell him. She'd be too afraid he'd try it himself. She'd be wrong, of course. Probably.

He realized that his Uncle Josh took it for granted that he was talked about in the family. He'd be awfully hurt if he knew that he was practically never mentioned at all. Edward felt resentful toward his parents for this.

"No," he said. "She never mentioned that."

"What sort of things does she tell you about me?"

"Oh . . . just things. You know. Like . . . well, she says I'm an awful lot like you."

"Does she?" said Uncle Josh, sounding pleased. "I'm flattered."

"So'm I," said Edward proudly. He was getting fonder of his uncle every second, and madder at his parents.

"Say . . . uh . . . Mr. . . ." Rod, who'd been petting Argess all this time, looked up at Edward's uncle inquiringly.

"Name's Bowdoin. But you might as well call me Uncle Josh, same as Edward here. Mister doesn't sit too comfortably in my ear."

"Okay, Uncle Josh," Rod said happily. "Thanks."

"Rod's an uncle, too," Edward said.

"Are you now," said Uncle Josh. "You made it early."

"Yup," said Rod. "I've got a nephew and a niece."

"That must make you proud."

"Yes," said Rod doubtfully. "Sometimes, anyway. But they're all moving in with me. The whole shebang, except my sister's husband. He's going to Saudi Arabia."

"Arabia, eh?" said Uncle Josh dreamily.

"So there they're all going to be, everybody on top of everybody."

"Sounds like a handy houseful."

"Handy," said Rod in a bitter voice. "You know what? I gotta give up my room. It's going to be the nursery."

"What are *you* going to do?" Edward asked in outrage.

"Sewing room. They're gonna shove my bed in the sewing room. If you ask me, they'll have to stand it against the wall."

"Be quite a trick, sleeping that way," said Uncle Josh.

"That's what I said," Rod told him, grinning a little. "I said what were they going to do, tie me to bed at night?"

"What did they say?" Edward asked.

"Said it would fit. In a pig's eye, it'll fit. Or maybe just. I'll have to jump from the hall into bed. And what about my desk? That won't go in at all. Dad says it's only for six months. Where'd they get that *only* is what I want to know."

"Oh, it can seem a long time," Uncle Josh agreed.

The two boys looked at each other, then at the man who was fiddling with Argess' ears and gazing off into space. "Arabia," he murmured. "What do you know."

The boys didn't have to speak to each other to know that they were in agreement. This was the most wonderful human being they had ever met. He talked to them the way they wanted to be talked to. Humorously, easily, as if everything they said was justified and everyone was equal. He didn't ask how old they were or whether they liked school. He thought it was outrageous that dogs should be chained, called responsibility "all this stuff," surrendered Argess to their care without a word. He went where he wanted to go, said what he wanted to say, and apparently didn't really do anything for a living.

Sitting beside Argess, they looked at Edward's uncle and hoped that they'd grow up to be exactly like him.

Then a morning came when Edward waited in vain for the clattering nails, the tug, the eager tongue. He lay under the sheet till he was stifled. Then he pushed it away and sat up, waiting. He wasn't allowing himself to think or be alarmed. He just waited.

And there was nothing. No sound of Argess belatedly on her way. No sound, he realized, of anything. He didn't hear his father's electric shaver, or his mother stirring about in the kitchen. He couldn't smell coffee. There wasn't a single thing to tell him it was morning, and yet—he looked at his clock to be sure—it was morning and time for everyone to be up and about. Time and way past for Argess to be here.

He got out of bed and moved into the hall in his bare feet. The door to Uncle Josh's room was closed and behind it all was quiet, so Argess couldn't be in there. He started for his parents' room, and then stopped to listen, because they were talking.

"How are we going to tell Edward?" his mother was saying. Her voice sounded tight and hurt.

"I don't know," Mr. Frost said. "I just don't know. Look, I don't understand this. He *can't* just have gone off, without a word, without an indication of where he was going or when he'd be back."

"He left that note."

"Note," said Mr. Frost. "What kind of a note is that? *It's been great, see you again.* You call that a message?"

"No. No, it isn't. But it's as much as he's ever left behind him. That's all he left last time, and you weren't this upset."

"Last time he hadn't gotten Edward to love him. And he hadn't brought a dog that Edward—that everyone loves. This is different, don't you see?"

"I see. Only Josh didn't. That's what nobody but me ever understands about Josh. He *doesn't* see. He just does what he wants. Why do you suppose I almost never talk of him? Because he can't be relied on at all, and he hurts people. He broke Mother's heart, and Dad's, when he left the first time, and he's gone on leaving just the same way ever since."

"But he *loved* Edward," Mr. Frost said, sounding angry and baffled. "I'm sure he did."

"No," said Mrs. Frost. "He's fond of him. But Josh is fond of lots of people and lots of places. Nothing ever holds him."

Edward, leaning against the wall, his eyes closed, remembered that his mother had said eavesdroppers sometimes got hurt. He hadn't believed her. I don't think I'll eavesdrop any more, he said to himself. Not any more, after this. He started back to his room, hearing his father's voice saying, "Well, then, why did he have to take the *dog?*"

Edward sat down on his bed and hunched a little against the pain inside him. Uncle Josh, who hadn't loved him, was gone. And Argess, who probably had, was gone. He tried to hate his uncle, but somehow he couldn't even do that. As his mother said, Uncle Josh just was the way he was. He sat there, remembering what a nice man he'd been to talk to, how gentle, how quick to understand. He knew all about birds, and the Grand Canyon, and he didn't ask silly questions.

I'm going to miss Uncle Josh, he thought. And then, though he was trying not to think of Argess, he thought of her, and he leaned slowly over till his face was in the pillow.

A little while later he felt his mother's hand on his shoulder, and he turned around. Both his parents were in his room, and nobody seemed to know what to say.

"You were listening to us?" Mrs. Frost said at last.

Edward nodded.

"I'm sorry."

"Look, Edward," Mr. Frost said, "we'll get you a—" He stopped, lifted his shoulders, and looked around the room as if a solution might be written on the walls somewhere.

Mrs. Frost sat on the edge of the bed. "Maybe I'd better change one thing I said. What I meant, Edward, was that your Uncle Josh loves you—but in his own way. His way isn't like other people's."

Edward gulped, sniffled, and nodded. "I know. His way is—" He didn't know what Uncle Josh's way was.

"Irresponsible," said Mrs. Frost. "He can love, but he can't be depended on."

"Then the loving doesn't matter much, does it?" Edward burst out.

"I don't know," said his mother. "All love matters, I guess. It's just that with someone like Josh people have to take what he can give and not look for what he can't." She stood up. . . . She hesitated, and looked at Edward. "I don't see anything else to do, do you?"

"No," Edward said dully. He got up.

9

Old Yeller

Fred Gipson

With his father away on a long cattle drive, fourteen-year-old Travis finds himself in charge of protecting his mother and his five-year-old brother, Arliss. When an ugly yellow dog is caught stealing meat, Travis wants to shoot it on the spot. But his mother intervenes on behalf of little Arliss, who immediately becomes attached to the dog. Eventually, Travis too is won over, and he and Yeller become fast friends. In the following scene, family and dog are endangered by a rabid wolf, and Travis is forced to make a hard decision.

It wasn't until dark came that I really began to get uneasy about Mama and Lisbeth. Then I could hardly stand it because they hadn't come home. I knew in my own mind why they hadn't: it had been late when they'd started out, they'd had a good long piece to go, and even with wood handy, it took considerable time to drag up enough for the size fire they needed.

And I couldn't think of any real danger to them. They weren't far enough away from the cabin to be lost. And if they were, Jumper knew the way home. Also, Jumper was gentle; there wasn't much chance that he'd scare and throw them off. On top of all that, they had Old Yeller along. Old Yeller might be pretty weak and crippled yet, but he'd protect them from just about anything that might come their way.

Still, I was uneasy. I couldn't help having the feeling that something was wrong. I'd have gone to see about them if it hadn't been for Little Arliss. It was past his suppertime; he was getting hungry and sleepy and fussy.

I took him and the speckled pup inside the kitchen and lit a candle. I settled them on the floor and gave them each a bowl of sweet milk into which I'd crumbled cold cornbread. In a little bit, both were eating out of the same bowl. Little Arliss knew better than that and I ought to have paddled him for doing it. But I didn't. I didn't say a word; I was too worried.

I'd just about made up my mind to put Little Arliss and the pup to bed and go look for Mama and Lisbeth when I heard a sound that took me to the door in a hurry. It was the sound of dogs fighting. The sound came from 'way out there in the dark; but the minute I stepped outside, I could tell that the fight was moving toward the cabin. Also, I recognized the voice of Old Yeller.

It was the sort of raging yell he let out when he was in a fight to the finish. It was the same savage roaring and snarling and squawling that he'd done the day he fought the killer hogs off me.

The sound of it chilled my blood. I stood, rooted to the ground, trying to think what it could be, what I ought to do.

Then I heard Jumper snorting keenly and Mama calling in a frightened voice. "Travis! Travis! Make a light, Son, and get your gun. And hurry!"

I came alive then. I hollered back at her, to let her know that I'd heard. I ran back into the cabin and got my gun. I couldn't think at first what would make the sort of light I needed, then recollected a clump of bear grass that Mama'd recently grubbed out, where she wanted to start a new fall garden. Bear grass has an oily sap that makes it burn bright and fierce for a long time. A pile of it burning would make a big light.

I ran and snatched up four bunches of the half-dried bear grass. The sharp ends of the stiff blades stabbed and stung my arms and chest as I grabbed them up. But I had no time to bother about that. I ran and dumped the bunches in a pile on the bare ground outside the yard fence, then hurried to bring a live coal from the fireplace to start them burning.

I fanned fast with my hat. The bear-grass blades started to smoking, giving off their foul smell. A little flame started, flickered and wavered for a moment, then bloomed suddenly and leaped high with a roar.

I jumped back, gun held ready, and caught my first glimpse of the screaming, howling battle that came wheeling into the circle of light. It was Old Yeller, all right, tangled with some animal as big and savage as he was.

Mama called from outside the light's rim. "Careful, Son. And take close aim; it's a big loafer wolf, gone mad."

My heart nearly quit on me. There weren't many of the gray loafer wolves in our part of the country, but I knew about them. They were big and savage enough to hamstring a horse or drag down a full-grown cow. And here was Old Yeller, weak and crippled, trying to fight a mad one!

I brought up my gun, then held fire while I hollered at Mama. "Y'all get in the cabin," I yelled. "I'm scared to shoot till I know you're out of the line of fire!"

I heard Mama whacking Jumper with a stick to make him go. I heard Jumper snort and the clatter of his hoofs as he went galloping in a wide circle to come up behind the cabin. But even after Mama called from the door behind me, I still couldn't fire. Not without taking a chance on killing Old Yeller.

I waited, my nerves on edge, while Old Yeller and the big wolf fought there in the firelight, whirling and leaping and snarling and slashing, their bared fangs gleaming white, their eyes burning green in the half light.

Then they went down in a tumbling roll that stopped with the big wolf on top, his huge jaws shut tight on Yeller's throat. That was my chance, and one that I'd better make good. As weak as Old Yeller was, he'd never break that throat hold.

There in the wavering light, I couldn't get a true bead on the wolf. I couldn't see my sights well enough. All I could do was guess-aim and hope for a hit.

I squeezed the trigger. The gunstock slammed back against my shoulder, and such a long streak of fire spouted from the gun barrel that it blinded me for a second; I couldn't see a thing.

Then I realized that all the growling and snarling had hushed. A second later, I was running toward the two still gray forms lying side by side.

For a second, I just knew that I'd killed Old Yeller, too. Then, about the time I bent over him, he heaved a big sort of sigh and struggled up to start licking my hands and wagging that stub tail.

I was so relieved that it seemed like all the strength went out of me. I slumped to the ground and was sitting there, shivering, when Mama came and sat down beside me.

She put one arm across my shoulders and held it there while she told me what had happened.

Like I'd figured, it had taken her and Lisbeth till dark to get the wood dragged up and the fire to going around the dead cow. Then they'd mounted old Jumper and headed for home. They'd been without water all this time and were thirsty. When they came to the crossing on Birdsong Creek, they'd dismounted to get a drink. And while they were lying down, drinking, the wolf came.

He was right on them before they knew it. Mama happened to look up and see the dark hulk of him come bounding toward them across a little clearing. He was snarling as he came, and Mama just barely had time to come to her feet and grab up a dead chinaberry pole before he sprang. She whacked him hard across the head, knocking him to the ground. Then Old Yeller was there, tying into him.

Mama and Lisbeth got back on Jumper and tore out for the house. Right after them came the wolf, like he had his mind fixed on catching them, and nothing else. But Old Yeller fought him too hard and too fast. Yeller wasn't big and strong enough to stop him, but he kept him slowed down and fought away from Jumper and Mama and Lisbeth.

"He had to've been mad, son," Mama wound up. "You know that no wolf in his right senses would have acted that way. Not even a big loafer wolf."

"Yessum," I said, "and it's sure a good thing that Old Yeller was along to keep him fought off." I shuddered at the thought of what could have happened without Old Yeller.

Mama waited a little bit, then said in a quiet voice: "It was a good thing for us, Son; but it wasn't good for Old Yeller."

The way she said that gave me a cold feeling in the pit of my stomach. I sat up straighter. "What do you mean?" I said. "Old Yeller's all right. He's maybe chewed up some, but he can't be bad hurt. See, he's done trotting off toward the house!"

Then it hit me what Mama was getting at. All my insides froze. I couldn't get my breath.

I jumped to my feet, wild with hurt and scare. "But Mama!" I cried out. "Old Yeller's just saved your life! He's saved my life. He's saved Little Arliss's life! We can't—"

Mama got up and put her arm across my shoulders again. "I know, Son," she said. "But he's been bitten by a mad wolf."

I stared off into the blackness of the night while my mind wheeled and darted this way and that, like a scared rat trying to find its way out of a trap.

"But Mama," I said. "We don't know for certain. We could wait and see. We could tie him or shut him up in the corncrib or some place till we know for sure!"

Mama broke down and went to crying then. She put her head on my shoulder and held me so tight that she nearly choked off my breath.

"We can't take a chance, Son," she sobbed. "It would be you or me or Little Arliss or Lisbeth next. I'll shoot him if you can't, but either way, we've got it to do. We just can't take the chance!"

It came clear to me then that Mama was right. We couldn't take the risk. And from everything I had heard, I knew that there was very little chance of Old Yeller's escaping the sickness. It was going to kill something inside me to do it, but I knew then that I had to shoot my big yeller dog.

Once I knew for sure I had it to do, I don't think I really felt anything. I was just numb all over, like a dead man walking.

Quickly, I left Mama and went to stand in the light of the burning bear grass. I reloaded my gun and called Old Yeller back from the house. I stuck the muzzle of the gun against his head and pulled the trigger.

Days went by, and I couldn't seem to get over it. I couldn't eat. I couldn't sleep. I couldn't cry. I was all empty inside, but hurting. Hurting worse than I'd ever hurt in my life. Hurting with a sickness there didn't seem to be any cure for. Thinking every minute of my big yeller dog, how we'd worked together and romped together, how he'd fought the she bear off Little Arliss, how he'd saved me from the killer hogs, how he'd fought the mad wolf off Mama and Lisbeth. Thinking that after all this, I'd had to shoot him the same as I'd done the roan bull and the spot heifer.

Mama tried to talk to me about it, and I let her. But while everything she said made sense, it didn't do a thing to that dead feeling I had.

Lisbeth talked to me. She didn't say much; she was too shy. But she pointed out that I had another dog, the speckled pup.

"He's part Old Yeller," she said. "And he was the best one of the bunch."

But that didn't help any either. The speckled pup might be part Old Yeller, but he wasn't Old Yeller. He hadn't saved all our lives and then been shot down like he was nothing.

Then one night it clouded up and rained till daylight. That seemed to wash away the hydrophobia plague. At least, pretty soon afterward, it died out completely.

But we didn't know that then. What seemed important to us about the rain was that the next morning after it fell, Papa came riding home through the mud.

The long ride to Kansas and back had Papa drawn down till he was as thin and knotty as a fence rail. But he had money in his pockets, a big shouting laugh for everybody, and a saddle horse for me.

The horse was a cat-stepping blue roan with a black mane and tail. Papa put me on him the first thing and made me gallop him in the clearing around the house. The roan had all the pride and fire any grown man would want in his best horse, yet was as gentle as a pet.

"Now, isn't he a dandy?" Papa asked.

I said, "Yessir!" and knew that Papa was right and that I ought to be proud and thankful. But I wasn't. I didn't feel one way or another about the horse.

Papa saw something was wrong. I saw him look a question at Mama and saw Mama shake her head. Then late that evening, just before supper, he called me off down to the spring, where we sat and he talked.

"Your mama told me about the dog," he said.

I said, "Yessir," but didn't add anything.

"That was rough," he said. "That was as rough a thing as I ever heard tell of happening to a boy. And I'm mighty proud to learn how my boy stood up to it. You couldn't ask any more of a grown man."

He stopped for a minute. He picked up some little pebbles and thumped them into the water, scattering a bunch of hairy-legged water bugs. The bugs darted across the water in all directions.

"Now the thing to do," he went on, "is to try to forget it and go on being a man."

"How?" I asked. "How can you forget a thing like that?"

He studied me for a moment, then shook his head. "I guess I don't quite mean that," he said. "It's not a thing you can forget. I don't guess it's a thing that you ought to forget. What I mean is, things like that happen. They may seem mighty cruel and unfair, but that's how life is a part of the time.

"But that isn't the only way life is. A part of the time, it's mighty good. And a man can't afford to waste all the good part, worrying about the bad parts. That makes it all bad. . . . You understand?"

"Yessir," I said. And I did understand. Only, it still didn't do me any good. I still felt just as dead and empty.

That went on for a week or better, I guess, before a thing happened that brought me alive again.

It was right at dinnertime. Papa had sent me out to the lot to feed Jumper and the horses. I'd just started back when I heard a commotion in the house. I heard Mama's voice lifted high and sharp. "Why, you thieving little whelp!" she cried out. Then I heard a shrieking yelp, and out the kitchen door came the speckled pup with a big chunk of cornbread clutched in his mouth. He raced around the house, running with his tail clamped. He was yelling and squawling like somebody was beating him to death. But that still didn't keep him from hanging onto that piece of cornbread that he'd stolen from Mama.

Inside the house, I heard Little Arliss. He was fighting and screaming his head off at Mama for hitting his dog. And above it all, I could hear Papa's roaring laughter.

Right then, I began to feel better. Sight of that little old pup, tearing out for the brush with that piece of cornbread seemed to loosen something inside me.

I felt better all day. I went back and rode my horse and enjoyed it. I rode 'way off out in the brush, not going anywhere especially, just riding and looking and beginning to feel proud of owning a real horse of my own.

Then along about sundown, I rode down into Birdsong Creek, headed for the house. Up at the spring, I heard a splashing and hollering. I looked ahead. Sure enough, it was Little Arliss. He was stripped naked and in our drinking water again. And right in there, romping with him, was that bread-stealing speckled pup.

I started to holler at them. I started to say: "*Arliss!* You get that nasty old pup out of our drinking water."

Then I didn't. Instead, I went to laughing. I sat there and laughed till I cried. When all the time I knew that I ought to go beat them to a frazzle for messing up our drinking water.

When finally I couldn't laugh and cry another bit, I rode on up to the lot and turned my horse in. Tomorrow, I thought, I'll take Arliss and that pup out for a squirrel hunt. The pup was still mighty little. But the way I figured it, if he was big enough to act like Old Yeller, he was big enough to start learning to earn his keep.

10

The Yearling

Marjorie Kinnan Rawlings

In the years following the Civil War, Jody Baxter and his parents live in the heart of the wild Florida scrub surrounded by bears, panthers, and quarrelsome neighbors. When Jody's father, Penny, is forced to shoot a doe, both father and son feel a responsibility to take care of the yearling fawn that is orphaned as a result.

The rattler struck him from under the grape-vine without warning. Jody saw the flash, blurred as a shadow, swifter than a martin, surer than the slashing claws of a bear. He saw his father stagger backward under the force of the blow. He heard him give a cry. He wanted to step back, too. He wanted to cry out with all his voice. He stood rooted to the sand and could not make a sound. It was lightning that had struck, and not a rattler. It was a branch that broke, it was a bird that flew, it was a rabbit running—

Penny shouted, "Git back! Hold the dogs!"

The voice released him. He dropped back and clutched the dogs by the scruff of their necks. He saw the mottled shadow lift its flat head, knee-high. The head swung from side to side, following his father's slow motions. He heard the rattles hum. The dogs heard. They winded. The fur stood stiff on their bodies. Old Julia whined and twisted out of his hand. She turned and slunk down the trail. Her long tail clung to her hindquarters. Rip reared on his hind feet, barking.

As slowly as a man in a dream, Penny backed away. The rattles sung. They were not rattles—Surely it was a locust humming. Surely it was a tree-frog singing—Penny lifted his gun to his shoulder and fired. Jody quivered. The rattler coiled and writhed in its spasms. The head was buried in the sand. The contortions moved down the length of the thick body, the rattles whirred feebly and were still. The coiling flattened into slow convolutions, like a low tide ebbing. Penny turned and stared at his son.

He said, "He got me."

He lifted his right arm and gaped at it. His lips lifted dry over his teeth. His throat worked. He looked dully at two punctures in the flesh. A drop of blood oozed from each.

He said, "He was a big un."

Jody let go his hold on Rip. The dog ran to the dead snake and barked fiercely. He made sorties and at last poked the coils with one paw. He quieted and snuffed about in the sand. Penny lifted his head from his staring. His face was like hickory ashes.

He said, "Ol' Death goin' to git me yit."

He licked his lips. He turned abruptly and began to push through the scrub in the direction of the clearing. The road would be shorter going, for it was open, but he headed blindly for home in a direct line. He plowed through the low scrub oaks, the gallberries, the scrub palmettos. Jody panted behind him. His heart pounded so hard that he could not see where he was going. He followed the sound of his father's crashing across the undergrowth. Suddenly the denseness ended. A patch of higher oaks made a shaded clearing. It was strange to walk in silence.

Penny stopped short. There was a stirring ahead. A doe-deer leaped to her feet. Penny drew a deep breath, as though breathing were for some reason easier. He lifted his shotgun and leveled it at the head. It flashed over Jody's mind that his father had gone mad. This was no moment to stop for game. Penny fired. The doe turned a somersault and dropped to the sand and kicked a little and lay still. Penny ran to the body and drew his knife from its scabbard. Now Jody knew his father was insane. Penny did not cut the throat, but slashed into the belly. He laid the carcass wide open. The pulse still throbbed in the heart. Penny slashed out the liver. Kneeling, he changed his knife to his left hand. He turned his right arm and stared again at the twin punctures. They were now closed. The forearm was thick-swollen and blackening. The sweat stood out on his forehead. He cut quickly across the wound. A dark blood gushed and he pressed the warm liver against the incision.

He said in a hushed voice, "I kin feel it draw—"

He pressed harder. He took the meat away and looked at it. It was a venomous green. He turned it and applied the fresh side.

He said, "Cut me out a piece o' the heart."

Jody jumped from his paralysis. He fumbled with the knife. He hacked away a portion.

Penny said, "Another."

He changed the application again and again.

He said, "Hand me the knife."

He cut a higher gash in his arm where the dark swelling rose the thickest. Jody cried out.

"Pa! You'll bleed to death!"

"I'd ruther bleed to death than swell. I seed a man die—"

The sweat poured down his cheeks.

"Do it hurt bad, Pa?"

"Like a hot knife was buried to the shoulder."

The meat no longer showed green when he withdrew it. The warm vitality of the doe's flesh was solidifying in death. He stood up.

He said quietly, "I cain't do it no more good. I'm goin' on home. You go to the Forresters and git 'em to ride to the Branch for Doc Wilson."

"Reckon they'll go?"

"We got to chance it. Call out to 'em quick, sayin', afore they chunk somethin' at you or mebbe shoot."

He turned back to pick up the beaten trail. Jody followed. Over his shoulder he heard a light rustling. He looked back. A spotted fawn stood peering from the edge of the clearing, wavering on uncertain legs. Its dark eyes were wide and wondering.

He called out, "Pa! The doe's got a fawn."

"Sorry, boy. I cain't he'p it. Come on."

An agony for the fawn came over him. He hesitated. It tossed its small head, bewildered. It wobbled to the carcass of the doe and leaned to smell it. It bleated.

Penny called, "Git a move on, young un."

Jody ran to catch up with him. Penny stopped an instant at the dim road.

"Tell somebody to take this road in to our place and pick me up in case I cain't make it in. Hurry."

Jody allowed his thoughts to drift back to the fawn. He could not keep it out of his mind. It stood in the back of it as close as he had held it, in his dreaming, in his arms. He slipped from the table and went to his father's bedside. Penny lay at rest. His eyes were open and clear, but the pupils were still dark and dilated.

Jody said, "How you comin', Pa?"

"Jest fine, son. Ol' Death gone thievin' elsewhere. But wa'n't it a close squeak!"

"I mean."

Penny said, "I'm proud of you, boy, the way you kept your head and done what was needed."

"Pa—"

"Yes, son."

"Pa, you recollect the doe and the fawn?"

"I cain't never forget 'em. The pore doe saved me, and that's certain."

"Pa, the fawn may be out there yit. Hit's hongry, and likely mighty skeert."

"I reckon so."

"Pa, I'm about growed and don't need no milk. How about me goin' out and seein' kin I find the fawn?"

"And tote it here?"

"And raise it."

Penny lay quiet, staring at the ceiling.

"Boy, you got me hemmed in."

"Hit won't take much to raise it, Pa. Hit'll soon git to where it kin make out on leaves and acorns."

"Dogged if you don't figger the farrest of ary young un I've ever knowed."

"We takened its mammy, and it wa'n't no-ways to blame."

"Shore don't seem grateful to leave it starve, do it? Son, I ain't got it in my heart to say 'No' to you. I never figgered I'd see daylight, come dawn today."

"Kin I ride back with Mill-wheel and see kin I find it?"

"Tell your Ma I said you're to go."

He sidled back to the table and sat down. His mother was pouring coffee for every one.

He said, "Ma, Pa says I kin go bring back the fawn."

She held the coffee-pot in mid-air.

"What fawn?"

"The fawn belonged to the doe we kilt, to use the liver to draw out the pizen and save Pa."

She gasped.

"Well, for pity sake—"

"Pa say hit'd not be grateful, to leave it starve."

Doc Wilson said, "That's right, Ma'am. Nothing in the world don't ever come quite free. The boy's right and his daddy's right."

Mill-wheel said, "He kin ride back with me. I'll he'p him find it."

She set down the pot helplessly.

"Well, if you'll give it your milk—We got nothin' else to feed it."

"That's what I aim to do. Hit'll be no time, and it not needin' nothin'."

The men rose from the table.

Doc said, "I don't look for nothing but progress, Ma'am, but if he takes a turn for the worse, you know where to find me."

She said, “Well. What do we owe you, Doc? We cain’t pay right now, but time the crops is made—”

“Pay for what? I’ve done nothing. He was safe before I got here. I’ve had a night’s lodging and a good breakfast. Send me some syrup when your cane’s ground.”

“You’re mighty good, Doc. We been scramblin’ so, I didn’t know folks could be so good.”

“Hush, woman. You got a good man there. Why wouldn’t folks be good to him?”

Buck said, “You reckon that ol’ horse o’ Penny’s kin keep ahead o’ me at the plow? I’m like to run him down.”

Doc said, “Get as much milk down Penny as he’ll take. Then give him greens and fresh meat, if you can get it.”

Buck said, “Me and Jody’ll tend to that.”

Mill-wheel said, “Come on, boy. We got to git ridin’.”

Ma Baxter asked anxiously, “You’ll not be gone long?”

Jody said, “I’ll be back shore, before dinner.”

“Reckon you’d not git home a-tall,” she said, “if ’twasn’t for dinner-time.”

Doc said, “That’s man-nature, Ma’am. Three things bring a man home again—his bed, his woman, and his dinner.”

Buck and Mill-wheel guffawed. Doc’s eye caught the cream-colored ’coonskin knapsack.

“Now ain’t that a pretty something? Wouldn’t I like such as that to tote my medicines?”

Jody had never before possessed a thing that was worth giving away. He took it from its nail, and put it in Doc’s hands.

“Hit’s mine,” he said. “Take it.”

“Why, I’d not rob you, boy.”

“I got no use for it,” he said loftily. “I kin git me another.”

“Now I thank you. Every trip I make, I’ll think, ‘Thank you Jody Baxter.’ ”

He skirted the carcass and parted the grass at the place where he had seen the fawn. It did not seem possible that it was only yesterday. The fawn was not there. He circled the clearing.

There was no sound, no sign. The buzzards clacked their wings, impatient to return to their business. He returned to the spot where the fawn had emerged and dropped to all fours, studying the sand for the small hoof-prints. The night's rain had washed away all tracks except those of cat and buzzards. But the cat-sign had not been made in this direction. Under a scrub palmetto he was able to make out a track, pointed and dainty as the mark of a ground-dove. He crawled past the palmetto.

Movement directly in front of him startled him so that he tumbled backward. The fawn lifted its face to his. It turned its head with a wide wondering motion and shook him through with the stare of its liquid eyes. It was quivering. It made no effort to rise or run. Jody could not trust himself to move.

He whispered, "It's me."

The fawn lifted its nose, scenting him. He reached out one hand and laid it on the soft neck. The touch made him delirious. He moved forward on all fours until he was close beside it. He put his arms around its body. A light convulsion passed over it but it did not stir. He stroked its sides as gently as though the fawn were a china deer and he might break it. Its skin was softer than the white 'coonskin knapsack. It was sleek and clean and had a sweet scent of grass. He rose slowly and lifted the fawn from the ground. It was no heavier than old Julia. Its legs hung limply. They were surprisingly long and he had to hoist the fawn as high as possible under his arm.

He was afraid that it might kick and bleat at sight and smell of its mother. He skirted the clearing and pushed his way into the thicket. It was difficult to fight through with his burden. The fawn's legs caught in the bushes and he could not lift his own with freedom. He tried to shield its face from prickling vines. Its head bobbed with his stride. His heart thumped with the marvel of its acceptance of him. He reached the trail and walked as fast as he could until he came to the intersection with the road home. He stopped to rest and set the fawn down on its dangling legs. It wavered on them. It looked at him and bleated.

He said, enchanted, "I'll tote you time I git my breath."

He remembered his father's saying that a fawn would follow that had been first carried. He started away slowly. The fawn stared after him. He came back to it and stroked it and walked away again. It took a few wobbling steps toward him and cried piteously. It was willing to follow him. It belonged to him. It was his own. He was light-headed with his joy. He wanted to fondle it, to run and romp with it, to call to it to come to him. He dared not alarm it. He picked it up and carried it in front of him over his two arms. It seemed to him that he walked without effort. He had the strength of a Forrester.

His arms began to ache and he was forced to stop again. When he walked on, the fawn followed him at once. He allowed it to walk a little distance, then picked it up again. The distance home was nothing. He could have walked all day and into the night, carrying it and watching it follow. He was wet with sweat but a light breeze blew through the June morning, cooling him. The sky was as clear as spring water in a blue china cup. He came to the clearing. It was fresh and green after the night's rain. He could see Buck Forrester following old Caesar at the plow in the cornfield. He thought he heard him curse the horse's slowness. He fumbled with the gate latch and was finally obliged to set down the fawn to manage it. It came to him that he would walk into the house, into Penny's bedroom, with the fawn walking behind him. But at the steps, the fawn balked and refused to climb them. He picked it up and went to his father. Penny lay with closed eyes.

Jody called, "Pa! Lookit!"

Penny turned his head. Jody stood beside him, the fawn clutched hard against him. It seemed to Penny that the boy's eyes were as bright as the fawn's. His face lightened, seeing them together.

He said, "I'm proud you found him."

"Pa, he wa'n't skeert o' me. He were layin' up right where his mammy had made his bed."

"The does learns 'em that, time they're borned. You kin step on a fawn, times, they lay so still."

"Pa, I toted him, and when I set him down, right off he follered me. Like a dog, Pa."

"Ain't that fine? Let's see him better."

Jody lifted the fawn high. Penny reached out a hand and touched its nose. It bleated and reached hopefully for his fingers.

He said, "Well, leetle feller. I'm sorry I had to take away your mammy."

"You reckon he misses her?"

"No. He misses his rations and he knows that. He misses somethin' else but he don't know jest what."

Ma Baxter came into the room.

"Look, Ma, I found him."

"I see."

"Ain't he purty, Ma? Lookit them spots all in rows. Lookit them big eyes. Ain't he purty?"

"He's powerful young. Hit'll take milk for him a long whiles. I don't know as I'd of give my consent, if I'd knowed he was so young."

Penny said, "Ory, I got one thing to say, and I'm sayin' it now, and then I'll have no more talk of it. The leetle fawn's as welcome in this house as Jody. It's hissen. We'll raise it without grudgment o' milk or meal. You got me to answer to, do I ever hear you quarrelin' about it. This is Jody's fawn jest like Julia's my dog."

11

The Glove and the Lions

Leigh Hunt

The lovely lady in Leigh Hunt's poem is not so lovely after all. Her vanity far outweighs her sense of responsibility.

King Francis was a hearty king, and loved a royal sport,
And one day, as his lions fought, sat looking at the court.
The nobles filled the benches, and the ladies in their pride,
And 'mongst them sat the Count de Lorge, with one for whom
he sighed:

And truly 'twas a gallant thing to see that crowning show,
Valor and love, and a king above, and the royal beasts below.
Ramped and roared the lions, with horrid laughing jaws;
They bit, they glared, gave blows like beams, a wind went with
their paws;

With wallowing might and stifled roar they rolled on one
another,
Till all the pit with sand and mane was in thunderous
smother.
The bloody foam above the bars came whisking through the
air;

Said Francis then, "Faith, gentlemen, we're better here than there."

De Lorge's love o'erheard the King, a beauteous lively dame,
With smiling lips and sharp bright eyes, which always seemed the same;
She thought, "The Count, my lover, is brave as brave can be;
He surely would do wondrous things to show his love of me;

King, ladies, lovers, all look on; the occasion is divine;
I'll drop my glove, to prove his love; great glory will be mine."
She dropped her glove, to prove his love, then looked at him and smiled;
He bowed, and in a moment leaped among the lions wild;

The leap was quick, return was quick, he has regained his place,
Then threw the glove, but not with love, right in the lady's face.
"By Heaven," said Francis, "rightly done!" and he rose from where he sat;
"No love," quoth he, "but vanity, sets love a task like that."

Loyalty

Like responsibility, loyalty is a way of showing that we care for others and that we are willing to stand by them in good times and bad. Animal stories often provide good examples of steadfast devotion. Zlateh the goat is one such example, and Rikki-tikki-tavi, the ferocious mongoose in Kipling's story, is another.

We owe loyalty to our friends and family because we are bound to them in a special way. We show loyalty by being faithful and dependable. This, of course, is never as easy as it sounds. Usually others need our loyalty most when they are facing difficult circumstances. It's easy to be a "fair-weather friend," but not as easy to be a friend-in-need. When our friends are sick or in trouble or under criticism, loyalty can be a difficult virtue to practice. This is why the marriage vow reminds us that our loyalty to our spouse is "for better or worse, for richer or poorer, in sickness and in health" and not just as long as the good times last.

This doesn't mean that we have to go along with everything our friend demands. The slogan "Friends don't let friends drive drunk" makes the point nicely. A true friend in this case does the opposite of what is requested. Loyalty sometimes means going against your friend's wishes. And this is true also of loyalty to country. We can be patriotic citizens and still disagree with our leaders. For example, in England those members of parliament who are in the minority are referred to as the "loyal opposition."

Just as there is a kind of false courage, there is also a kind of false or misplaced loyalty. We need to guard against blind loyalty to our peers. As always, we have an obligation to exercise good judgment in our activities, and it is not virtuous to support our group when it engages in wrongdoing. In cases like this, we usually find that we have a higher loyalty—to family, to humanity, to God—and it is this higher obligation that most deserves our allegiance.

12

Zlateh the Goat

Isaac Bashevis Singer

Aaron and his goat, Zlateh, reluctantly set off on a journey that will end at the butcher's. To make matters worse, along the way they are caught in a whirling blizzard.

At Hanukkah time the road from the village to the town is usually covered with snow, but this year the winter had been a mild one. Hanukkah had almost come, yet little snow had fallen. The sun shone most of the time. The peasants complained that because of the dry weather there would be a poor harvest of winter grain. New grass sprouted, and the peasants sent their cattle out to pasture.

For Reuven the furrier it was a bad year, and after long hesitation he decided to sell Zlateh the goat. She was old and gave little milk. Feivel the town butcher had offered eight gulden for her. Such a sum would buy Hanukkah candles, potatoes and oil for pancakes, gifts for the children, and other holiday necessaries for the house. Reuven told his oldest boy Aaron to take the goat to town.

Aaron understood what taking the goat to Feivel meant, but he had to obey his father. Leah, his mother, wiped the tears from her eyes when she heard the news. Aaron's younger sisters, Anna and Miriam, cried loudly. Aaron put on his quilted jacket and a cap with earmuffs, bound a rope around Zlateh's neck, and took along two slices of bread with cheese to eat on the road. Aaron was supposed to deliver the goat by evening, spend the night at the butcher's, and return the next day with the money.

While the family said good-bye to the goat, and Aaron placed the rope around her neck, Zlateh stood as patiently and good-naturedly as ever. She licked Reuven's hand. She shook her small white beard. Zlateh trusted human beings. She knew that they always fed her and never did her any harm.

When Aaron brought her out on the road to town, she seemed somewhat astonished. She'd never been led in that direction before. She looked back at him questioningly, as if to say, "Where are you taking me?" But after a while she seemed to come to the conclusion that a goat shouldn't ask questions. Still, the road was different. They passed new fields, pastures, and huts with thatched roofs. Here and there a dog barked and came running after them, but Aaron chased it away with his stick.

The sun was shining when Aaron left the village. Suddenly the weather changed. A large black cloud with a bluish center appeared in the east and spread itself rapidly over the sky. A cold wind blew in with it. The crows flew low, croaking. At first it looked as if it would rain, but instead it began to hail as in summer. It was early in the day, but it became dark as dusk. After a while the hail turned to snow.

In his twelve years Aaron had seen all kinds of weather, but he had never experienced a snow like this one. It was so dense it shut out the light of the day. In a short time their path was completely covered. The wind became as cold as ice. The road to town was narrow and winding. Aaron no longer knew where he was. He could not see through the snow. The cold soon penetrated his quilted jacket.

At first Zlateh didn't seem to mind the change in weather. She too was twelve years old and knew what winter meant. But when her legs sank deeper and deeper into the snow, she began to turn her head and look at Aaron in wonderment. Her mild eyes seemed to ask, "Why are we out in such a storm?" Aaron hoped that a peasant would come along with his cart, but no one passed by.

The snow grew thicker, falling to the ground in large, whirling flakes. Beneath it Aaron's boots touched the softness of a plowed field. He realized that he was no longer on the road. He had gone astray. He could no longer figure out which was east or west, which way was the village, the town. The wind whistled, howled, whirled the snow about in eddies. It looked as if white imps were playing tag on the fields. A white dust rose above the ground. Zlateh stopped. She could walk no longer. Stubbornly she anchored her cleft hooves in the earth and bleated as if pleading to be taken home. Icicles hung from her white beard, and her horns were glazed with frost.

Aaron did not want to admit the danger, but he knew just the same that if they did not find shelter they would freeze to death. This was no ordinary storm. It was a mighty blizzard. The snowfall had reached his knees. His hands were numb, and he could no longer feel his toes. He choked when he breathed. His nose felt like wood, and he rubbed it with snow. Zlateh's bleating began to sound like crying. Those humans in whom she had so much confidence had dragged her into a trap. Aaron began to pray to God for himself and for the innocent animal.

Suddenly he made out the shape of a hill. He wondered what it could be. Who had piled snow into such a huge heap? He moved toward it, dragging Zlateh after him. When he came near it, he realized that it was a large haystack which the snow had blanketed.

Aaron realized immediately that they were saved. With great effort he dug his way through the snow. He was a village boy and knew what to do. When he reached the hay, he hollowed out a nest for himself and the goat. No matter how cold it may be outside, in the hay it is always warm. And hay was food for Zlateh. The moment she smelled it she became contented and began to eat. Outside the snow continued to fall. It quickly covered the passageway Aaron had dug. But a boy and an animal need to breathe, and there was hardly any air in their hideout.

Aaron bored a kind of a window through the hay and snow and carefully kept the passage clear.

Zlateh, having eaten her fill, sat down on her hind legs and seemed to have regained her confidence in man. Aaron ate his two slices of bread and cheese, but after the difficult journey he was still hungry. He looked at Zlateh and noticed her udders were full. He lay down next to her, placing himself so that when he milked her he could squirt the milk into his mouth. It was rich and sweet. Zlateh was not accustomed to being milked that way, but she did not resist. On the contrary, she seemed eager to reward Aaron for bringing her to a shelter whose very walls, floor, and ceiling were made of food.

Through the window Aaron could catch a glimpse of the chaos outside. The wind carried before it whole drifts of snow. It was completely dark, and he did not know whether night had already come or whether it was the darkness of the storm. Thank God that in the hay it was not cold. The dried hay, grass, and field flowers exuded the warmth of the summer sun. Zlateh ate frequently; she nibbled from above, below, from the left and right. Her body gave forth an animal warmth, and Aaron cuddled up to her. He had always loved Zlateh, but now she was like a sister. He was alone, cut off from his family, and wanted to talk. He began to talk to Zlateh. "Zlateh, what do you think about what has happened to us?" he asked.

"Maaaa," Zlateh answered.

"If we hadn't found this stack of hay, we would both be frozen stiff by now," Aaron said.

"Maaaa," was the goat's reply.

"If the snow keeps on falling like this, we may have to stay here for days," Aaron explained.

"Maaaa," Zlateh bleated.

"What does 'Maaaa' mean?" Aaron asked. "You'd better speak up clearly."

"Maaaa. Maaaa," Zlateh tried.

"Well, let it be 'Maaaa' then," Aaron said patiently. "You can't speak, but I know you understand. I need you and you need me. Isn't that right?"

"Maaaa."

Aaron became sleepy. He made a pillow out of some hay, leaned his head on it, and dozed off. Zlateh too fell asleep.

When Aaron opened his eyes, he didn't know whether it was morning or night. The snow had blocked up his window. He tried to clear it, but when he had bored through to the length of his arm, he still hadn't reached the outside. Luckily he had his stick with him and was able to break through to the open air. It was still dark outside. The snow continued to fall and the wind wailed, first with one voice and then with many. Sometimes it had the sound of devilish laughter. Zlateh too awoke, and when Aaron greeted her, she answered, "Maaaa." Yes, Zlateh's language consisted of only one word, but it meant many things. Now she was saying, "We must accept all that God gives us—heat, cold, hunger, satisfaction, light, and darkness."

Aaron had awakened hungry. He had eaten up his food, but Zlateh had plenty of milk.

For three days Aaron and Zlateh stayed in the haystack. Aaron had always loved Zlateh, but in these three days he loved her more and more. She fed him with her milk and helped him keep warm. She comforted him with her patience. He told her many stories, and she always cocked her ears and listened. When he patted her, she licked his hand and his face. Then she said, "Maaaa," and he knew it meant, I love you too.

The snow fell for three days, though after the first day it was not as thick and the wind quieted down. Sometimes Aaron felt that there could never have been a summer, that the snow had always fallen, ever since he could remember. He, Aaron, never had a father or mother or sisters. He was a snow child, born of the snow, and so was Zlateh. It was so quiet in the hay that his ears rang in the stillness. Aaron and Zlateh slept all night and a good part of the day. As for Aaron's dreams, they were all about warm weather. He dreamed of green fields, trees covered with blossoms, clear brooks, and singing birds. By the third night the snow had stopped, but Aaron did not dare to find his way home in the darkness. The sky became clear and the moon shone, casting silvery nets on the snow. Aaron dug his way out and looked at the world. It was all white, quiet, dreaming dreams of heavenly splendor. The stars were large and close. The moon swam in the sky as in a sea.

On the morning of the fourth day Aaron heard the ringing of sleigh bells. The haystack was not far from the road. The peasant who drove the sleigh pointed out the way to him—not to the town and Feivel the butcher, but home to the village. Aaron had decided in the haystack that he would never part with Zlateh.

Aaron's family and their neighbors had searched for the boy and the goat but had found no trace of them during the storm. They feared they were lost. Aaron's mother and sisters cried for him; his father remained silent and gloomy. Suddenly one of the neighbors came running to their house with the news that Aaron and Zlateh were coming up the road.

There was great joy in the family. Aaron told them how he had found the stack of hay and how Zlateh had fed him with her milk. Aaron's sisters kissed and hugged Zlateh and gave her a special treat of chopped carrots and potato peels, which Zlateh gobbled up hungrily.

Nobody ever again thought of selling Zlateh, and now that the cold weather had finally set in, the villagers needed the services of Reuven the furrier once more. When Hanukkah came, Aaron's mother was able to fry pancakes every evening, and Zlateh got her portion too. Even though Zlateh had her own pen, she often came to the kitchen, knocking on the door with her horns to indicate that she was ready to visit, and she was always admitted. In the evening Aaron, Miriam, and Anna played dreidel. Zlateh sat near the stove watching the children and the flickering of the Hanukkah candles.

Once in a while Aaron would ask her, "Zlateh, do you remember the three days we spent together?"

And Zlateh would scratch her neck with a horn, shake her white bearded head, and come out with the single sound which expressed all her thoughts, and all her love.

13

A Secret for Two

Quentin Reynolds

Here is a story of friendship that ends with a surprise.

Montreal is a very large city, but, like all large cities, it has some very small streets. Streets, for instance, like Prince Edward Street, which is only four blocks long, ending in a cul-de-sac. No one knew Prince Edward Street as well as did Pierre Dupin, for Pierre had delivered milk to the families on the street for thirty years now.

During the past fifteen years the horse which drew the milk wagon used by Pierre was a large white horse named Joseph. In Montreal, especially in that part of Montreal which is very French, the animals, like children, are often given the names of saints. When the big white horse first came to the Provincale Milk Company, he didn't have a name. They told Pierre that he could use the white horse henceforth. Pierre stroked the softness of the horse's neck; he stroked the sheen of its splendid belly and he looked into the eyes of the horse.

"This is a kind horse, a gentle and a faithful horse," Pierre said, "and I can see a beautiful spirit shining out of the eyes of the horse. I will name him after good St. Joseph, who was also kind and gentle and faithful and a beautiful spirit."

Within a year Joseph knew the milk route as well as Pierre. Pierre used to boast that he didn't need reins—he never touched them. Each morning Pierre arrived at the stables of the Provincale Milk Company at five o'clock. The wagon would be loaded and Joseph hitched to it. Pierre would call *"Bon jour, vieil ami,"* as he climbed into his seat, and Joseph would turn his head and other drivers would say that the horse would smile at Pierre. Then Jacques, the foreman, would say, "All right, Pierre, go on," and Pierre would call softly to Joseph, *"Avance, mon ami,"* and this splendid combination would stalk proudly down the street.

The wagon, without any direction from Pierre, would roll three blocks down St. Catherine Street, then turn right two blocks along Roslyn Avenue; then left, for that was Prince Edward Street. The horse would stop at the first house, allow Pierre perhaps thirty seconds to get down from his seat and put a bottle of milk at the front door and would then go on, skipping two houses and stopping at the third. So down the length of the street. Then Joseph, still without any direction from Pierre, would turn around and come back along the other side. Yes, Joseph was a smart horse.

Pierre would boast at the stable of Joseph's skill, "I never touch the reins. He knows just where to stop. Why, a blind man could handle my route with Joseph pulling the wagon."

So it went for years—always the same. Pierre and Joseph both grew old together, but gradually, not suddenly. Pierre's huge walrus mustache was pure white now and Joseph didn't lift his knees so high or raise his head quite as much. Jacques, the foreman of the stables, never noticed that they were both getting old until Pierre appeared one morning carrying a heavy walking stick. "Hey, Pierre," Jacques laughed. "Maybe you got the gout, hey?" *"Mais oui, Jacques,"* Pierre said a bit uncertainly. "One grows old. One's legs get tired."

"You should teach that horse to carry the milk to the front door for you," Jacques told him. "He does everything else."

He knew every one of the forty families he served on Prince Edward Street. The cooks knew that Pierre could neither read nor write, so instead of following the usual custom of leaving a note in an empty bottle if an additional quart of milk was needed they would sing out when they heard the rumble of his wagon wheels over the cobbled street, "Bring an extra quart this morning, Pierre." "So you have company for dinner tonight," he would call back gayly.

Pierre had a remarkable memory. When he arrived back at the stable he'd always remember to tell Jacques, "The Paquins took an extra quart this morning; the Lemoines bought a pint of cream."

Jacques would note these things in a little book he always carried. Most of the drivers had to make out the weekly bills and collect the money, but Jacques, liking Pierre, had always excused him from this task. All Pierre had to do was arrive at five in the morning, walk to his wagon, which was always in the same spot at the curb, and deliver his milk. He returned some two hours later, got down stiffly from his seat, called a cheery, "*Au 'voir*" to Jacques and then limped slowly down the street.

One morning the president of the Provincale Milk Company come to inspect the early morning deliveries. Jacques pointed Pierre out to him and said: "Watch how he talks to that horse. See how the horse listens and how he turns his head toward Pierre? See the look in that horse's eyes? You know, I think those two share a secret. I have often noticed it. It is as though they both sometimes chuckle at us as they go off on their route. Pierre is a good man, *Monsieur* President, but he gets old. Would it be too bold of me to suggest that he be retired and be given perhaps a small pension?" he added anxiously.

"But of course," the president laughed. "I know his record. He has been on this route now for thirty years and never once has there been a complaint. Tell him it is time he rested. His salary will go on just the same."

But Pierre refused to retire. He was panic-stricken by the thought of not driving Joseph every day. "We are two old men," he said to Jacques. "Let us wear out together. When Joseph is ready to retire—then I, too, will quit."

Jacques, who was a kind man, understood. There was something about Pierre and Joseph which made a man smile tenderly. It was as though each drew some hidden strength from the other. When Pierre was sitting in his seat, and when Joseph was hitched to the wagon, neither seemed old. But when they finished their work, then Pierre would limp down the street slowly, seeming very old indeed, and the horse's head would drop and he would walk very wearily back to his stall.

Then one morning Jacques had dreadful news for Pierre when he arrived. It was a cold morning and still pitch-dark. The air was like iced wine that morning and the snow which had fallen during the night glistened like a million diamonds piled together.

Jacques said, "Pierre, your horse, Joseph, did not wake up this morning. He was very old, Pierre, he was twenty-five and that is like being seventy-five for a man."

"Yes," Pierre said, slowly, "Yes. I am seventy-five. And I cannot see Joseph again."

"Of course you can," Jacques soothed. "He is over in his stall, looking very peaceful. Go over and see him."

Pierre took one step forward, then turned. "No . . . no . . . you don't understand, Jacques."

Jacques clapped him on the shoulder. "We'll find another horse just as good as Joseph. Why, in a month you'll teach him to know your route as well as Joseph did. We'll . . ."

The look in Pierre's eyes stopped him. For years Pierre had worn a heavy cap, the peak of which came low over his eyes, keeping the bitter morning wind out of them. Now Jacques looked into Pierre's eyes and he saw something which startled him. He saw a dead, lifeless look in them. The eyes were mirroring the grief that was in Pierre's heart and his soul. It was as though his heart and soul had died.

"Take today off, Pierre," Jacques said, but already Pierre was hobbling off down the street, and had one been near one would have seen tears streaming down his cheeks and have heard half-smothered sobs. Pierre walked to the corner and stepped into the street. There was a warning yell from the driver of a huge truck that was coming fast and there was the scream of brakes, but Pierre apparently heard neither.

Five minutes later an ambulance driver said, "He's dead. Was killed instantly."

Jacques and several of the milk wagon drivers had arrived and they looked down at the still figure.

"I couldn't help it," the driver of the truck protested; "he walked right into my truck. He never saw it, I guess. Why, he walked into it as though he were blind."

The ambulance doctor bent down. "Blind? Of course the man was blind. Look at his eyes. See those cataracts? This man has been blind for five years." He turned to Jacques, "You say he worked for you? Didn't you know he was blind?"

"No . . . no . . ." Jacques said, softly. "None of us knew. Only one knew—a friend of his named Joseph. . . . It was a secret, I think, just between those two."

14

"Rikki-Tikki-Tavi"

Rudyard Kipling

Set in British colonial India, this is the story of a mongoose who goes to heroic lengths to protect the humans whose home he shares.

This is the story of the great war that Rikki-tikki-tavi fought single-handed, through the bath-rooms of the big bungalow in Segowlee cantonment. Darzee, the tailor-bird, helped him, and Chuchundra, the musk-rat, who never comes out into the middle of the floor, but always creeps round by the wall, gave him advice; but Rikki-tikki did the real fighting.

He was a mongoose, rather like a little cat in his fur and his tail, but quite like a weasel in his head and his habits. His eyes and the end of his restless nose were pink; he could scratch himself anywhere he pleased, with any leg, front or back, that he chose to use; he could fluff up his tail till it looked like a bottle-brush, and his war-cry, as he scuttled through the long grass, was: *"Rikk-tikk-tikki-tikki-tchk!"*

One day, a high summer flood washed him out of the burrow where he lived with his father and mother, and carried him, kicking and clucking, down a road-side ditch. He found a little wisp of grass floating there, and clung to it till he lost his senses. When he revived, he was lying in the hot sun on the middle of a garden path, very draggled indeed, and a small boy was saying: "Here's a dead mongoose. Let's have a funeral."

"No," said his mother; "let's take him in and dry him. Perhaps he isn't really dead."

They took him into the house, and a big man picked him up between his finger and thumb, and said he was not dead but half choked; so they wrapped him in cotton-wool, and warmed him, and he opened his eyes and sneezed.

"Now," said the big man (he was an Englishman who had just moved into the bungalow), "don't frighten him, and we'll see what he'll do."

It is the hardest thing in the world to frighten a mongoose, because he is eaten up from nose to tail with curiosity. The motto of all the mongoose family is, 'Run and find out'; and Rikki-tikki was a true mongoose. He looked at the cotton-wool, decided that it was not good to eat, ran all round the table, sat up and put his fur in order, scratched himself, and jumped on the small boy's shoulder.

"Don't be frightened, Teddy," said his father. "That's his way of making friends."

"Ouch! He's tickling under my chin," said Teddy.

Rikki-tikki looked down between the boy's collar and neck, snuffed at his ear, and climbed down to the floor, where he sat rubbing his nose.

"Good gracious," said Teddy's mother, "and that's a wild creature! I suppose he's so tame because we've been kind to him."

"All mongooses are like that," said her husband. "If Teddy doesn't pick him up by the tail, or try to put him in a cage, he'll run in and out of the house all day long. Let's give him something to eat."

They gave him a little piece of raw meat. Rikki-tikki liked it immensely, and when it was finished he went out into the veranda and sat in the sunshine and fluffed up his fur to make it dry to the roots. Then he felt better.

"There are more things to find out about in this house," he said to himself, "than all my family could find out in all their lives. I shall certainly stay and find out."

He spent all that day roaming over the house. He nearly drowned himself in the bath-tubs, put his nose into the ink on a writing-table, and burnt it on the end of the big man's cigar, for he climbed up in the big man's lap to see how writing was done. At nightfall he ran into Teddy's nursery to watch how kerosene-lamps were lighted, and when Teddy went to bed Rikki-tikki climbed up too; but he was a restless companion, because he had to get up and attend to every noise all through the night, and find out what made it. Teddy's mother and father came in, the last thing, to look at their boy, and Rikki-tikki was awake on the pillow. "I don't like that," said Teddy's mother; "he may bite the child." "He'll do no such thing," said the father. "Teddy's safer with that little beast than if he had a bloodhound to watch him. If a snake came into the nursery now—"

But Teddy's mother wouldn't think of anything so awful.

Early in the morning Rikki-tikki came to early breakfast in the veranda riding on Teddy's shoulder, and they gave him banana and some boiled egg; and he sat on all their laps one after the other, because every well-brought-up mongoose always hopes to be a house-mongoose some day and have rooms to run about in, and Rikki-tikki's mother (she used to live in the General's house at Segowlee) had carefully told Rikki what to do if ever he came across white men.

Then Rikki-tikki went out into the garden to see what was to be seen. It was a large garden, only half cultivated, with bushes as big as summer-houses of Marshall Niel roses, lime and orange trees, clumps of bamboos, and thickets of high grass. Rikki-tikki licked his lips. "This is a splendid hunting-ground," he said, and his tail grew bottle-brushy at the thought of it, and he scuttled up and down the garden, snuffing here and there till he heard very sorrowful voices in a thorn-bush.

It was Darzee, the tailor-bird, and his wife. They had made a beautiful nest by pulling two big leaves together and stitching them up the edges with fibres, and had filled the hollow with cotton and downy fluff. The nest swayed to and fro, as they sat on the rim and cried.

"What is the matter?" asked Rikki-tikki.

"We are very miserable," said Darzee. "One of our babies fell out of the nest yesterday, and Nag ate him."

"H'm!" said Rikki-tikki, "that is very sad—but I am a stranger here. Who is Nag?"

Darzee and his wife only cowered down in the nest without answering, for from the thick grass at the foot of the bush there came a low hiss—a horrid cold sound that made Rikki-tikki jump back two clear feet. Then inch by inch out of the grass rose up the head and spread hood of Nag, the big black cobra, and he was five feet long from tongue to tail. When he had lifted one-third of himself clear of the ground, he stayed balancing to and fro exactly as a dandelion-tuft balances in the wind, and he looked at Rikki-tikki with the wicked snake's eyes that never change their expression, whatever the snake may be thinking of.

"Who is Nag?" said he. "*I* am Nag. The great god Brahm put his mark upon all our people when the first cobra spread his hood to keep the sun off Brahm as he slept. Look, and be afraid!"

He spread out his hood more than ever, and Rikki-tikki saw the spectacle-mark on the back of it that looks exactly like the eye part of a hook-and-eye fastening. He was afraid for the minute; but it is impossible for a mongoose to stay frightened for any length of time, and though Rikki-tikki had never met a live cobra before, his mother had fed him on dead ones, and he knew that all a grown mongoose's business in life was to fight and eat snakes. Nag knew that too, and at the bottom of his cold heart he was afraid.

"Well," said Rikki-tikki, and his tail began to fluff up again, "marks or no marks, do you think it is right for you to eat fledglings out of a nest?"

Nag was thinking to himself, and watching the least little movement in the grass behind Rikki-tikki. He knew that mongooses in the garden meant death sooner or later for him and his family, but he wanted to get Rikki-tikki off his guard. So he dropped his head a little, and put it on one side.

"Let us talk," he said. "You eat eggs. Why should not I eat birds?"

"Behind you! Look behind you!" sang Darzee.

Rikki-tikki knew better than to waste time in staring. He jumped up in the air as high as he could go, and just under him whizzed by the head of Nagaina, Nag's wicked wife. She had crept up behind him as he was talking, to make an end of him; and he heard her savage hiss as the stroke missed. He came down almost across her back, and if he had been an old mongoose he would have known that then was the time to break her back with one bite; but he was afraid of the terrible lashing return-stroke of the cobra. He bit, indeed, but did not bite long enough, and he jumped clear of the whisking tail, leaving Nagaina torn and angry.

"Wicked, wicked Darzee!" said Nag, lashing up as high as he could reach towards the nest in the thorn-bush; but Darzee had built it out of reach of snakes, and it only swayed to and fro.

Rikki-tikki felt his eyes growing red and hot (when a mongoose's eyes grow red, he is angry), and he sat back on his tail and hind legs like a little kangaroo, and looked all round him, and chattered with rage. But Nag and Nagaina had disappeared into the grass. When a snake misses its stroke, it never says anything or gives any sign of what it means to do next. Rikki-tikki did not care to follow them, for he did not feel sure that he could manage two snakes at once. So he trotted off to the gravel path near the house, and sat down to think. It was a serious matter for him.

If you read the old books of natural history, you will find they say that when the mongoose fights the snake and happens to get bitten, he runs off and eats some herb that cures him. That is not true. The victory is only a matter of quickness of eye and quickness of foot—snake's blow against mongoose's jump—and as no eye can follow the motion of a snake's head when it strikes, that makes things much more wonderful than any magic herb. Rikki-tikki knew he was a young mongoose, and it made him all the more pleased to think that he had managed to escape a blow from behind. It gave him confidence in himself, and when Teddy came running down the path, Rikki-tikki was ready to be petted.

But just as Teddy was stooping, something flinched a little in the dust, and a tiny voice said: "Be careful. I am death!" It was Karait, the dusty brown snakeling that lies for choice on the dusty earth; and his bite is as dangerous as the cobra's. But he is so small that nobody thinks of him, and so he does the more harm to people.

Rikki-tikki's eyes grew red again, and he danced up to Karait with the peculiar rocking, swaying motion that he had inherited from his family. It looks very funny, but it is so perfectly balanced a gait that you can fly off from it at any angle you please; and in dealing with snakes this is an advantage. If Rikki-tikki had only known, he was doing a much more dangerous thing than fighting Nag, for Karait is so small, and can turn so quickly, that unless Rikki bit him close to the back of the head, he would get the return-stroke in his eye or lip. But Rikki did not know: his eyes were all red, and he rocked back and forth, looking for a good place to hold. Karait struck out. Rikki jumped sideways and tried to run in, but the wicked little dusty grey head lashed within a fraction of his shoulder, and he had to jump over the body, and the head followed his heels close.

Teddy shouted to the house: "Oh, look here! Our mongoose is killing a snake"; and Rikki-tikki heard a scream from Teddy's mother. His father ran out with a stick, but by the time he came up, Karait had lunged out once too far, and Rikki-tikki had sprung, jumped on the snake's back, dropped his head far between his fore-legs, bitten as high up the back as he could get hold, and rolled away. That bite paralysed Karait, and Rikki-tikki was just going to eat him up from the tail, after the custom of his family at dinner, when he remembered that a full meal makes a slow mongoose, and if he wanted all his strength and quickness ready, he must keep himself thin.

He went away for a dust-bath under the castor-oil bushes, while Teddy's father beat the dead Karait. "What is the use of that?" thought Rikki-tikki. "I have settled it all"; and then Teddy's mother picked him up from the dust and hugged him, crying that he had saved Teddy from death, and Teddy's father said that he was a providence, and Teddy looked on with big scared eyes. Rikki-tikki was rather amused at all the fuss, which, of course, he did not understand. Teddy's mother might just as well have petted Teddy for playing in the dust. Rikki was thoroughly enjoying himself.

That night, at dinner, walking to and fro among the wine-glasses on the table, he could have stuffed himself three times over with nice things; but he remembered Nag and Nagaina, and though it was very pleasant to be patted and petted by Teddy's mother, and to sit on Teddy's shoulder, his eyes would get red from time to time, and he would go off into his long war-cry of *"Rikk-tikk-tikki-tikki-tchk!"*

Teddy carried him off to bed, and insisted on Rikki-tikki sleeping under his chin. Rikki-tikki was too well-bred to bite or scratch, but as soon as Teddy was asleep he went off for his nightly walk round the house, and in the dark he ran up against Chuchundra, the musk-rat, creeping round by the wall. Chuchundra is a broken-hearted little beast. He whimpers and cheeps all the night, trying to make up his mind to run into the middle of the room, but he never gets there.

"Don't kill me," said Chuchundra, almost weeping. "Rikki-tikki, don't kill me!"

"Do you think a snake-killer kills musk-rats?" said Rikki-tikki scornfully.

"Those who kill snakes get killed by snakes," said Chuchundra, more sorrowfully than ever. "And how am I to be sure that Nag won't mistake me for you some dark night?"

"There's not the least danger," said Rikki-tikki; "but Nag is in the garden, and I know you don't go there."

"My cousin Chua, the rat, told me—" said Chuchundra, and then he stopped.

"Told you what?"

"H'sh! Nag is everywhere, Rikki-tikki. You should have talked to Chua in the garden."

"I didn't—so you must tell me. Quick, Chuchundra, or I'll bite you!"

Chuchundra sat down and cried till the tears rolled off his whiskers. "I am a very poor man," he sobbed. "I never had spirit enough to run out into the middle of the room. H'sh! I mustn't tell you anything. Can't you *hear,* Rikki-tikki?"

Rikki-tikki listened. The house was as still as still, but he thought he could just catch the faintest *scratch-scratch* in the world—a noise as faint as that of a wasp walking on a windowpane—the dry scratch of a snake's scales on brickwork.

"That's Nag or Nagaina," he said to himself, "and he is crawling into the bath-room sluice. You're right, Chuchundra; I should have talked to Chua."

He stole off to Teddy's bath-room, but there was nothing there, and then to Teddy's mother's bath-room. At the bottom of the smooth plaster wall there was a brick pulled out to make a sluice for the bath-water, and as Rikki-tikki stole in by the masonry curb where the bath is put, he heard Nag and Nagaina whispering together outside in the moonlight.

"When the house is emptied of people," said Nagaina to her husband, "*he* will have to go away, and then the garden will be our own again. Go in quietly, and remember that the big man who killed Karait is the first one to bite. Then come out and tell me, and we will hunt for Rikki-tikki together."

"But are you sure that there is anything to be gained by killing the people?" said Nag.

"Everything. When there were no people in the bungalow, did we have any mongoose in the garden? So long as the bungalow is empty, we are king and queen of the garden; and remember that as soon as our eggs in the melon-bed hatch (as they may tomorrow), our children will need room and quiet."

"I had not thought of that," said Nag. "I will go, but there is no need that we should hunt for Rikki-tikki afterward. I will kill the big man and his wife, and the child if I can, and come away quietly. Then the bungalow will be empty, and Rikki-tikki will go."

Rikki-tikki tingled all over with rage and hatred at this, and then Nag's head came through the sluice, and his five feet of cold body followed it. Angry as he was, Rikki-tikki was very frightened as he saw the size of the big cobra. Nag coiled himself up, raised his head, and looked into the bath-room in the dark, and Rikki could see his eyes glitter.

"Now, if I kill him here, Nagaina will know; and if I fight him on the open floor, the odds are in his favour. What am I to do?" said Rikki-tikki-tavi.

Nag waved to and fro, and then Rikki-tikki heard him drinking from the biggest water-jar that was used to fill the bath. "That is good," said the snake. "Now, when Karait was killed, the big man had a stick. He may have that stick still, but when he comes in to bathe in the morning he will not have a stick. I shall wait here till he comes. Nagaina—do you hear me?—I shall wait here in the cool till daytime."

There was no answer from outside, so Rikki-tikki knew Nagaina had gone away. Nag coiled himself down, coil by coil, round the bulge at the bottom of the water-jar, and Rikki-tikki stayed still as death. After an hour he began to move, muscle by muscle, toward the jar. Nag was asleep, and Rikki-tikki looked at his big back, wondering which would be the best place for a good hold. "If I don't break his back at the first jump," said Rikki, "he can still fight; and if he fights—O, Rikki!" He looked at the thickness of the neck below the hood, but that was too much for him; and a bite near the tail would only make Nag savage.

"It must be the head," he said at last; "the head above the hood; and when I am once there, I must not let go."

Then he jumped. The head was lying a little clear of the water-jar, under the curve of it; and, as his teeth met, Rikki braced his back against the bulge of the red earthenware to hold down the head. This gave him just one second's purchase, and he made the most of it. Then he was battered to and fro as a rat is shaken by a dog—to and fro on the floor, up and down, and round in great circles; but his eyes were red, and he held on as the body cart-whipped over the floor, upsetting the tin dipper and the soap-dish and the flesh-brush, and banged against the tin side of the bath. As he held he closed his jaws tighter and tighter, for he made sure he would be banged to death, and, for the honour of his family, he preferred to be found with his teeth locked. He was dizzy, aching, and felt shaken to pieces when something went off like a thunderclap just behind him; a hot wind knocked him senseless, and red fire singed his fur. The big man had been wakened by the noise, and had fired both barrels of a shot-gun into Nag just behind the hood.

Rikki-tikki held on with his eyes shut, for now he was quite sure he was dead; but the head did not move, and the big man picked him up and said: "It's the mongoose again, Alice; the little chap has saved *our* lives now." Then Teddy's mother came in with a very white face, and saw what was left of Nag, and Rikki-tikki dragged himself to Teddy's bedroom and spent half the rest of the night shaking himself tenderly to find out whether he really was broken into forty pieces, as he fancied.

When morning came he was very stiff, but well pleased with his doings. "Now I have Nagaina to settle with, and she will be worse than five Nags, and there's no knowing when the eggs she spoke of will hatch. Goodness! I must go and see Darzee," he said.

Without waiting for breakfast, Rikki-tikki ran to the thorn-bush where Darzee was singing a song of triumph at the top of his voice. The news of Nag's death was all over the garden, for the sweeper had thrown the body on the rubbish-heap.

"Oh, you stupid tuft of feathers!" said Rikki-tikki angrily. "Is this the time to sing?"

"Nag is dead—is dead—is dead!" sang Darzee. "The valiant Rikki-tikki caught him by the head and held fast. The big man brought the bang-stick, and Nag fell in two pieces! He will never eat my babies again."

"All that's true enough; but where's Nagaina?" said Rikki-tikki, looking carefully round him.

"Nagaina came to the bath-room sluice and called for Nag," Darzee went on; "and Nag came out on the end of a stick—the sweeper picked him up on the end of a stick and threw him upon the rubbish-heap. Let us sing about the great, the red-eyed Rikki-tikki!" and Darzee filled his throat and sang.

"If I could get up to your nest, I'd roll all your babies out!" said Rikki-tikki. "You don't know when to do the right thing at the right time. You're safe enough in your nest there, but it's war for me down here. Stop singing a minute, Darzee."

"For the great, the beautiful Rikki-tikki's sake I will stop," said Darzee. "What is it, O Killer of the terrible Nag?"

"Where is Nagaina, for the third time?"

"On the rubbish-heap by the stables, mourning for Nag. Great is Rikki-tikki with the white teeth."

"Bother my white teeth! Have you ever heard where she keeps her eggs?"

"In the melon-bed, on the end nearest the wall, where the sun strikes nearly all day. She hid them there weeks ago."

"And you never thought it worth while to tell me? The end nearest the wall, you said?"

"Rikki-tikki, you are not going to eat her eggs?"

"Not eat exactly; no. Darzee, if you have a grain of sense you will fly off to the stables and pretend that your wing is broken, and let Nagaina chase you away to this bush. I must get to the melon-bed, and if I went there now she'd see me."

Darzee was a feather-brained little fellow who could never hold more than one idea at a time in his head; and just because he knew that Nagaina's children were born in eggs like his own, he didn't think at first that it was fair to kill them. But his wife was a sensible bird, and she knew that cobra's eggs meant young cobras later on; so she flew off from the nest, and left Darzee to keep the babies warm, and continue his song about the death of Nag. Darzee was very like a man in some ways.

She fluttered in front of Nagaina by the rubbish-heap, and cried out: "Oh, my wing is broken! The boy in the house threw a stone at me and broke it." Then she fluttered more desperately than ever.

Nagaina lifted up her head and hissed: "You warned Rikki-tikki when I would have killed him. Indeed and truly, you've chosen a bad place to be lame in." And she moved toward Darzee's wife, slipping along over the dust.

"The boy broke it with a stone!" shrieked Darzee's wife.

"Well, it may be some consolation to you when you're dead to know that I shall settle accounts with the boy. My husband lies on the rubbish-heap this morning, but before night the boy in the house will lie very still. What is the use of running away? I am sure to catch you. Little fool, look at me!"

Darzee's wife knew better than to do *that,* for a bird who looks at a snake's eyes gets so frightened that she cannot move. Darzee's wife fluttered on, piping sorrowfully, and never leaving the ground, and Nagaina quickened her pace.

Rikki-tikki heard them going up the path from the stables, and he raced for the end of the melon-patch near the wall. There, in the warm litter about the melons, very cunningly hidden, he found twenty-five eggs, about the size of a bantam's eggs, but with whitish skin instead of shell.

"I was not a day too soon," he said; for he could see the baby cobras curled up inside the skin, and he knew that the minute they were hatched they could each kill a man or a mongoose. He bit off the tops of the eggs as fast as he could, taking care to crush the young cobras, and turned over the litter from time to time to see whether he had missed any. At last there were only three eggs left, and Rikki-tikki began to chuckle to himself, when he heard Darzee's wife screaming:

"Rikki-tikki, I led Nagaina toward the house, and she has gone into the veranda, and—oh, come quickly—she means killing!"

Rikki-tikki smashed two eggs, and tumbled backward down the melon-bed with the third egg in his mouth, and scuttled to the veranda as hard as he could put foot to the ground. Teddy and his mother and father were there at early breakfast; but Rikki-tikki saw that they were not eating anything. They sat stone-still, and their faces were white. Nagaina was coiled up on the matting by Teddy's chair, within easy striking distance of Teddy's bare leg, and she was swaying to and fro singing a song of triumph.

"Son of the big man that killed Nag," she hissed, "stay still. I am not ready yet. Wait a little. Keep very still, all you three. If you move I strike, and if you do not move I strike. Oh, foolish people, who killed my Nag!"

Teddy's eyes were fixed on his father, and all his father could do was to whisper: "Sit still, Teddy. You mustn't move. Teddy, keep still."

Then Rikki-tikki came up and cried: "Turn round, Nagaina; turn and fight!"

"All in good time," said she, without moving her eyes. "I will settle my account with you presently. Look at your friends, Rikki-tikki. They are still and white; they are afraid. They dare not move, and if you come a step nearer I strike."

"Look at your eggs," said Rikki-tikki, "in the melon-bed near the wall. Go and look, Nagaina."

The big snake turned half round, and saw the egg on the veranda. "Ah-h! Give it to me," she said.

Rikki-tikki put his paws one on each side of the egg, and his eyes were blood-red. "What price for a snake's egg? For a young cobra? For a young king-cobra? For the last—the very last of the brood? The ants are eating all the others down by the melon-bed."

Nagaina spun clear round, forgetting everything for the sake of the one egg; and Rikki-tikki saw Teddy's father shoot out a big hand, catch Teddy by the shoulder, and drag him across the little table with the tea-cups, safe and out of reach of Nagaina.

"Tricked! Tricked! Tricked! *Rikk-tck-tck!*" chuckled Rikki-tikki. "The boy is safe, and it was I—I—I that caught Nag by the hood last night in the bath-room." Then he began to jump up and down, all four feet together, his head close to the floor. "He threw me to and fro, but he could not shake me off. He was dead before the big man blew him in two. I did it. *Rikki-tikki-tck-tck!* Come then, Nagaina. Come and fight with me. You shall not be a widow long."

Nagaina saw that she had lost her chance of killing Teddy, and the egg lay between Rikki-tikki's paws. "Give me the egg, Rikki-tikki. Give me the last of my eggs, and I will go away and never come back," she said, lowering her hood.

"Yes, you will go away, and you will never come back; for you will go to the rubbish-heap with Nag. Fight, widow! The big man has gone for his gun! Fight!"

Rikki-tikki was bounding all round Nagaina, keeping just out of reach of her stroke, his little eyes like hot coals. Nagaina gathered herself together, and flung out at him. Rikki-tikki jumped up and backward. Again and again and again she struck, and each time her head came with a whack on the matting of the veranda, and she gathered herself together like a watch-spring. Then Rikki-tikki danced in a circle to get behind her, and Nagaina spun round to keep her head to his head, so that the rustle of her tail on the matting sounded like dry leaves blown along by the wind.

He had forgotten the egg. It still lay on the veranda, and Nagaina came nearer and nearer to it, till at last, while Rikki-tikki was drawing breath, she caught it in her mouth, turned to the veranda steps, and flew like an arrow down the path, with Rikki-tikki behind her. When the cobra runs for her life, she goes like a whip-lash flicked across a horse's neck.

Rikki-tikki knew that he must catch her, or all the trouble would begin again. She headed straight for the long grass by the thorn-bush, and as he was running Rikki-tikki heard Darzee still singing his foolish little song of triumph. But Darzee's wife was wiser. She flew off her nest as Nagaina came along, and flapped her wings about Nagaina's head. If Darzee had helped they might have turned her; but Nagaina only lowered her hood and went on. Still, the instant's delay brought Rikki-tikki up to her, and as she plunged into the rat-hole where she and Nag used to live, his little white teeth were clenched on her tail, and he went down with her—and very few mongooses, however wise and old they may be, care to follow a cobra into its hole. It was dark in the hole; and Rikki-tikki never knew when it might open out and give Nagaina room to turn and strike at him. He held on savagely, and struck out his feet to act as brakes on the dark slope of the hot, moist earth.

Then the grass by the mouth of the hole stopped waving, and Darzee said: "It is all over with Rikki-tikki! We must sing his death-song. Valiant Rikki-tikki is dead! For Nagaina will surely kill him underground."

So he sang a very mournful song that he made up on the spur of the minute, and just as he got to the most touching part the grass quivered again, and Rikki-tikki, covered with dirt, dragged himself out of the hole leg by leg, licking his whiskers. Darzee stopped with a little shout. Rikki-tikki shook some of the dust out of his fur and sneezed. "It is all over," he said. "The widow will never come out again." And the red ants that live between the grassstems heard him, and began to troop down one after another to see if he had spoken the truth.

Rikki-tikki curled himself up in the grass and slept where he was—slept and slept till it was late in the afternoon, for he had done a hard day's work.

"Now," he said, when he awoke, "I will go back to the house. Tell the Coppersmith, Darzee, and he will tell the garden that Nagaina is dead."

The Coppersmith is a bird who makes a noise exactly like the beating of a little hammer on a copper pot; and the reason he is always making it is because he is the town-crier to every Indian garden, and tells all the news to everybody who cares to listen. As Rikki-tikki went up the path, he heard his "attention" notes like a tiny dinner-gong; and then the steady "*Ding-dong-tock!* Nag is dead—*dong!* Nagaina is dead! *Ding-dong-tock!*" That set all the birds in the garden singing, and the frogs croaking; for Nag and Nagaina used to eat frogs as well as little birds.

When Rikki got to the house, Teddy and Teddy's mother (she still looked very white, for she had been fainting) and Teddy's father came out and almost cried over him; and that night he ate all that was given him till he could eat no more, and went to bed on Teddy's shoulder, where Teddy's mother saw him when she came to look late at night.

"He saved our lives and Teddy's life," she said to her husband. "Just think, he saved all our lives!"

Rikki-tikki woke up with a jump, for all the mongooses are light sleepers.

"Oh, it's you!" said he. "What are you bothering for? All the cobras are dead; and if they weren't, I'm here."

Rikki-tikki had a right to be proud of himself; but he did not grow too proud, and he kept that garden as a mongoose should keep it, with tooth and jump and spring and bite, till never a cobra dared show its head inside the walls.

Perseverance

Most of the characters we meet in fiction are not superheroes of the type we meet in cartoons and comic books. Like us, they encounter doubts and confusion, failure and setbacks. The path to virtue is not an easy one, and we shouldn't expect our own path to be free of difficulties. One thing you notice in these stories, in both the human and animal characters, is perseverance. They fail time and again before they succeed, but they keep on trying.

And this is something you discover about real-life heroes too. For example, we remember Ulysses Grant as president of the United States and as a victorious Civil War general. But how many know that Grant failed at most of the things he attempted in the early part of his life? He tried his hand at one business endeavor after another and failed again and again. It's the same story with other great men and women. George Washington lost more battles than he won. Anne Frank wrote her diary under the constant threat of arrest. Alexander Solzhenitsyn wrote *The Gulag Archipelago* in the prison camps of Siberia. After being turned down by the king of Portugal, Christopher Columbus pleaded his case for six years at the court of Ferdinand and Isabella. Anne Sullivan persisted for months in her attempt to break through to Helen Keller.

Adversity can wear us down and make us want to give up, but if we persist in our goals, we usually find that we become better people for it. In the movie *Conan the Barbarian,* there is a scene in which the boy Conan is enslaved and put to work pushing the spokes of an enormously heavy gristmill. After years of pushing, the determined boy grows amazingly strong—strong enough to break the chains of his captivity. A similar process can occur in our lives on the moral level. When we push against an obstacle, we may not move it at first—we may not move it at all—but in the process we become morally stronger. And that strength will serve us well when we meet the next obstacle, and the next.

15

A Rare Provider

Carol Ryrie Brink

Caddie Woodlawn is the strong-willed, fearless heroine of *Magical Melons*, a collection of stories about a pioneer family living on a Wisconsin farm. Ten-year-old Caddie spends much of her time romping through forest and field, but in this story she takes on a quieter task.

It was early in the winter of 1863 that Alex McCormick got as far as Dunnville in western Wisconsin with his flock of about a thousand sheep. He had intended going farther west to the open grazing land; but the roads of that time were poor, and suddenly winter had overtaken him before he reached his goal. Snow had fallen in the morning, and now, as evening drew near, a low shaft of sunlight broke through the clouds and made broad golden bands across the snow. Where the shadows fell, the snow looked as blue and tranquil as a summer lake; but it was very cold.

Caddie Woodlawn and her younger brother, Warren, were perched on the rail fence in front of their father's farm, watching the sunset over the new snow while they waited for supper. Tom, who was two years older than Caddie, stood beside them with his elbows on the top rail, and beside him sat Nero, their dog.

"Red sky at night,
Sailor's delight,"

Tom said, wagging his head like a weather prophet.

"Yah," said Warren, "fair, but a lot colder tonight. I'd hate to have to spend the night out on the road."

"Listen!" said Caddie, holding up a finger. "There's a funny noise off over the hill. Do you hear something?"

"It sounds like bells," said Warren. "We didn't miss any of the cows tonight, did we?"

"No," said Tom. "Our bells don't sound like that. Besides, Nero wouldn't let a cow of ours get lost—even if *we* did."

Nero usually wagged his tail appreciatively when his name was mentioned, but now his ears were cocked forward as if he, too, were listening to something far away.

"It's sheep!" said Caddie after a moment's pause. "Listen! They're all saying 'Baa-baa-baa!' If it isn't sheep, I'll eat my best hat."

"The one with the feather?" asked Warren incredulously.

"It must be sheep!" said Tom.

Pouring down the road like a slow gray flood came the thousand sheep of Alex McCormick. A couple of shaggy Scotch sheep dogs ran about them, barking and keeping them on the road. They were a sorry-looking lot, tired and thin and crying from the long days of walking, and their master, who rode behind on a lame horse, was not much better. He was a tall Scotsman, his lean face browned like an Indian's and in startling contrast to his faded blond hair and beard. His eyes were as blue as the shadows on the snow, and they burned strangely in the dark hollows of his hungry-looking face.

"Will ye tell your Daddy I'd like to speak wi' him?" he called as he came abreast of the three children.

Tom dashed away, with a whoop, for Father, and soon the whole Woodlawn household had turned out to witness the curious sight of nearly a thousand weary sheep milling about in the open space before the farm. They had cows and horses and oxen, but none of the pioneer farmers in the valley had yet brought in sheep.

Caddie and Warren stood upon the top rail, balancing themselves precariously and trying to count the sheep. Nero circled about, uncertain whether or not to be friendly with the strange dogs and deeply suspicious of the plaintive bleatings and baaings of the sheep.

Suddenly Caddie hopped off the fence in the midst of the sheep. "Look, mister! There's something wrong with this one."

One of the ewes had dropped down in her tracks and looked as if she might be dying. But Mr. McCormick and Father were deep in conversation and paid no attention to her.

"Here, Caddie! Tom! Warren!" called Father. "We've got to help Mr. McCormick find shelter for his sheep tonight. Run to the neighbors and ask them if they can spare some barn or pasture room and come and help us."

The three children started off across the fields in different directions. As she raced across the light snow toward the Silbernagle farm, Caddie saw tracks ahead of her and, topping the first rise, she saw her little sister Hetty already on her way to tell Lida Silbernagle. Hetty's bonnet and her red knitted mittens flew behind her by their strings, for Hetty never bothered with her bonnet or mittens when there was news to be spread. So Caddie veered north toward the Bunns'.

In a pioneer community everyone must work together for the common good and, although Alex McCormick was a stranger to them all, the men from the neighboring farms had soon gathered to help him save his weary sheep from the cold. With a great deal of shouting, barking, and bleating the flock was divided into small sections and driven off to different farms, where the sheep could shelter under haystacks or sheds through the cold night.

When the last sheep were being driven off, Caddie remembered the sick ewe and ran to see what had become of her. She still lay where she had fallen, her eyes half closed with weariness, her breath coming so feebly that it seemed as if she scarcely lived at all.

"Oh, look, Mr. McCormick!" called Caddie. "You ought to tend to this one or she'll be a goner."

"Hoots!" said the Scotsman. "I've no time to waste on a dead one with hundreds of live ones still on their legs and like to freeze to death the night."

"I've got lots of time, if you haven't, Mr. McCormick," volunteered Caddie.

"Verra good," said the Scotsman. "I'll give her to ye, lassie, if ye can save her life."

"Really?" cried Caddie, and then, "It's a bargain!"

In a moment she had enlisted the services of Tom and Warren, and they were staggering along under the dead weight of the helpless sheep. Their father watched them with a twinkle of amusement in his eye.

"And what are you going to do with that?" he asked.

"It's nothing but a sick sheep," said Tom, "but Caddie thinks she can save it."

"Oh, Father," cried Caddie, "may I put her in the box stall and give her something to eat? She's just worn out and starved—that's all."

Father nodded and smiled.

"I'll look around at her later," he said.

But when Father had time later to visit the box stall, he found Caddie sitting with a lantern beside her ewe and looking very disconsolate.

"Father, I know she's hungry; but I can't make her eat. I don't know what to do."

Mr. Woodlawn knelt beside the animal and felt her all over for possible injuries. Then he opened her mouth and ran his finger gently over her gums.

"Well, Caddie," he said, "I guess you'll have to make her a set of false teeth."

"False teeth!" echoed Caddie. Then she stuck her own fingers in the ewe's mouth. "She hasn't any teeth!" she cried. "No wonder she couldn't chew hay! Whatever shall we do?"

Mr. Woodlawn looked thoughtfully into his small daughter's worried face.

"Well," he said, "it would be quite a task, and I don't know whether you want to undertake it."

"Yes, I do," said Caddie. "Tell me what."

"Mother has more of those small potatoes than she can use this winter. Get her to cook some of them for you until they are quite soft, and mix them with bran and milk into a mash. I think you can pull your old sheep through on that. But it will be an everyday job, like taking care of a baby. You'll find it pretty tiresome."

"Oh! But, Father, it's better than having her die!"

That evening Mr. McCormick stayed for supper with them. It was not often that they had a stranger from outside as their guest, and their eager faces turned toward him around the lamplit table. Father and Mother at each end of the table, with the six children ranged around; and Robert Ireton, the hired man, and Katie Conroy, the hired girl, there, too—they made an appreciative audience. Mr. McCormick's tongue, with its rich Scotch burr, was loosened to relate for them the story of his long journey from the East with his sheep. He told how Indians had stolen some and wolves others; how the herdsman he had brought with him had caught a fever and died on the way, and was buried at the edge of an Indian village; how they had forded streams and weathered a tornado.

While the dishes were being cleared away, the Scotsman took Hetty and little Minnie on his knees and told them about the little thatched home in Scotland where he had been born. Then he opened a wallet, which he had inside his buckskin shirt, to show them some treasure which he kept there. They all crowded around to see, and it was only a bit of dried heather which had come from Scotland.

As the stranger talked, Caddie's mind kept going to the box stall in the barn; and something warm and pleasant sang inside her.

"She ate the potato mash," she thought. "If I take good care of her she'll live, and it will be all because of me! I love her more than any pet I've got—except, of course, Nero."

The next day the muddy, trampled place where the sheep had been was white with fresh snow, and Mr. McCormick set out for Dunnville to try to sell as many of his sheep as he could. Winter had overtaken him too soon, and after all his long journey he found himself still far from open grazing land and without sheds or shelter to keep the sheep over the winter. But Dunnville was a small place, and he could sell only a very small part of his huge flock. When he had disposed of all he could, he made an agreement with Mr. Woodlawn and the other farmers that they might keep as many of his sheep as they could feed and shelter over the winter, if they would give him half of the wool and half of the lambs in the spring.

"How about mine?" asked Caddie.

Mr. McCormick laughed.

"Nay, lassie," he said. "You've earned the old ewe fair an' square, and everything that belongs to her."

The old ewe was on her feet now, and baaing and nuzzling Caddie's hand whenever Caddie came near her. That was a busy winter for Caddie. Before school in the morning and after school in the evening, there were always mashes of vegetables and bran to be cooked up for Nanny.

"You'll get tired doing that," said Tom.

"Nanny!" scoffed Warren. "That's a name for a goat."

"No," said Caddie firmly. "That's a name for Caddie Woodlawn's sheep, and you see if I get tired of feeding her!"

When the days began to lengthen and grow warmer toward the end of February, Caddie turned Nanny out during the day with the other sheep. At first she tied a red woolen string about Nanny's neck; for, even if one loves them, sheep are very much alike, and Caddie did not want to lose her own. But really that was quite unnecessary, for as soon as Nanny saw her coming with a pan of mash and an iron spoon she broke away from the others and made a beeline for Caddie. At night she came to the barn and waited for Caddie to let her in.

One morning in March, when Caddie had risen early to serve Nanny's breakfast before she went to school, Robert came out of the barn to meet her. She had flung Mother's shawl on over her pinafore, and the pan of warm mash which she carried steamed cozily in the chill spring air.

For once Robert was neither singing nor whistling at his work, and he looked at Caddie with such a mixture of sorrow and glad tidings on his honest Irish face that Caddie stopped short.

"Something's happened!" she cried.

"Aye. Faith, an' you may well say so, Miss Caddie," said Robert seriously.

Caddie's heart almost stopped beating for a moment. Something had happened to Nanny! In a daze of apprehension she ran into the barn.

"You're not to feel too grieved now, mavourneen," said Robert, coming after her. "You did more for the poor beast than any other body would have done."

But words meant nothing to Caddie now, for in solemn truth the thin thread of life which she had coaxed along in the sick sheep all winter had finally ebbed away and Nanny was dead. Caddie flung away the pan of mash and knelt down beside the old sheep. She could not speak or make a sound, but the hot tears ran down her cheeks and tasted salty on her lips. Her heart felt ready to burst with sorrow.

"Wurra! Wurra! Wurra!" said Robert sympathetically, leaning over the side of the stall and looking down on them. "But 'tis an ill wind blows nobody good. Why don't ye look around an' see the good the ill wind has been a-blowing of you?"

Caddie shook her head, squeezing her eyes tight shut to keep the tears from flowing so fast.

"Look!" he urged again.

Robert had come into the stall and thrust something soft and warm under her hand. The something soft and warm stirred, and a faint small voice said, "Ma-a-a-a!"

"Look!" said Robert. "Its Ma is dead and, faith, if 'tis not a-callin' *you* Ma! It knows which side its bread is buttered on."

Caddie opened her eyes in astonishment. Her tears had suddenly ceased to flow, for Robert had put into her arms something so young and helpless and so lovable that half of her sorrow was already swept away.

"It's a lamb!" said Caddie, half to herself, and then to Robert, "Is it—Nanny's?"

"Aye," said Robert, "it is that. But Nanny was too tired to mother it. 'Sure an' 'tis all right for me to go to sleep an' leave it,' says Nanny to herself, 'for Caddie Woodlawn is a rare provider.'"

Caddie wrapped the shawl around her baby and cradled the small shivering creature in her arms.

"Potato mash won't do," she was saying to herself.

"Warm milk is what it needs, and maybe Mother will give me one of Baby Joe's bottles to make the feeding easier."

The lamb cuddled warmly and closely against her. "Ma-a-a-a!" it said.

"Oh, yes, I will be!" Caddie whispered back.

16

Island of the Blue Dolphins

Scott O'Dell

When her tribe is forced to flee their island, Karana, seeing her little brother left behind on the beach, dives into the water and returns to him. In the weeks that follow, the two begin to learn to fish and gather food, but when a pack of wild dogs kills Ramo, the girl is left entirely alone. The following passage recounts her attempt to leave the island and her fortunate encounter with the animals that gave her island its name.

Summer is the best time on the Island of the Blue Dolphins. The sun is warm then and the winds blow milder out of the west, sometimes out of the south.

It was during these days that the ship might return and now I spent most of my time on the rock, looking out from the high headland into the east, toward the country where my people had gone, across the sea that was never-ending.

Once while I watched I saw a small object which I took to be the ship, but a stream of water rose from it and I knew that it was a whale spouting. During those summer days I saw nothing else.

The first storm of winter ended my hopes. If the white men's ship were coming for me it would have come during the time of good weather. Now I would have to wait until winter was gone, maybe longer.

The thought of being alone on the island while so many suns rose from the sea and went slowly back into the sea filled my heart with loneliness. I had not felt so lonely before because I was sure that the ship would return as Matasaip had said it would. Now my hopes were dead. Now I was really alone. I could not eat much, nor could I sleep without dreaming terrible dreams.

The storm blew out of the north, sending big waves against the island and winds so strong that I was unable to stay on the rock. I moved my bed to the foot of the rock and for protection kept a fire going throughout the night. I slept there five times. The first night the dogs came and stood outside the ring made by the fire. I killed three of them with arrows, but not the leader, and they did not come again.

On the sixth day, when the storm had ended, I went to the place where the canoes had been hidden, and let myself down over the cliff. This part of the shore was sheltered from the wind and I found the canoes just as they had been left. The dried food was still good, but the water was stale, so I went back to the spring and filled a fresh basket.

I had decided during the days of the storm, when I had given up hope of seeing the ship, that I would take one of the canoes and go to the country that lay toward the east. I remembered how Kimki, before he had gone, had asked the advice of his ancestors who had lived many ages in the past, who had come to the island from that country, and likewise the advice of Zuma, the medicine man who held power over the wind and the seas. But these things I could not do, for Zuma had been killed by the Aleuts, and in all my life I had never been able to speak with the dead, though many times I had tried.

Yet I cannot say that I was really afraid as I stood there on the shore. I knew that my ancestors had crossed the sea in their canoes, coming from that place which lay beyond. Kimki, too, had crossed the sea. I was not nearly so skilled with a canoe as these men, but I must say that whatever might befall me on the endless waters did not trouble me. It meant far less than the thought of staying on the island alone, without a home or companions, pursued by wild dogs, where everything reminded me of those who were dead and those who had gone away.

Of the four canoes stored there against the cliff, I chose the smallest, which was still very heavy because it could carry six people. The task that faced me was to push it down the rocky shore and into the water, a distance four or five times its length.

This I did by first removing all the large rocks in front of the canoe. I then filled in all these holes with pebbles and along this path laid down long strips of kelp, making a slippery bed. The shore was steep and once I got the canoe to move with its own weight, it slid down the path and into the water.

The sun was in the west when I left the shore. The sea was calm behind the high cliffs. Using the two-bladed paddle I quickly skirted the south part of the island. As I reached the sandspit the wind struck. I was paddling from the back of the canoe because you can go faster kneeling there, but I could not handle it in the wind.

Kneeling in the middle of the canoe, I paddled hard and did not pause until I had gone through the tides that run fast around the sandspit. There were many small waves and I was soon wet, but as I came out from behind the spit the spray lessened and the waves grew long and rolling. Though it would have been easier to go the way they slanted, this would have taken me in the wrong direction. I therefore kept them on my left hand, as well as the island, which grew smaller and smaller, behind me.

At dusk I looked back. The Island of the Blue Dolphins had disappeared. This was the first time that I felt afraid.

There were only hills and valleys of water around me now. When I was in a valley I could see nothing and when the canoe rose out of it, only the ocean stretching away and away.

Night fell and I drank from the basket. The water cooled my throat.

The sea was black and there was no difference between it and the sky. The waves made no sound among themselves, only faint noises as they went under the canoe or struck against it. Sometimes the noises seemed angry and at other times like people laughing. I was not hungry because of my fear.

The first star made me feel less afraid. It came out low in the sky and it was in front of me, toward the east. Other stars began to appear all around, but it was this one I kept my gaze upon. It was in the figure that we call a serpent, a star which shone green and which I knew. Now and then it was hidden by mist, yet it always came out brightly again.

Without this star I would have been lost, for the waves never changed. They came always from the same direction and in a manner that kept pushing me away from the place I wanted to reach. For this reason the canoe made a path in the black water like a snake. But somehow I kept moving toward the star which shone in the east.

This star rose high and then I kept the North Star on my left hand, the one we call "the star that does not move." The wind grew quiet. Since it always died down when the night was half over, I knew how long I had been traveling and how far away the dawn was.

About this time I found that the canoe was leaking. Before dark I had emptied one of the baskets in which food was stored and used it to dip out the water that came over the sides. The water that now moved around my knees was not from the waves.

I stopped paddling and worked with the basket until the bottom of the canoe was almost dry. Then I searched around, feeling in the dark along the smooth planks, and found the place near the bow where the water was seeping through a crack as long as my hand and the width of a finger. Most of the time it was out of the sea, but it leaked whenever the canoe dipped forward in the waves.

The places between the planks were filled with black pitch which we gather along the shore. Lacking this, I tore a piece of fiber from my skirt and pressed it into the crack, which held back the water.

Dawn broke in a clear sky and as the sun came out of the waves I saw that it was far off on my left. During the night I had drifted south of the place I wished to go, so I changed my direction and paddled along the path made by the rising sun.

There was no wind on this morning and the long waves went quietly under the canoe. I therefore moved faster than during the night.

I was very tired, but more hopeful than I had been since I left the island. If the good weather did not change I would cover many leagues before dark. Another night and another day might bring me within sight of the shore toward which I was going.

Not long after dawn, while I was thinking of this strange place and what it would look like, the canoe began to leak again. This crack was between the same planks, but was a larger one and close to where I was kneeling.

The fiber I tore from my skirt and pushed into the crack held back most of the water which seeped in whenever the canoe rose and fell with the waves. Yet I could see that the planks were weak from one end to the other, probably from the canoe being stored so long in the sun, and that they might open along their whole length if the waves grew rougher.

It was suddenly clear to me that it was dangerous to go on. The voyage would take two more days, perhaps longer. By turning back to the island I would not have nearly so far to travel.

Still I could not make up my mind to do so. The sea was calm and I had come far. The thought of turning back after all this labor was more than I could bear. Even greater was the thought of the deserted island I would return to, of living there alone and forgotten. For how many suns and how many moons?

The canoe drifted idly on the calm sea while these thoughts went over and over in my mind, but when I saw the water seeping through the crack again, I picked up the paddle. There was no choice except to turn back toward the island.

I knew that only by the best of fortune would I ever reach it.

The wind did not blow until the sun was overhead. Before that time I covered a good distance, pausing only when it was necessary to dip water from the canoe. With the wind I went more slowly and had to stop more often because of the water spilling over the sides, but the leak did not grow worse.

This was my first good fortune. The next was when a swarm of dolphins appeared. They came swimming out of the west, but as they saw the canoe they turned around in a great circle and began to follow me. They swam up slowly and so close that I could see their eyes, which are large and the color of the ocean. Then they swam on ahead of the canoe, crossing back and forth in front of it, diving in and out, as if they were weaving a piece of cloth with their broad snouts.

Dolphins are animals of good omen. It made me happy to have them swimming around the canoe, and though my hands had begun to bleed from the chafing of the paddle, just watching them made me forget the pain. I was very lonely before they appeared, but now I felt that I had friends with me and did not feel the same.

The blue dolphins left me shortly before dusk. They left as quickly as they had come, going on into the west, but for a long time I could see the last of the sun shining on them. After night fell I could still see them in my thoughts and it was because of this that I kept on paddling when I wanted to lie down and sleep.

More than anything, it was the blue dolphins that took me back home.

Fog came with the night, yet from time to time I could see the star that stands high in the west, the red star called Magat which is part of the figure that looks like a crawfish and is known by that name. The crack in the planks grew wider so I had to stop often to fill it with fiber and to dip out the water.

The night was very long, longer than the night before. Twice I dozed kneeling there in the canoe, though I was more afraid than I had ever been. But the morning broke clear and in front of me lay the dim line of the island like a great fish sunning itself on the sea.

I reached it before the sun was high, the sandspit and its tides that bore me into the shore. My legs were stiff from kneeling and as the canoe struck the sand I fell when I rose to climb out. I crawled through the shallow water and up the beach. There I lay for a long time, hugging the sand in happiness.

I was too tired to think of the wild dogs. Soon I fell asleep.

17

Lassie Come-Home

Eric Knight

Lassie is a purebred collie, beloved of Joe Carraclough, her young Yorkshire master. But hard times and lack of work force Joe's father to sell Lassie to the wealthy Duke of Rudling. When Lassie is taken far away to northern Scotland by the Duke, it looks as if Joe has seen the last of her. But Lassie has other ideas.

Sam Carraclough had spoken the truth early that year when he told his son Joe that it was a long way from Greenall Bridge in Yorkshire to the Duke of Rudling's place in Scotland. And it is just as many miles coming the other way, a matter of four hundred miles.

But that would be for a man, traveling straight by road or by train. For an animal how far would it be—an animal that must circle and quest at obstacles, wander and err, backtrack and sidetrack till it found a way?

A thousand miles it would be—a thousand miles through strange terrain it had never crossed before, with nothing but instinct to tell direction.

Yes, a thousand miles of mountain and dale, of highland and moor, plowland and path, ravine and river and beck and burn; a thousand miles of tor and brae, of snow and rain and fog and sun; of wire and thistle and thorn and flint and rock to tear the feet—who could expect a dog to win through that?

Yet, if it were almost a miracle, in his heart Joe Carraclough tried to believe in that miracle—that somehow, wonderfully, inexplicably, his dog would be there some day; there, waiting by the school gate. Each day as he came out of school, his eyes would turn to the spot where Lassie had always waited. And each day there was nothing there, and Joe Carraclough would walk home slowly, silently, stolidly as did the people of his country.

Always, when school ended, Joe tried to prepare himself—told himself not to be disappointed, because there could be no dog there. Thus, through the long weeks, Joe began to teach himself not to believe in the impossible. He had hoped against hope so long that hope began to die.

But if hope can die in a human, it does not in an animal. As long as it lives, the hope is there and the faith is there. And so, coming across the schoolyard that day, Joe Carraclough would not believe his eyes. He shook his head and blinked, and rubbed his fists in his eyes, for he thought what he was seeing was a dream. There, walking the last few yards to the school gate was—his dog!

He stood, for the coming of the dog was terrible—her walk was a thing that tore at her breath. Her head and her tail were down almost to the pavement. Each footstep forward seemed a separate effort. It was a crawl rather than a walk. But the steps were made, one by one, and at last the animal dropped in her place by the gate and lay still.

Then Joe roused himself. Even if it were a dream, he must do something. In dreams one must try.

He raced across the yard and fell to his knees, and then, when his hands were touching and feeling fur, he knew it was reality. His dog had come to meet him!

But what a dog was this—no prize collie with fine tricolor coat glowing, with ears lifted gladly over the proud, slim head with its perfect black mask. It was not a dog whose bright eyes were alert, and who jumped up to bark a glad welcome. This was a dog that lay, weakly trying to lift a head that would no longer lift; trying to move a tail that was torn and matted with thorns and burrs, and managing to do nothing very much except to whine in a weak, happy, crying way. For she knew that at last the terrible driving instinct was at peace. She was at the place. She had kept her lifelong rendezvous, and hands were touching her that had not touched her for so long a time.

By the Labor Exchange, Ian Cawper stood with the other out-of-work miners, waiting until it was tea time so that they could all go back to their cottages.

You could have picked out Ian, for he was much the biggest man even among the many big men that Yorkshire grows. In fact, he was reputed to be the biggest and strongest man in all that Riding of Yorkshire. A big man, but gentle and often very slow of thinking and speech.

And so Ian was a few seconds behind the others in realizing that something of urgency was happening in the village. Then he too saw it—a boy struggling, half running, along the main street, his voice lifted in excitement, a great bundle of something in his arms.

The men stirred and moved forward. Then, when the boy was nearer, they heard his cry:

"She's come back! She's come back!"

The men looked at each other and blew out their breath and then stared at the bundle the boy was carrying. It was true. Sam Carraclough's collie had walked back home from Scotland.

"I must get her home, quick!" the boy was saying. He staggered on.

Ian Cawper stepped forward.

"Here," he said. "Run on ahead, tell 'em to get ready."

His great arms cradled the dog—arms that could have carried ten times the weight of this poor, thin animal.

"Oh, hurry, Ian!" the boy cried, dancing in excitement.

"I'm hurrying, lad. Go on ahead."

So Joe Carraclough raced along the street, turned up the side street, ran down the garden path, and burst into the cottage:

"Mother! Father!"

"What is it, lad?"

Joe paused. He could hardly get the words out—the excitement was choking up in his throat, hot and stifling. And then the words were said:

"Lassie! She's come home! Lassie's come home!"

He opened the door, and Ian Cawper, bowing his head to pass under the lintel, carried the dog to the hearth and laid her there.

There were many things that Joe Carraclough was to remember from that evening. He was never to forget the look that passed over his father's face as he first knelt beside the dog that had been his for so many years, and let his hands travel over the emaciated frame. He was to remember how his mother moved about the kitchen, not grumbling or scolding now, but silently and with a sort of terrific intensity, poking the fire quickly, stirring the condensed milk into warm water, kneeling to hold the dog's head and lift open the jowl.

Not a word did his parents speak to him. They seemed to have forgotten him altogether. Instead, they both worked over the dog with a concentration that seemed to put them in a separate world.

Joe watched how his father spooned in the warm liquid; he saw how it drooled out again from the unswallowing dog's jowls and dribbled down onto the rug. He saw his mother warm up a blanket and wrap it round the dog. He saw them try again and again to feed her. He saw his father rise at last.

"It's no use, lass," he said to his mother.

Between his mother and father many questions and answers passed unspoken except through their eyes.

"Pneumonia," his father said at last. "She's not strong enough now . . ."

For a while his parents stood, and then it was his mother who seemed to be somehow wonderfully alive and strong.

"I won't be beat!" she said. "I just won't be beat."

She pursed her lips, and as if this grimace had settled something, she went to the mantlepiece and took down a vase. She turned it over and shook it. The copper pennies came into her hand. She held them out to her husband, not explaining nor needing to explain what was needed. But he stared at the money.

"Go on, lad," she said. "I were saving it for insurance, like."

"But how'll we . . ."

"Hush," the woman said.

Then her eyes flickered over her son, and Joe knew that they were aware of him again for the first time in an hour. His father looked at him, at the money in the woman's hand, and at last at the dog. Suddenly he took the money. He put on his cap and hurried out into the night. When he came back he was carrying bundles—eggs and a small bottle of brandy—precious and costly things in that home.

Joe watched as they were beaten together, and again and again his father tried to spoon some into the dog's mouth. Then his mother blew in exasperation. Angrily she snatched the spoon. She cradled the dog's head on her lap, she lifted the jowls, and poured and stroked the throat—stroked it and stroked it, until at last the dog swallowed.

"Aaaah!"

It was his father, breathing a long, triumphant exclamation. And the firelight shone gold on his mother's hair as she crouched there, holding the dog's head—stroking its throat, soothing it with soft, loving sounds.

Joe did not clearly remember about it afterwards, only a faint sensation that he was being carried to bed at some strange hour of darkness.

And in the morning when he rose, his father sat in his chair, but his mother was still on the rug, and the fire was still burning warm. The dog, swathed in blankets, lay quiet.

"Is she—dead?" Joe asked.

His mother smiled weakly.

"Shhh," she said. "She's just sleeping. And I suppose I ought to get breakfast—but I'm that played out—if I nobbut had a nice strong cup o' tea . . ."

And that morning, strangely enough, it was his father who got the breakfast, boiling the water, brewing the tea, cutting the bread. It was his mother who sat in the rocking chair, waiting until it was ready.

That evening when Joe came home from school, Lassie still lay where he had left her when he went off to school. He wanted to sit and cradle her, but he knew that ill dogs are best left alone. All evening he sat, watching her, stretched out, with the faint breathing the only sign of life. He didn't want to go to bed.

"Now she'll be all right," his mother cried. "Go to bed—she'll be all right."

"Are you sure she'll get better, Mother?"

"Ye can see for yourself, can't you? She doesn't look any worse, does she?"

"But are you sure she's going to be better?"

The woman sighed.

"Of course—I'm sure—now go to bed and sleep."

And Joe went to bed, confident in his parents.

That was one day. There were others to remember. There was the day when Joe returned and, as he walked to the hearth, there came from the dog lying there a movement that was meant to be a wag of the tail.

There was another day when Joe's mother sighed with pleasure, for as she prepared the bowl of milk, the dog stirred, lifted herself unsteadily, and waited. And when the bowl was set down, she put down her head and lapped, while her pinched flanks quivered.

And finally there was that day when Joe first realized that—even now—his dog was not to be his own again. So again the cottage rang with cries and protests, and again a woman's voice was lifted, tired and shrilling:

"Is there never to be any more peace and quiet in my home?"

And long after Joe had gone to bed, he heard the voices continuing—his mother's clear and rising and falling; his father's in a steady, reiterative monotone, never changing, always coming to one sentence:

"But even if he would sell her back, where'd Ah get the brass to buy her—where's the money coming fro'? Ye know we can't get it."

To Joe Carraclough's father, life was laid out in straight rules. When a man could get work, he worked his best and got the best wage he could. If he raised a dog, he raised the best one he could. If he had a wife and children, he took care of them the best he could.

In this out-of-work collier's mind, there were no devious exceptions and evasions concerning life and its codes. Like most simple men, he saw all these things clearly. Lying, cheating, stealing—they were wrong, and you couldn't make them right by twisting them round in your mind.

So it was that, when he was faced with any problem, he so often brought it smack up against elemental truths.

"Honest is honest, and there's no two ways about it," he would say.

He had a habit of putting it like that. "Truth is truth." Or, "Cheating is cheating."

And the matter of Lassie came up against this simple, direct code of morals. He had sold the dog and taken the money and spent it. Therefore the dog did not belong to him any more, and no matter how you argued you could not change that.

But a man has to live with his family, too. When a woman starts to argue . . . well . . .

That next morning when Joe came down to breakfast, while his mother served the oatmeal with pursed lips, his father coughed and spoke as if he had rehearsed a set speech over in his mind many times that night:

"Joe, lad. We've decided upon it—that is, thy mother and me—that Lassie can stay here till she's all better.

"That's all right, because I believe true in ma heart that nobody could nurse her better and wi' more care nor we're doing. So that's honest. But when she's better, well . . .

"Now ye have her for a little while yet, so be content. And don't plague us, lad. There's enough things to worry us now wi'out more. So don't plague us no more—and try to be a man about it—and be content."

With the young, "for a little while" has two shapes. Seen from one end, it is a great, yawning stretch of time extending into the unlimitable future. From the other, it is a ghastly span of days that has been cruelly whisked away before the realization comes.

Joe Carraclough knew that it was the latter that morning when he went to school and heard a mighty, booming voice. As he turned to look, he saw in an automobile a fearsome old man and a girl with her flaxen hair cascading from under a beret. And the old man, with his ferocious white moustaches looking like an animal's misshapen fangs, was waving an ugly blackthorn stick to the danger of the car, the chauffeur, and the world in general, and shouting at him:

"Hi! Hi, there! Yes, I mean you, m' lad! Damme, Jenkins, will you make this smelly contraption stand still a moment? Whoa, there, Jenkins! Whoa! Why we ever stopped using horses is more than any sane man can understand. Country's going to pot, that's what! Here, m' lad! Come here!"

For a moment Joe thought of running—doing anything to get all these things he feared out of his sight, so that they might, miraculously, be out of his mind, too. But a machine can go faster than a boy, and then, too, Joe had in him the blood of men who might think slowly and stick to old ideas and bear trouble patiently—but who do not run away. So he stood sturdily on the pavement and remembered his manners as his mother had taught him, and said:

"Yes, sir?"

"You're Whosis—What's-his-name's lad, aren't you?"

Joe's eyes had turned to the girl. She was the one he had seen long ago when he was putting Lassie in the Duke's kennels. Her face was not hearty-red like his own. It was blue-white.

On the hand that clutched the edge of the car the veins stood out clear-blue. That hand looked thin. He was thinking that, as his mother would say, she could do with some plumduff.

She was looking at him, too. Something made him draw himself up proudly.

"My father is Sam Carraclough," he said firmly.

"I know, I know," the old man shouted impatiently. "I never forget a name. Never! Used to know every last soul in this village. Too many of you growing up now—younger generation. And, by gad, they're all of them not worth one of the old bunch—not the whole kit and caboodle. The modern generation, why . . ."

He halted, for the girl beside him was tugging his sleeve.

"What is it? Eh? Oh, yes. I was just coming to it. Where's your father, m' lad? Is he home?"

"No, sir."

"Where is he?"

"He's off over Allerby, sir."

"Allerby, what's he doing there?"

"A mate spoke for him at the pit, I think, and he's gone to see if there's a chance of getting taken on."

"Oh, yes—yes, of course. When'll he be back?"

"I don't know, sir. I think about tea."

"Don't mumble! Not till tea. Damme, very inconvenient—very! Well, I'll drop round about five-ish. You tell him to stay home and I want to see him—it's important. Tell him to wait."

Then the car was gone, and Joe hurried to school. There was never such a long morning as that one. The minutes in the classroom crawled past as the lessons droned on.

Joe had only one desire—to have it become noon. And when at last the leaden moments that were years were gone, he raced home and burst through the door. It was the same cry—for his mother.

"Mother, Mother!"

"Goodness, don't knock the door down. And close it—anyone would think you were brought up in a barn. What's the matter?"

"Mother, he's coming to take Lassie away!"

"Who is?"

"The Duke . . . he's coming . . ."

"The Duke? How in the world does he know that she's . . ."

"I don't know. But he stopped me this morning. He's coming at tea time . . ."

"Coming here? Are ye sure?"

"Yes, he said he'd come at tea. Oh, Mother, please . . ."

"Now, Joe. Don't start! Now I warn ye!"

"Mother, you've got to listen. Please, please!"

"You hear me? I said . . ."

"No, Mother. Please help me. Please!"

The woman looked at her son and heaved a sigh of weariness and exasperation. Then she threw up her hands in despair.

"Eigh, dearie me! Is there never to be any more peace in this house? Never?"

She sank into her chair and looked at the floor. The boy went to her and touched her arm.

"Mother—do something," the boy pleaded. "Can't we hide her? He'll be here at five. He told me to tell Father he'd be here at five. Oh, Mother . . ."

"Nay, Joe. Thy father won't . . ."

"Won't you beg him? Please, please! Beg Father to . . ."

"Joe!" his mother cried angrily. Then her voice became patient again. "Now, Joe, it's no use. So stop thy plaguing. It's just that thy father won't lie. That much I'll give him. Come good, come bad, he'll not lie."

"But just this once, Mother."

The woman shook her head sadly and sat by the fire, staring into it as if she would find peace there. Her son went to her and touched her bare forearm.

"Please, Mother. Beg him. Just this once. Just one lie wouldn't hurt him. I'll make it up to him, I will. I will, truly!"

The words began to race from his mouth quickly.

"I'll make it up to both of you. When I'm growed up, I'll get a job. I'll earn money. I'll buy him things—I'll buy you things, too. I'll buy you both anything you ever want, if you'll only please, please . . ."

And then, for the first time in all his trouble, Joe Carraclough became a child, his sturdiness gone, and the tears choked his voice. His mother could hear his sobs, and she patted his hand, but she would not look at him. From the magic of the fire she seemed to read deep wisdom, and she spoke slowly.

"Tha mustn't, Joe," she said, her words soft. "Tha mustn't want like that. Tha must learn never to want anything i' life so hard as tha wants Lassie. It doesn't do."

It was then that she felt her son's hand trembling with impatience, and his voice rising clear.

"Ye don't understand, Mother. Ye don't understand. It ain't me that wants her. It's her that wants us—so terrible bad. That's what made her come home all that way. She wants us, so terrible bad."

It was then that Mrs. Carraclough looked at her son at last. She could see his face, contorted, and the tears rolling openly down his cheeks. And yet, in that moment of childishness, it was as if he were suddenly all the more grown up. Mrs. Carraclough felt as if time had jumped, and she were seeing this boy, this son of her own, for the first time in many years.

She stared at him and then she clasped her hands together. Her lips pressed together in a straight line and she got up.

"Joe, come and eat, then. And go back to school and be content. I'll talk to thy father."

She lifted her head, and her voice sounded firm.

"Yes—I'll talk to him, all right. I'll talk to Mr. Samuel Carraclough. I will indeed!"

At five that afternoon, the Duke of Rudling, fuming and muttering in his bad-tempered way, got out of a car that had stopped by a cottage gate. And behind the gate was a boy, who stood sturdily, his feet apart, as if to bar the way.

"Well, well, m' lad! Did ye tell him?"

"Go away," the boy said fiercely. "Go away! Thy tyke's net here."

For once in his life the Duke of Rudling stepped backward. He stared at the boy in amazement.

"Well, drat my buttons, Priscilla," he breathed. "Th' lad's touched. He is—he's touched!"

"Thy tyke's net here. Away wi' thee," the boy said stoutly. And it seemed as if in his determination he spoke in the broadest dialect he could command.

"What's he saying?" Priscilla asked.

"He's saying my dog isn't here. Drat my buttons, are you going deaf, Priscilla? I'm supposed to be deaf, and I can hear him all right. Now, ma lad, what tyke o' mine's net here?"

The Duke, when he answered, also turned to the broadest tones of Yorkshire dialect, as he always did to the people of the cottages—a habit which many of the members of the Duke's family deplored deeply.

"Coom, coom, ma lad. Speak up! What tyke's net here?"

As he spoke he waved his cane ferociously and advanced. Joe Carraclough stepped back from the fearful old man, but he still barred the path.

"No tyke o' thine," he cried stoutly.

But the Duke continued to advance. The words raced from Joe's mouth with a torrent of despair.

"Us hasn't got her. She's not here. She couldn't be here. No tyke could ha' done it. No tyke could come all them miles. It's not Lassie—it's—it's just another one that looks like her. It isn't Lassie."

"Well, bless my heart and soul," puffed the Duke. "Bless my heart and soul. Where's thy father, lad?"

Joe shook his head grimly. But behind him the cottage door opened and his mother's voice spoke.

"If it's Sam Carraclough ye're looking for—he's out in the shed, and been shut up there half the afternoon."

"What's this lad talking about—a dog o' mine being here?"

"Nay, ye're mistaken," the woman said stoutly.

"I'm mistaken?" roared the Duke.

"Yes. He didn't say a tyke o' thine was here. He said it wasn't here."

"Drat my buttons," the Duke sputtered angrily. "Don't twist my words up."

Then his eyes narrowed, and he stepped a pace forward.

"Well, if he said a dog of mine *isn't,* perhaps you'll be good enough to tell me just *which* dog of mine it is that isn't here. Now," he finished triumphantly. "Come, come! Answer me!"

Joe, watching his mother, saw her swallow and then look about her as if for help. She pressed her lips together. The Duke stood waiting for his answer, peering out angrily from beneath his jutting eyebrows. Then Mrs. Carraclough drew a breath to speak.

But her answer, truth or lie, was never spoken. For they all heard the rattle of a chain being drawn from a door, and then the voice of Sam Carraclough said clearly:

"This, I give ye my word, is th' only tyke us has here. So tell me, does it look like any dog that belongs to thee?"

Joe's mouth was opening for a last cry of protest, but as his eyes fell on the dog by his father, the exclamation died. And he stared in amazement.

There he saw his father, Sam Carraclough, the collie fancier, standing with a dog at his heels the like of which few men had ever seen before, or would wish to see. It was a dog that sat patiently at his left heel, as any well-trained dog should do—just as Lassie used to do. But this dog—it was ridiculous to think of it at the same moment as Lassie.

For where Lassie's skull was aristocratic and slim, this dog's head was clumsy and rough. Where Lassie's ears stood in the grace of twin-lapped symmetry, this dog had one screw ear and the other standing up Alsatian fashion, in a way that would give any collie breeder the cold shivers.

More than that. Where Lassie's coat faded to delicate sable, this curious dog had ugly splashes of black; and where Lassie's apron was a billowing expanse of white, this dog had muddy puddles of off-color, blue-merle mixture. Lassie had four white paws, and this one had only one white, two dirty-brown, and one almost black. Lassie's tail flowed gracefully behind her, and this dog's tail looked like something added as an afterthought.

And yet, as Joe Carraclough looked at the dog beside his father, he understood. He knew that if a dog coper could treat a dog with cunning so that its bad points came to look like good ones, he could also reverse the process and make all its good ones look like bad ones—especially if that man were his father, one of the most knowing of dog fanciers in all that Riding of Yorkshire.

In that moment, he understood his father's words, too. For in dog-dealing, as in horse-dealing, the spoken word is a binding contract, and once it is given, no real dog-man will attempt to go back on it.

And that was how his father, in his patient, slow way, had tried to escape with honor. He had not lied. He had not denied anything. He had merely asked a question:

"Tell me, does this dog look like any dog that belongs to thee?"

And the Duke had only to say:

"Why, that's not my dog," and forever after, it would not be his.

So the boy, his mother and his father, gazed steadily at the old man, and waited with held breath as he continued to stare at the dog.

But the Duke of Rudling knew many things too—many, many things. And he was not answering. Instead he was walking forward slowly, the great cane now tapping as he leaned on it. His eyes never left the dog for a second. Slowly, as if he were in a dream, he knelt down, and his hand made one gentle movement. It picked up a forepaw and turned it slightly. So he knelt by the collie, looking with eyes that were as knowing about dogs as any man in Yorkshire. And those eyes did not waste themselves upon twisted ears or blotched markings or rough head. Instead, they stared steadily at the underside of the paw, seeing only the five black pads, crossed and recrossed with half-healed scars where thorns had torn and stones had lacerated.

Then the Duke lifted his head, but for a long time he knelt, gazing into space, while they waited. When he did get up, he spoke, not using Yorkshire dialect any more, but speaking as one gentleman might address another.

"Sam Carraclough," he said. "This is no dog of mine. 'Pon my soul and honor, she never belonged to me. No! Not for a single second did she ever belong to me!"

Then he turned and walked down the path, thumping his cane and muttering: "Bless my soul! I wouldn't ha' believed it! Bless my soul! Four hundred miles! I wouldn't ha' believed it."

It was at the gate that his granddaughter tugged his sleeve.

"What you came for," she whispered. "Remember?"

The Duke seemed to come from his dream, and then he suddenly turned into his old self again.

"Don't whisper! What's that? Oh, yes, of course. You don't need to tell me—I hadn't forgotten!"

He turned and made his voice terrible.

"Carraclough! Carraclough! Drat my buttons, where are ye? What're ye hiding for?"

"I'm still here, sir."

"Oh, yes. Yes. Of course. There you are. You working?"

"Eigh, now—working," Joe's father said. That was the best he could manage.

"Yes, working—working! A job! A job! Do you have one?" the Duke fumed.

"Well, now—it's this road . . ." began Carraclough.

As he fumbled his words, Mrs. Carraclough came to his rescue, as good housewives will in Yorkshire—and in most other parts of the world.

"My Sam's not exactly working, but he's got three or four things that he's been considering. Sort of investigating, as ye might say. But—he hasn't quite said yes or no to any of them yet."

"Then he'd better say no, and quickly," snapped the Duke. "I need somebody up at my kennels. And I think, Carraclough . . ." His eyes turned to the dog still sitting at the man's heel. "I think you must know—a lot—about dogs. So there. That's settled."

"Nay, hold on," Carraclough said. "Ye see, I wouldn't like to think I got a chap into trouble and then took his job. Ye see, Mr. Hynes couldn't help . . ."

"Hynes!" snorted the Duke. "Hynes? Utter nincompoop. Had to sack him. Didn't know a dog from a ringtailed filly. Should ha' known no Londoner could ever run a kennel for a Yorkshireman's taste. Now, I want you for the job."

"Nay, there's still summat," Mrs. Carraclough protested.

"What now?"

"Well, how much would this position be paying?"

The Duke puffed his lips.

"How much do you want, Carraclough?"

"Seven pounds a week, and worth every penny," Mrs. Carraclough cut in, before her husband could even get round to drawing a preparatory breath.

But the Duke was a Yorkshireman, too, and that meant he would scorn himself if he missed a chance to be "practical," as they say, where money is concerned.

"Five," he roared. "And not a penny more."

"Six pounds, ten," bargained Mrs. Carraclough.

"Six even," offered the Duke cannily.

"Done," said Mrs. Carraclough, as quick as a hawk's swoop. They both glowed, self-righteously pleased with themselves. Mrs. Carraclough would have been willing to settle for three pounds a week in the first place—and as for the Duke, he felt he was getting a man for his kennels who was beyond price.

"Then it's settled," the Duke said.

"Well, almost," the woman said. "I presume, of course . . ." She liked the taste of what she considered a very fine word, so she repeated it. ". . . I presume that means we get the cottage on the estate, too."

"Ye drive a fierce bargain, ma'am," said the Duke, scowling. "But ye get it—on one condition." He lifted his voice and roared. "On condition that as long as ye live on my land, you never allow that thick-skulled, screw-lugged, gay-tailed eyesore of an excuse for a collie on my property. Now, what do ye say?"

He waited, rumbling and chuckling happily to himself as Sam Carraclough stooped, perplexed. But it was the boy who answered gladly: "Oh, no, sir. She'll be down at school waiting for me most o' the time. And, anyway, in a day or so we'll have her fixed up so's ye'd never recognize her."

"I don't doubt that," puffed the Duke, as he stumped toward his car. "I don't doubt ye could do exactly that. Hmm . . . Well, I never . . ."

It was afterwards in the car that the girl edged close to the old man.

"Now don't wriggle," he protested. "I can't stand anyone wriggling."

"Grandfather," she said. "You are kind—I mean about their dog."

The old man coughed and cleared his throat.

"Nonsense," he growled. "Nonsense. When you grow up, you'll understand that I'm what people call a hard-hearted Yorkshire realist. For five years I've sworn I'd have that dog. And now I've got her."

Then he shook his head slowly.

"But I had to buy the man to get her. Ah, well. Perhaps that's not the worst part of the bargain."

Self-Sacrifice

The ultimate self-sacrifice is giving up one's life for another, but there are many other kinds as well. There is the kind we show by giving up our free time in order to help someone less fortunate. There is the kind that a father or mother shows by giving up an important meeting in order to attend a daughter's dance recital. There is the kind we show when we give money we have saved for new clothes to a charitable cause instead. And there is the kind demonstrated by Stone Fox when he gives up his opportunity to win the sled race.

Of course, self-sacrifice often involves more than a single act of generosity. A doctor may sacrifice years from his career in order to work with impoverished people. A young man or woman may give up part of his or her life to work for the Peace Corps or as a missionary. A parent may give up opportunities for self-fulfillment year after year in order to create better opportunities for a child.

The idea of self-sacrifice has not been popular in recent years. There has been so much emphasis on "self" and "self-fulfillment" in our culture that self-denial has been made to look stupid and foolish. If one's own self is the most important thing in the universe, then it doesn't make sense to give up free time or deny oneself pleasures for the sake of others. It even used to be thought that high self-esteem would make people more moral.

But social scientists are questioning that now. They point out, for instance, that violent criminals have very high self-esteem and tend to feel superior to others—especially after they have just committed a crime. Habitual criminals often have childish personalities centered mainly on their own needs, wants, and desires. It rarely occurs to them to think about the needs of others.

Practicing acts of self-sacrifice helps us to mature beyond this childish state of selfishness. It's also helpful to remind ourselves that others—our parents, relatives, and teachers—have sacrificed much for us. The best way to pay them back is to be willing to spend our time and energy to help others. We should also remember all those men and women who gave freely of their lives for the sake of creating a better, more just society. The lives of men and women such as Martin Luther King, Jr., Clara Barton, and Susan B. Anthony remind us that societies, like families, work best when altruism, not "look out for number one," is our guiding principle.

If you look up "self-sacrifice" in the thesaurus, you will find synonyms such as "generous," "chivalrous," "handsome," "princely," "noble," and "heroic." When we practice self-sacrifice, these noble qualities become part of our character. And, unlike the self-centered person, we will have good reason to feel good about ourselves.

18

Stone Fox

John Reynolds Gardiner

Every February the National Dogsled Races are held in Jackson, Wyoming. Stone Fox, the legendary Indian who has never lost a dogsled race, is one of the contestants. He plans to use his winnings to buy back land for his people. Ten-year-old Willy needs to win so he can save his grandfather's farm from the tax man. But how can Willy and his dog, Searchlight, hope to compete against the experienced teams driven by Stone Fox and the other sledders?

The Race

Searchlight sprang forward with such force that little Willy couldn't hang on. If it weren't for a lucky grab, he would have fallen off the sled for sure.

In what seemed only seconds, little Willy and Searchlight had traveled down Main Street, turned onto North Road, and were gone. Far, far ahead of the others. They were winning. At least for the moment.

Stone Fox started off dead last. He went so slowly down Main Street that everyone was sure something must be wrong.

Swish! Little Willy's sled flew by the schoolhouse on the outskirts of town, and then by the old deserted barn.

Swish! Swish! Swish! Other racers followed in hot pursuit.

"Go, Searchlight! Go!" little Willy sang out. The cold wind pressed against his face, causing his good eye to shut almost completely. The snow was well packed. It was going to be a fast race today. The fastest they had ever run.

The road was full of dangerous twists and turns, but little Willy did not have to slow down as the other racers did. With only one dog and a small sled, he was able to take the sharp turns at full speed without risk of sliding off the road or losing control.

Therefore, with each turn, little Willy pulled farther and farther ahead.

Swish! The sled rounded a corner, sending snow flying. Little Willy was smiling. This was fun!

About three miles out of town the road made a half circle around a frozen lake. Instead of following the turn, little Willy took a shortcut right across the lake. This was tricky going, but Searchlight had done it many times before.

Little Willy had asked Mayor Smiley if he was permitted to go across the lake, not wanting to be disqualified. "As long as you leave town heading north and come back on South Road," the mayor had said, "anything goes!"

None of the other racers attempted to cross the lake. Not even Stone Fox. The risk of falling through the ice was just too great.

Little Willy's lead increased.

Stone Fox was still running in last place. But he was picking up speed.

At the end of five miles, little Willy was so far out in front that he couldn't see anybody behind him when he looked back.

He knew, however, that the return five miles, going back into town, would not be this easy. The trail along South Road was practically straight and very smooth, and Stone Fox was sure to close the gap. But by how much? Little Willy didn't know.

Doc Smith's house flew by on the right. The tall trees surrounding her cabin seemed like one solid wall.

Grandfather's farm was coming up next.

When Searchlight saw the farmhouse, she started to pick up speed. "No, girl," little Willy yelled. "Not yet."

As they approached the farmhouse, little Willy thought he saw someone in Grandfather's bedroom window. It was difficult to see with only one good eye. The someone was a man. With a full beard.

It couldn't be. But it was! It was Grandfather!

Grandfather was sitting up in bed. He was looking out the window.

Little Willy was so excited he couldn't think straight. He started to stop the sled, but Grandfather indicated no, waving him on. "Of course," little Willy said to himself. "I must finish the race. I haven't won yet."

"Go, Searchlight!" little Willy shrieked. "Go girl!"

Grandfather was better. Tears of joy rolled down little Willy's smiling face. Everything was going to be all right.

And then Stone Fox made his move.

One by one he began to pass the other racers. He went from last place to eighth. Then from eighth place to seventh. Then from seventh to sixth. Sixth to fifth.

He passed the others as if they were standing still.

He went from fifth place to fourth. Then to third. Then to second.

Until only little Willy remained.

But little Willy still had a good lead. In fact, it was not until the last two miles of the race that Stone Fox got his first glimpse of little Willy since the race had begun.

The five Samoyeds looked magnificent as they moved effortlessly across the snow. Stone Fox was gaining, and he was gaining fast. And little Willy wasn't aware of it.

Look back, little Willy! Look back!

But little Willy didn't look back. He was busy thinking about Grandfather. He could hear him laughing . . . and playing his harmonica . . .

Finally little Willy glanced back over his shoulder. He couldn't believe what he saw! Stone Fox was nearly on top of him!

This made little Willy mad. Mad at himself. Why hadn't he looked back more often? What was he doing? He hadn't won yet. Well, no time to think of that now. He had a race to win.

"Go, Searchlight! Go, girl!"

But Stone Fox kept gaining. Silently. Steadily.

"Go, Searchlight! Go!"

The lead Samoyed passed little Willy and pulled up even with Searchlight. Then it was a nose ahead. But that was all. Searchlight moved forward, inching *her* nose ahead. Then the Samoyed regained the lead. Then Searchlight . . .

When you enter the town of Jackson on South Road, the first buildings come into view about a half a mile away. Whether Searchlight took those buildings to be Grandfather's farmhouse again, no one can be sure, but it was at this time that she poured on the steam.

Little Willy's sled seemed to lift up off the ground and fly. Stone Fox was left behind.

But not that far behind.

The Finish Line

The crowd cheered madly when they saw little Willy come into view at the far end of Main Street, and even more madly when they saw that Stone Fox was right on his tail.

"Go, Searchlight! Go!"

Searchlight forged ahead. But Stone Fox was gaining!

"Go, Searchlight! Go!" little Willy cried out.

Searchlight gave it everything she had.

She was a hundred feet from the finish line when her heart burst. She died instantly. There was no suffering.

The sled and little Willy tumbled over her, slid along the snow for a while, then came to a stop about ten feet from the finish line. It had started to snow—white snowflakes landed on Searchlight's dark fur as she lay motionless on the ground.

The crowd became deathly silent.

Lester's eyes looked to the ground. Miss Williams had her hands over her mouth. Mr. Foster's cigar lay on the snow. Doc

Smith started to run out to little Willy, but stopped. Mayor Smiley looked shocked and helpless. And so did Hank and Dusty, and so did the city slickers, and so did Clifford Snyder, the tax man.

Stone Fox brought his sled to a stop alongside little Willy. He stood tall in the icy wind and looked down at the young challenger, and at the dog that lay limp in his arms.

"Is she dead, Mr. Stone Fox? Is she dead?" little Willy asked, looking up at Stone Fox with his one good eye.

Stone Fox knelt down and put one massive hand on Searchlight's chest. He felt no heartbeat. He looked at little Willy, and the boy understood.

Little Willy squeezed Searchlight with all his might. "You did real good, girl. Real good. I'm real proud of you. You rest now, just rest." Little Willy began to brush the snow off Searchlight's back.

Stone Fox stood up slowly.

No one spoke. No one moved. All eyes were on the Indian, the one called Stone Fox, the one who had never lost a race, and who now had another victory within his grasp.

But Stone Fox did nothing.

He just stood there. Like a mountain.

His eyes shifted to his own dogs, then to the finish line, then back to little Willy, holding Searchlight.

With the heel of his moccasin Stone Fox drew a long line in the snow. Then he walked back over to his sled and pulled out his rifle.

Down at the end of Main Street, the other racers began to appear. As they approached, Stone Fox fired his rifle into the air. They came to a stop.

Stone Fox spoke.

"Anyone crosses this line—I shoot."

And there wasn't anybody who didn't believe him.

Stone Fox nodded to the boy.

The town looked on in silence as little Willy, carrying Searchlight, walked the last ten feet and across the finish line.

19

North to Freedom

Anne S. Holm

When twelve-year-old David manages to escape from a prison camp, his only thought is to evade "them"—his communist captors. Having known nothing but prison life, David is fearful and suspicious of everyone he encounters. As he makes his way across Europe, he gradually awakens to the beauty of trust and friendship. When, by a twist of fate, David again finds himself in the clutches of "them," his deliverance comes from an unexpected source—the shepherd dog he had earlier befriended.

Perhaps it happened because he was in too much of a hurry. He was able to plan his route from the maps he found in railway stations, and he had become quite good at working out how long a particular stretch of the journey would take if he got a lift or if he had to walk. He knew that it would not take him many days now to reach Denmark. Perhaps it happened, too, because for hours at a time he could now forget his fears—almost, but not quite. He had had fear too well drilled into him for him ever to be completely free of it. But it was not so bad now, for now he was sure the man really had intended him to get to Denmark. There had been no trap. And the children's parents had not given him away either. There was only the farmer, and David thought he was too stupid to imagine David might have run away from *them*.

A search was being made for him of course; the man's influence was limited, and he would not have been able to prevent it. But no one knew *where* to look for him. And now Denmark was almost within reach . . . Denmark and the woman who was his mother.

He must have been walking for half an hour before he was suddenly aware of his fear and knew he should have sensed danger earlier. It was dusk, and he had been too preoccupied with finding a good place to sleep.

He knew at once that something was wrong. That building farther down the hillside . . . and the men standing idly about . . .

He called to King softly, in a whisper.

He had returned to *them!*

He lay as still as death behind a bush. It was lucky King always did as he was told and was now also lying perfectly still by his side. David's thoughts ran on. . . . How had it happened? There was no doubt about it; he was back among *them*. David knew the signs. He was only too familiar with the way *they* looked. It must have happened when the dog ran off over the fields. David would sometimes play with the dog. It would run off with a stone or a stick in its mouth, intending David to chase it. David thought it was rather pointless, really, and not very amusing, but the dog liked it, and so David would join in to please it.

But he ought to have known something was wrong as soon as they had got back to the road, and now that he thought of it, he realized the three people they had met on the way should have aroused his suspicions. People always looked like that where *they* were—like prisoners in a concentration camp, weary, gray-faced, apprehensive . . . dejected and sorrowful, as though they had forgotten life could be good . . . dull-eyed and apathetic, as if they no longer thought about anything.

The dog looked at him questioningly and began quietly whimpering. David placed his hand over its muzzle and it stopped, but it continued to look at him. The bush was too thin, its new green leaves too small. David quite forgot how beautiful he had thought spring was only that morning, with its small new bright-green leaves. His one thought now was that anyone could look through the bush and see him lying on the ground—and he was David, the boy who had fled from *them*.

In their barracks they would have a list of everybody who was under suspicion and should be arrested on sight. *Their* guards always had a list like that. On that list would be found: "David. A thin boy with brown hair, escaped from concentration camp." And under the heading "Recognition Marks" would be: "It is obvious from the appearance of his eyes that he is not an ordinary boy but only a prisoner."

If the men had not been talking so loudly, they would have heard him already. . . . They were much too close to him, and he would never be able to get away. Even if he waited until it was quite dark, they would hear him as soon as he moved.

His flight would end where it began—at the point of a rifle, for he would not stop when they shouted to him. If he stopped, they would not shoot, but they would interrogate him instead and send him back to the camp. And there, strong and healthy as he was, he would be a terribly long time dying.

No, when they called to him, he would run, and then the shot would be fired—the one that had been waiting for him ever since that night when he had walked calmly toward the tree on the way to the mine outside the camp. But this time he would not be able to walk calmly away from them. He knew now how wonderful life could be, and his desire to live would spur him on. He would run—he knew it—and it would be a victory for *them*.

David remembered all the pain and bitterness he had ever known—and how much he could remember in such a short time! He recalled, too, all the good things he had learned about since he had gained his freedom—beauty and laughter, music and kind people . . . Maria . . . and a tree smothered in pink blossom . . . a dog to walk by his side . . . and a place to aim for . . .

This would be the end of it all. David tried to feel glad that he had known so much that was good and beautiful before the bullet found its mark, but he could not; it was too difficult. He pressed his face into the dog's long coat so that no one should hear him and wept. He wept quite quietly, but the dog grew uneasy and wanted to whimper again.

David stopped crying. "God," he whispered, "God of the green pastures and the still waters, I've one promise of help left, but it's too late now. You can't do anything about this. I don't mean to be rude, because I know You're very strong and You could make those men down there want to walk away for a bit. But they won't. They don't know You, You see, and they're not afraid of You. But they are afraid of the commandant because he'll have them shot if they leave their posts. So You can see there's nothing You can do now. But please don't think I'm blaming You. It was my own fault for not seeing the danger in time. I shall run. . . . Perhaps You'll see they aim straight so it doesn't hurt before I die. I'm so frightened of things that hurt. No, I forgot. I've only one promise of help left, and it's more important You should help the dog get away and find some good people to live with. Perhaps *they'll* shoot straight anyway, but if they don't, it can't be helped. You must save the dog because it once tried to protect me. Thank You for being my God; I'm glad I chose You. And now I must run, for if I leave it any longer, I shan't have the courage to die. I am David. Amen."

The dog kept nudging him. It wanted them to go back the way they had come, away from the spot where it sensed danger lurking.

"No," David whispered, "we can't go back . . . it's too late. You must keep still, King . . . and when they've hit me, perhaps you can get away by yourself . . ."

The dog licked his cheek eagerly, impatiently nudging him again and moving restlessly as if it wanted to go on. It nudged him once more . . . and then jumped up before David could stop it.

In one swift second David understood what the dog wanted. It did not run back the way they had come. . . . It was a sheep dog, and it had sensed danger. . . . It was going to take David's place!

Barking loudly, it sprang toward the men . . .

"Run!" something inside him told David. "Run . . . run!" That was what the dog wanted him to do.

So he ran. . . . He hesitated a moment and then ran more quickly than he had ever run in all his life. As he ran, he heard the men shouting and running, too, but in a different direction. . . . One of them yelled with pain—then came the sound of a shot and a strange loud bark from the dog.

David knew the dog was dead.

He went on running. He was some distance away now, and they had not heard him. But he ran on until he had left far behind the field where they had left the road an hour before. Then he threw himself down in a ditch sobbing and gasping painfully for breath.

He felt as if he would never be able to stop crying, never. God of the pastures and waters, so strong that He could influence a person's thoughts, had let the dog run forward, although He knew it would be shot. "Oh, You shouldn't have done it!" David sobbed again and again. "The dog that followed me . . . and I was never able to look after it properly because I was only David. . . . I couldn't even give it enough to eat, and it had to steal to get food. . . . The dog came with me of its own free will and then had to die just because of it . . ."

Then David suddenly realized he was wrong. It was not because it had followed him that the dog was dead. The dog had gone with him freely, and it had met its death freely . . . in order to protect David from *them*. It was a sheep dog, and it knew what it was doing. It had shown David what it wanted him to do, and then it had diverted the danger from him and faced it itself . . . because it wanted to.

Its very bark as it sprang forward had seemed to say, "Run, run!" And all the while David was running, he had known he must not turn back and try to save it. He must not let the dog's action be in vain; he had to accept it.

Had God of the green pastures and the still waters entered into the dog and made it do it, or had it just done it because it wanted to? Oh, but he never wanted anyone to suffer for his sake . . . and the dog had given its life . . . and he had never been able to do anything for it. So one could get something for nothing after all?

David stood still in the big city and looked around him.

On shop signs and posters were words not altogether unfamiliar to him, but by and large the language was quite strange. "Denmark," he told himself. "I'm in Denmark."

He scarcely knew how he came to be there. Since the night he had realized that the dog had died for him, he felt as if nothing had really penetrated his thoughts.

He had gotten lifts most of the way, and the drivers had shared their food with him. They were all concerned about him and remarked how ill he looked. He had felt better sitting in a truck. All the time he was walking, he thought he could see the dog running along just in front of him, although he knew it could not be true.

He had met several Danish truck drivers in Germany, all quiet men with little to say, and they had all been kind to him.

And he had come to Denmark. He had come straight across the frontier with one of them. . . . He had been traveling in a big truck, and the driver had stowed him away inside. He had told him it was against the law, but he said he had boys of his own at home, and he could not bring himself to hand David over to the customs officers in the state he was in. He said the officers would be kind enough to him, but there would be no end of paperwork to go through, and what David needed was to get to the family he spoke about as quickly as possible and get into a good warm bed.

In a town called Kolding the truck driver had gotten hold of a friend who, he said, would take David on to Copenhagen. David had begun to pick up a little of the language. The two men had said something about "Passport or no passport, a bit of a lad like him can't have anything serious against him, and you can see with half an eye he can't hold out much longer."

David had watched the countryside passing by. There were no mountains, no big rivers. Everything was small and compact. But bright and cheerful, too—the houses, the people, the woods, everything. David had never imagined woods could look like these, their coloring bright and delicate like sunshine on one of Maria's dresses. There was beauty in Denmark, too, but beauty of a different kind. But all the while he felt too tired to look at it properly.

He had been on a ship, too. . . . The driver bought him a ticket, and so he did not even have to hide. But when they came to the big city called Copenhagen, David tried to pull himself together. The driver said if David could just give him the address, he would put him down at the right place.

But he could not, of course. He had told the driver it was in his bundle in the back of the truck. It was not the truth, and when the man realized he had no address, he would be suspicious. David knew by this time that nothing very serious would happen to him here, because it was a free country, but you could not be too careful. . . . If they found a strange boy with nowhere to go, they might consider it their duty to hand him over to the police, especially if he were not Danish. One thing David had really gotten into his head during all the days that had passed since the dog's death—he must reach the woman in Denmark, for if it should turn out that the dog had given its life for him and all to no purpose, it would be too awful to think about, as if the dog's sacrifice had been despised. And that must never be.

David had watched the driver make a telephone call. He had gone into a little glassed-in box affair, and there were books where you could find the numbers you wanted to call and people's addresses. He only had to slip away while the driver was not looking and find another telephone kiosk.

They pulled up on a large square, and the driver said something to him that David pretended not to understand. The man was going to buy what he called a "hot dog" to give him. As soon as he left the truck, David dropped to the ground on the other side. He quickly ran to the back of the truck, opened it, and snatched up his bundle. There were crowds of people, and it was easy enough to hide among them.

It was hardly the thing to do when the driver had been so kind to him, but there was no other way out. David felt as certain as if he had been told that he would very soon come to the end of his strength, and before that happened, he must try to find the woman.

He ran along street after street, turning corners all the time, until he felt safe. He had no difficulty in finding a telephone kiosk, and there were the directories all in order!

He found six people called Hjort Fengel, but there was only one with an "E" in front of the name. And the address was Strandvejen 758.

It must be a long street, and David decided to ask. . . . There were many people who could understand you if you spoke English. He stood there for a moment or two with the book in his hand and looked about him. But before he could make up his mind whom to ask, a woman spoke to him. She asked if she could help him in any way. David answered politely in English, and she understood what he said.

She told him the address was a very long way off. Then she looked at him and said, "But I'm going that way myself. I can take you most of the way in the car . . ."

She asked him what country he came from, and David told her he was French, since he could not very well say he came from nowhere at all. She seemed to realize he was tired, for after that she said very little, and David sat looking out of the window. Soon they came to the sea, and David thought it was almost as blue as it was in Italy, where he had made his home among the rocks. That seemed a very long time ago now, and he found it difficult to remember so far back.

David stood for a long time looking at number 758. Everything smelled fresh and pleasant. There were trees everywhere with white and yellow and lilac-colored blossoms. The sun was shining, the leaves were bright green, and the sea was a deep blue. Denmark was beautiful, too —perhaps all countries were beautiful where *they* weren't.

A few yards would take him to the door, and yet David thought he would never get there. His legs could carry him no farther, and he was on the point of collapsing. He had thought for some time that perhaps if the woman who lived there would tell him what to do next and where to go, he would be able to manage, but now he knew he couldn't. If his happiest dreams came true, he could go on living; if not, he had come to the end.

French was the language he spoke best. David picked up his bundle, walked to the door, and rang the bell, and when the woman opened it, he knew she was the woman in the photograph, the woman whose eyes had seen so much and yet could smile.

Then David said in French, "Madame . . . I am David. I am . . ."

He could say no more. The woman looked into his face and said clearly and distinctly, "David . . . my son David . . ."

20

The Dog of Pompeii

Louis Untermeyer

In A.D. 79 the bustling Roman city of Pompeii was destroyed by volcanic eruption, and thousands perished amid the fire and choking fumes. Taking an actual archaeological find as his starting point, Untermeyer weaves this story of one boy's escape.

Tito and his dog Bimbo lived (if you could call it living) under the wall where it joined the inner gate. They really didn't live there; they just slept there. They lived anywhere. Pompeii was one of the gayest of the old Latin towns, but although Tito was never an unhappy boy, he was not exactly a merry one. The streets were always lively with shining chariots and bright red trappings; the open-air theaters rocked with laughing crowds; sham-battles and athletic sports were free for the asking in the great stadium. Once a year the Caesar visited the pleasure-city and the fire-works lasted for days; the sacrifices in the Forum were better than a show. But Tito saw none of these things. He was blind—had been blind from birth. He was known to everyone in the poorer quarters. But no one could say how old he was, no one remembered his parents, no one could tell where he came from. Bimbo was another mystery.

As long as people could remember seeing Tito—about twelve or thirteen years—they had seen Bimbo. Bimbo had never left his side. He was not only dog, but nurse, pillow, playmate, mother and father to Tito.

Did I say Bimbo never left his master? (Perhaps I had better say comrade, for if any one was the master, it was Bimbo.) I was wrong. Bimbo did trust Tito alone exactly three times a day. It was a fixed routine, a custom understood between boy and dog since the beginning of their friendship, and the way it worked was this: Early in the morning, shortly after dawn, while Tito was still dreaming, Bimbo would disappear. When Tito woke, Bimbo would be sitting quietly at his side, his ears cocked, his stump of a tail tapping the ground, and a fresh-baked bread—more like a large round roll—at his feet. Tito would stretch himself; Bimbo would yawn; then they would breakfast. At noon, no matter where they happened to be, Bimbo would put his paw on Tito's knee and the two of them would return to the inner gate. Tito would curl up in the corner (almost like a dog) and go to sleep, while Bimbo, looking quite important (almost like a boy) would disappear again. In half an hour he'd be back with their lunch. Sometimes it would be a piece of fruit or a scrap of meat, often it was nothing but a dry crust. But sometimes there would be one of those flat rich cakes, sprinkled with raisins and sugar, that Tito liked so much. At supper time the same thing happened, although there was a little less of everything, for things were hard to snatch in the evening with the streets full of people. Besides, Bimbo didn't approve of too much food before going to sleep. A heavy supper made boys too restless and dogs too stodgy—and it was the business of a dog to sleep lightly with one ear open and muscles ready for action.

But, whether there was much or little, hot or cold, fresh or dry, food was always there. Tito never asked where it came from and Bimbo never told him. There was plenty of rainwater in the hollows of soft stones; the old egg-woman at the corner sometimes gave him a cupful of strong goat's milk; in the grape-season the fat wine-maker let him have drippings of the mild juice. So there was no danger of going hungry or thirsty. There was plenty of everything in Pompeii, if you knew where to find it—and if you had a dog like Bimbo.

The Forum was the favorite promenade for rich and poor. What with the priests arguing with the politicians, servants doing the day's shopping, tradesmen crying their wares, women displaying the latest fashions from Greece and Egypt, children playing hide-and-seek among the marble columns, knots of soldiers, sailors, peasants from the provinces—to say nothing of those who merely came to lounge and look on—the square was crowded to its last inch. His ears even more than his nose guided Tito to the place where the talk was loudest. It was in front of the Shrine of the Household Gods that, naturally enough, the householders were arguing.

"I tell you," rumbled a voice which Tito recognized as bathmaster Rufus's, "there won't be another earthquake in my lifetime or yours. There may be a tremble or two, but earthquakes, like lightnings, never strike twice in the same place."

"Do they not?" asked a thin voice Tito had never heard. It had a high, sharp ring to it and Tito knew it as the accent of a stranger. "How about the two towns of Sicily that have been ruined three times within fifteen years by the eruptions of Mount Etna? And were they not warned? And does that column of smoke above Vesuvius mean nothing?"

"That?" Tito could hear the grunt with which one question answered another. "That's always there. We use it for our weather-guide. When the smoke stands up straight we know we'll have fair weather; when it flattens out it's sure to be foggy; when it drifts to the east—"

"Yes, yes," cut in the edged voice. "I've heard about your mountain barometer. But the column of smoke seems hundreds of feet higher than usual and it's thickening and spreading like a shadowy tree. They say in Naples—"

"Oh, Naples!" Tito knew this voice by the little squeak that went with it. It was Atillio, the cameo-cutter. "*They* talk while we suffer. Little help we got from them last time. Naples commits the crimes and Pompeii pays the price. It's become a proverb with us. Let them mind their own business."

"Yes," grumbled Rufus, "and others, too."

"Very well, my confident friends," responded the thin voice which now sounded curiously flat. "We also have a proverb—and it is this: Those who will not listen to men must be taught by the gods. I say no more. But I leave a last warning. Remember the holy ones. Look to your temples. And when the smoke-tree above Vesuvius grows to the shape of an umbrella-pine, look to your lives."

Tito could hear the air whistle as the speaker drew his toga about him and the quick shuffle of feet told him the stranger had gone.

"Now what," said the cameo-cutter, "did he mean by that?"

"I wonder," grunted Rufus, "I wonder."

The next morning there were *two* of the beloved raisin and sugar cakes for his breakfast. Bimbo was unusually active and thumped his bit of a tail until Tito was afraid he would wear it out. The boy could not imagine whether Bimbo was urging him to some sort of game or was trying to tell something. After a while, he ceased to notice Bimbo. He felt drowsy. Last night's late hours had tired him. Besides, there was a heavy mist in the air—no, a thick fog rather than a mist—a fog that got into his throat and scraped it and made him cough. He walked as far as the marine gate to get a breath of the sea. But the blanket of haze had spread all over the bay and even the salt air seemed smoky.

He went to bed before dusk and slept. But he did not sleep well. He had too many dreams—dreams of ships lurching in the Forum, of losing his way in a screaming crowd, of armies marching across his chest, of being pulled over every rough pavement of Pompeii.

He woke early. Or, rather, he was pulled awake. Bimbo was doing the pulling. The dog had dragged Tito to his feet and was urging the boy along. Somewhere. Where, Tito did not know.

His feet stumbled uncertainly; he was still half asleep. For a while he noticed nothing except the fact that it was hard to breathe. The air was hot. And heavy. So heavy that he could taste it. The air, it seemed, had turned to powder, a warm powder that stung his nostrils and burned his sightless eyes.

Then he began to hear sounds. Peculiar sounds. Like animals under the earth. Hissings and groanings and muffled cries that a dying creature might make dislodging the stones of his underground cave. There was no doubt of it now. The noises came from underneath. He not only heard them—he could feel them. The earth twitched; the twitching changed to an uneven shrugging of the soil. Then, as Bimbo half-pulled, half-coaxed him across, the ground jerked away from his feet and he was thrown against a stone-fountain.

The water—hot water—splashing in his face revived him. He got to his feet, Bimbo steadying him, helping him on again. The noises grew louder; they came closer. The cries were even more animal-like than before, but now they came from human throats. A few people, quicker of foot and more hurried by fear, began to rush by. A family or two—then a section—then, it seemed, an army broken out of bounds. Tito, bewildered though he was, could recognize Rufus as he bellowed past him, like a water-buffalo gone mad. Time was lost in a nightmare.

It was then the crashing began. First a sharp crackling, like a monstrous snapping of twigs; then a roar like the fall of a whole forest of trees; then an explosion that tore earth and sky. The heavens, though Tito could not see them, were shot through with continual flickerings of fire. Lightnings above were answered by thunders beneath. A house fell. Then another. By a miracle the two companions had escaped the dangerous side-streets and were in a more open space. It was the Forum. They rested here awhile—how long he did not know.

Tito had no idea of the time of day. He could *feel* it was black—an unnatural blackness. Something inside—perhaps the lack of breakfast and lunch—told him it was past noon. But it didn't matter. Nothing seemed to matter. He was getting drowsy, too drowsy to walk. But walk he must. He knew it. And Bimbo knew it, the sharp tugs told him so. Nor was it a moment too soon.

The sacred ground of the Forum was safe no longer. It was beginning to rock, then to pitch, then to split. As they stumbled out of the square, the earth wriggled like a caught snake and all the columns of the temple of Jupiter came down. It was the end of the world—or so it seemed.

To walk was not enough now. They must run. Tito was too frightened to know what to do or where to go. He had lost all sense of direction. He started to go back to the inner gate; but Bimbo, straining his back to the last inch, almost pulled his clothes from him. What did the creature want? Had the dog gone mad?

Then, suddenly, he understood. Bimbo was telling him the way out—urging him there. The sea gate of course. The sea gate—and then the sea. Far from falling buildings, heaving ground. He turned, Bimbo guiding him across open pits and dangerous pools of bubbling mud, away from buildings that had caught fire and were dropping their burning beams. Tito could no longer tell whether the noises were made by the shrieking sky or the agonized people. He and Bimbo ran on—the only silent beings in a howling world.

New dangers threatened. All Pompeii seemed to be thronging toward the marine gate and, squeezing among the crowds, there was the chance of being trampled to death. But the chance had to be taken. It was growing harder and harder to breathe. What air there was choked him. It was all dust now—dust and pebbles, pebbles as large as beans. They fell on his head, his hands—pumice-stones from the black heart of Vesuvius. The mountain was turning itself inside out. Tito remembered a phrase that the stranger had said in the Forum two days ago: "Those who will not listen to men must be taught by the gods." The people of Pompeii had refused to heed the warnings; they were being taught now—if it was not too late.

Suddenly it seemed too late for Tito. The red hot ashes blistered his skin, the stinging vapors tore his throat. He could not go on. He staggered toward a small tree at the side of the road and fell. In a moment Bimbo was beside him. He coaxed. But there was no answer. He licked Tito's hands, his feet, his face. The boy did not stir. Then Bimbo did the last thing he could—

the last thing he wanted to do. He bit his comrade, bit him deep in the arm. With a cry of pain, Tito jumped to his feet, Bimbo after him. Tito was in despair, but Bimbo was determined. He drove the boy on, snapping at his heels, worrying his way through the crowd; barking, baring his teeth, heedless of kicks or falling stones. Sick with hunger, half-dead with fear and sulphur-fumes, Tito pounded on, pursued by Bimbo. How long he never knew. At last he staggered through the marine gate and felt soft sand under him. Then Tito fainted. . . .

Someone was dashing sea-water over him. Someone was carrying him toward a boat.

"Bimbo," he called. And then louder, "Bimbo!" But Bimbo had disappeared.

Voices jarred against each other. "Hurry-hurry!" "To the boats!" "Can't you see the child's frightened and starving!" "He keeps calling for someone!" "Poor boy, he's out of his mind." "Here, child—take this!"

They tucked him in among them. The oar-locks creaked; the oars splashed; the boat rode over toppling waves. Tito was safe. But he wept continually.

"Bimbo!" he wailed. "Bimbo! Bimbo!"

He could not be comforted.

Eighteen hundred years passed. Scientists were restoring the ancient city; excavators were working their way through the stones and trash that had buried the entire town. Much had already been brought to light—statues, bronze instruments, bright mosaics, household articles; even delicate paintings had been preserved by the fall of ashes that had taken over two thousand lives. Columns were dug up and the Forum was beginning to emerge.

It was at a place where the ruins lay deepest that the Director paused.

"Come here," he called to his assistant. "I think we've discovered the remains of a building in good shape. Here are four huge mill-stones that were most likely turned by slaves or mules—and here is a whole wall standing with shelves inside it. Why! It must have been a bakery. And here's a curious thing. What do you think I found under this heap where the ashes were thickest? The skeleton of a dog!"

"Amazing!" gasped his assistant. "You'd think a dog would have had sense enough to run away at the time. And what is that flat thing he's holding between his teeth? It can't be a stone."

"No. It must have come from this bakery. You know it looks to me like some sort of cake hardened with the years. And, bless me, if those little black pebbles aren't raisins. A raisin-cake almost two thousand years old! I wonder what made him want it at such a moment?"

"I wonder," murmured the assistant.

21

Lad: A Dog

Albert Payson Terhune

Lad has always been indifferent to guests at his master's home until a lame and sickly five-year-old girl arrives. Despite the objections of the girl's foolish and fussy mother, Lad becomes her constant companion.

On a hot morning in early June, when the Mistress and the Master had driven over to the village for the mail, the child's mother wheeled the invalid chair to a tree-roofed nook down by the lake—a spot whose deep shade and lush long grass promised more coolness than did the veranda.

It was just the spot a city dweller would have chosen for a nap—and just the spot through which no countryman would have cared to venture, at that dry season, without wearing high boots.

Here, not three days earlier, the Master had killed a copperhead snake. Here, every summer, during the late June mowing, The Place's scythe-wielders moved with glum caution. And seldom did their progress go unmarked by the scythe-severed body of at least one snake.

The Place, for the most part, lay on hillside and plateau, free from poisonous snakes of all kinds, and usually free from mosquitoes as well. The lawn, close-shaven, sloped down to the lake. To one side of it, in a narrow stretch of bottom land, a row of weeping willows pierced the loose stone lake wall.

Here, the ground was seldom bone-dry. Here, the grass grew rankest. Here, also, driven to water by the drought, abode eft, lizard and an occasional snake, finding coolness and moisture in the long grass, and a thousand hiding places amid the stone crannies or the lake wall.

If either the Mistress or the Master had been at home on this morning, the guest would have been warned against taking Baby there at all. She would have been doubly warned against the folly which she now proceeded to commit—of lifting the child from the wheel chair, and placing her on a spread rug in the grass, with her back to the low wall.

The rug, on its mattress of lush grasses, was soft. The lake breeze stirred the lower boughs of the willows. The air was pleasantly cool here, and had lost the dead hotness that brooded over the higher ground.

The guest was well pleased with her choice of a resting place. Lad was not.

The big dog had been growingly uneasy from the time the wheel chair approached the lake wall. Twice he put himself in front of it; only to be ordered aside. Once the wheels hit his ribs with jarring impact. As Baby was laid upon her grassy bed, Lad barked loudly and pulled at one end of the rug with his teeth.

The guest shook her parasol at him and ordered him back to the house. Lad obeyed no orders, save those of his two deities. Instead of slinking away, he sat down beside the child; so close to her that his ruff pressed against her shoulder. He did not lie down as usual, but sat—tulip ears erect, dark eyes cloudy with trouble, head turning slowly from side to side, nostrils pulsing.

To a human, there was nothing to see or hear or smell—other than the cool beauty of the nook, the soughing of the breeze in the willows, the soft fragrance of a June morning. To a dog, there were faint rustling sounds that were not made by the breeze. There were equally faint and elusive scents that the human nose could not register. Notably, a subtle odor as of crushed cucumbers. (If ever you have killed a pit viper, you know that smell.)

The dog was worried. He was uneasy. His uneasiness would not let him sit still. It made him fidget and shift his position and, once or twice, growl a little under his breath.

Presently, his eyes brightened, and his brush began to thud gently on the rug edge. For, a quarter mile above, The Place's car was turning in from the highway. In it were the Mistress and the Master, coming home with the mail. Now everything would be all right. And the onerous duties of guardianship would pass to more capable hands.

As the car rounded the corner of the house and came to a stop at the front door, the guest caught sight of it. Jumping up from her seat on the rug, she started toward it in quest of mail. So hastily did she rise that she dislodged one of the wall's small stones and sent it rattling down into a wide crevice between two larger rocks.

She did not heed the tinkle of stone on stone; nor a sharp little hiss that followed, as the falling missile smote the coils of a sleeping copperhead snake in one of the wall's lowest cavities. But Lad heard it. And he heard the slithering of scales against rock sides, as the snake angrily sought new sleeping quarters.

The guest walked away, all ignorant of what she had done. And, before she had taken three steps, a triangular grayish-ruddy head was pushed out from the bottom of the wall.

Twistingly, the copperhead glided out onto the grass at the very edge of the rug. The snake was short, and thick, and dirty, with a distinct and intricate pattern interwoven on its rough upper body. The head was short, flat, wedge-shaped. Between eye and nostril, on either side, was the sinister "pinhole," that is the infallible mark of the poison-sac serpent. . . .

Out from its wall cranny oozed the reptile. Along the fringe of the rug it moved for a foot or two; then paused uncertain—perhaps momentarily dazzled by the light. It stopped within a yard of the child's wizened little hand that rested idle on the rug. Baby's other arm was around Lad, and her body was between him and the snake.

Lad, with a shiver, freed himself from the frail embrace and got nervously to his feet.

There are two things—and perhaps *only* two things—of which the best type of thoroughbred collie is abjectly afraid and from which he will run for his life. One is a mad dog. The other is a poisonous snake. Instinct, and the horror of death, warn him violently away from both.

At stronger scent, and then at sight of the copperhead, Lad's stout heart failed him. Gallantly had he attacked human marauders who had invaded The Place. More than once, in dashing fearlessness, he had fought with dogs larger than himself. With a d'Artagnan-like gaiety of zest, he had tackled and deflected a bull that had charged head down at the Mistress.

Commonly speaking, he knew no fear. Yet now he was afraid; tremulously, quakingly, *sickly* afraid. Afraid of the deadly thing that was halting within three feet of him, with only the Baby's fragile body as a barrier between.

Left to himself, he would have taken, incontinently, to his heels. With the lower animal's instinctive appeal to a human in moments of danger, he even pressed closer to the helpless child at his side, as if seeking the protection of her humanness. A great wave of cowardice shook the dog from foot to head.

The Master had alighted from the car and was coming down the hill, toward his guest, with several letters in his hand. Lad cast a yearning look at him. But the Master, he knew, was too far away to be summoned in time by even the most imperious bark.

And it was then that the child's straying gaze fell on the snake.

With a gasp and a shudder, Baby shrank back against Lad. At least, the upper half of her body moved away from the peril. Her legs and feet lay inert. The motion jerked the rug's fringe an inch or two, disturbing the copperhead. The snake coiled, and drew back its three-cornered head, the forklike maroon tongue playing fitfully.

With a cry of panic fright at her own impotence to escape, the child caught up a picture book from the rug beside her, and flung it at the serpent. The fluttering book missed its mark. But it served its purpose by giving the copperhead reason to believe itself attacked.

Back went the triangular head, farther than ever; and then flashed forward. The double move was made in the minutest fraction of a second.

A full third of the squat reddish body going with the blow, the copperhead struck. It struck for the thin knee, not ten inches away from its own coiled body. The child screamed again in mortal terror.

Before the scream could leave the fear-chalked lips, Baby was knocked flat by a mighty and hairy shape that lunged across her toward her foe.

And the copperhead's fangs sank deep in Lad's nose.

He gave no sign of pain, but leaped back. As he sprang his jaws caught Baby by the shoulder. The keen teeth did not so much as bruise her soft flesh as he half-dragged, half-threw her into the grass behind him.

Athwart the rug again, Lad launched himself bodily upon the coiled snake.

As he charged, the swift-striking fangs found a second mark—this time in the side of his jaw.

An instant later the copperhead lay twisting and writhing and thrashing impotently among the grass roots, its back broken, and its body sheared almost in two by a slash of the dog's saberlike tusk.

The fight was over. The menace was past. The child was safe.

And, in her rescuer's muzzle and jaw were two deposits of mortal poison.

Lad stood panting above the prostrate and crying Baby. His work was done; and instinct told him at what cost. But his idol was unhurt and he was happy. He bent down to lick the convulsed little face in mute plea for pardon for his needful roughness toward her.

But he was denied even this tiny consolation. Even as he leaned downward he was knocked prone to earth by a blow that all but fractured his skull.

At the child's first terrified cry, her mother had turned back. Nearsighted and easily confused, she had seen only that the dog had knocked her sick baby flat and was plunging across her body. Next, she had seen him grip Baby's shoulder with his teeth and drag her, shrieking, along the ground.

That was enough. The primal mother instinct (that is sometimes almost as strong in woman as in lioness—or cow) was aroused. Fearless of danger to herself, the guest rushed to her child's rescue. As she ran she caught her thick parasol by the ferrule and swung it aloft.

Down came the agate handle of the sunshade on the head of the dog. The handle was as large as a woman's fist, and was composed of a single stone, set in four silver claws.

As Lad staggered to his feet after the terrific blow felled him, the impromptu weapon arose once more in air, descending this time on his broad shoulders.

Lad did not cringe—did not seek to dodge or run—did not show his teeth. This mad assailant was a woman. Moreover, she was a guest, and as such, sacred under the Guest Law which he had mastered from puppyhood.

Had a man raised his hand against Lad—a man other than the Master or a guest—there would right speedily have been a case for a hospital, if not for the undertaker. But, as things now were, he could not resent the beating.

His head and shoulders quivered under the force and the pain of the blows. But his splendid body did not cower. And the woman, wild with fear and mother love, continued to smite with all her random strength.

Then came the rescue.

At the first blow the child had cried out in fierce protest at her pet's ill-treatment. Her cry went unheard.

"Mother!" she shrieked, her high treble cracked with anguish. "Mother! Don't! Don't! He kept the snake from eating me! He—!"

The frantic woman still did not heed. Each successive blow seemed to fall upon the little onlooker's own bare heart. And Baby, under the stress, went quite mad.

Scrambling to her feet, in crazy zeal to protect her beloved playmate, she tottered forward three steps, and seized her mother by the skirt.

At the touch the woman looked down. Then her face went yellow-white; and the parasol clattered unnoticed to the ground.

For a long instant the mother stood thus, her eyes wide and glazed, her mouth open, her cheeks ashy—staring at the swaying child who clutched her dress for support and who was sobbing forth incoherent pleas for the dog.

The Master had broken into a run and into a flood of wordless profanity at sight of his dog's punishment. Now he came to an abrupt halt and was glaring dazedly at the miracle before him.

The child had risen and had walked.

The child had *walked!*—she whose lower motive centers, the wise doctors had declared, were hopelessly paralyzed—she who could never hope to twitch so much as a single toe or feel any sensation from the hips downward!

Small wonder that both guest and Master seemed to have caught, for the moment, some of the paralysis that so magically departed from the invalid!

And yet—as a corps of learned physicians later agreed—there was no miracle—no magic—about it. Baby's was not the first, nor the thousandth case in pathologic history, in which paralyzed sensory powers had been restored to their normal functions by means of a shock.

The child had had no malformation, no accident, to injure the spine or the coordination between limbs and brain. A long illness had left her powerless. Country air and new interest in life had gradually built up wasted tissues. A shock had reestablished communication between brain and lower body—a communication that had been suspended; not broken.

When, at last, there was room in any of the human minds for aught but blank wonder and gratitude, the joyously weeping mother was made to listen to the child's story of the fight with the snake—a story corroborated by the Master's find of the copperhead's half-severed body.

"I'll—I'll get down on my knees to that heaven-sent dog," sobbed the guest, "and apologize to him. Oh, I wish some of you would beat me as I beat him! I'd feel so much better! Where is he?"

The question brought no answer. Lad had vanished. Nor could eager callings and searchings bring him to view. The Master, returning from a shout-punctuated hunt through the forest, made Baby tell her story all over again. Then he nodded.

"I understand," he said, feeling a ludicrously unmanly desire to cry. "I see how it was. The snake must have bitten him, at least once. Probably oftener, and he knew what that meant. Lad knows everything—*knew* everything I mean. If he had known a little less he'd have been human. But—if he'd been human, he probably wouldn't have thrown away his life for Baby."

"Thrown away his life," repeated the guest. "I—I don't understand. Surely I didn't strike him hard enough to—"

"No," returned the Master, "but the snake did."

"You mean, he has—?"

"I mean it is the nature of all animals to crawl away, alone, into the forest to die. They are more considerate than we. They try to cause no further trouble to those they have loved. Lad got his death from the copperhead's fangs. He knew it. And while we were all taken up with the wonder of Baby's cure, he quietly went away—to die."

The Mistress got up hurriedly and left the room. She loved the great dog, as she loved few humans. The guest dissolved into a flood of sloppy tears.

"And I beat him," she wailed. "I beat him—horribly! And all the time he was dying from the poison he had saved my child from! Oh, I'll never forgive myself for this, the longest day I live."

"The longest day is a long day," dryly commented the Master. "And self-forgiveness is the easiest of all lessons to learn. After all, Lad was only a dog. That's why he is dead."

The Place's atmosphere tingled with jubilation over the child's cure. Her uncertain, but always successful, efforts at walking were an hourly delight.

But, through the general joy, the Mistress and the Master could not always keep their faces bright. Even the guest mourned frequently, and loudly, and eloquently the passing of Lad. And Baby was openly inconsolable at the loss of her chum.

At dawn on the morning of the fourth day, the Master let himself silently out of the house, for his usual before-breakfast cross-country tramp—a tramp on which, for years, Lad had always been his companion. Heavy-hearted, the Master prepared to set forth alone.

As he swung shut the veranda door behind him, Something arose stiffly from a porch rug—Something the Master looked at in a daze of unbelief.

It was a dog—yet no such dog as had ever before sullied the cleanness of The Place's well-scoured veranda.

The animal's body was lean to emaciation. The head was swollen—though, apparently, the swelling had begun to recede. The fur, from spine to toe, from nose to tail tip, was one solid and shapeless mass of caked mud.

The Master sat down very suddenly on the veranda floor beside the dirt-encrusted brute and caught it in his arms, sputtering disjointedly:

"Lad!—*Laddie!*—Old *friend!* You're alive again! You're—you're—*alive!*"

Yes, Lad had known enough to creep away to the woods to die. But, thanks to the wolf strain in his collie blood, he had also known how to do something far wiser than die.

Three days of self-burial, to the very nostrils, in the mysteriously healing ooze of the marshes, behind the forest, had done for him what such mud baths have done for a million wild creatures. It had drawn out the viper poison and had left him whole again—thin, shaky on the legs, slightly swollen of head—but *whole.*

"He's—he's awfully dirty, though! Isn't he?" commented the guest, when an idiotic triumph yell from the Master had summoned the whole family, in sketchy attire, to the veranda. "Awfully dirty and—"

"Yes," curtly assented the Master, Lad's head between his caressing hands. "'Awfully dirty.' That's why he's still alive."

Self-Discipline

Most of us would like to be more virtuous, but we wouldn't be human if we didn't want to be happy too. Fortunately, we can have both. In fact, Aristotle said that virtue was the surest way to a happy life. The virtue of self-discipline is a good example of what he meant. People who lack it aren't, as a rule, very happy. A child throwing a temper tantrum isn't happy, and neither is an adult who loses his temper (for a good example of an adult temper tantrum, see the story "The King and His Hawk"). In addition, people who can't control themselves usually bring a lot of sadness into the lives of others. For example, adults who can't control their drinking or gambling often create great unhappiness for their families. On the other hand, parents who set limits for themselves and their children generally lead happier lives and their children are happier and more self-confident. Of course, the best policy is to get to the stage where you start to set limits on yourself. As you get older, your goal should be to become your own teacher and trainer.

Self-discipline also brings more freedom. This is something our society had to learn the hard way. Starting in the 1960s, a lot of people got the idea that goodness didn't really require hard work or self-control. "We are all naturally good," they said, "and all we have to do is be ourselves or just do what feels right." By simply following our natural impulses, they argued, we would become freer and happier. As a result of listening to this advice, many people gave up the struggle to shape their character. As a society, we became morally lazy, thinking that good feelings and good intentions were a substitute for good deeds. We can see now that this approach hasn't worked. Instead of gaining more freedom, many people lost control over their lives to various addictions such as drug use and compulsive gambling.

Self-disciplined people, on the other hand, are much freer. They have more choices because they have trained themselves to do things that undisciplined people can't do. Think of it this way: You can't choose to compete in the Boston Marathon unless you've trained yourself as a long-distance runner. Likewise, you can't choose to pick up a trumpet and play a tune unless you've practiced diligently. A psychologist who is also a musician noted that several of his friends—all accomplished and respected musicians—had been made to practice as youngsters. "They are able to do what they want to today," he said, "because they weren't free to do what they wanted when they were young." As a result of learning self-discipline when young, they grew up with the freedom to invent and improvise, to take pleasure in their own music, and to give pleasure to others. In a similar way self-discipline allows us to have more choices about our own behavior. When we have self-control, we're no longer slaves to our first impulse. We have the freedom to choose what's really in our own best interest.

22

The King and His Hawk

Retold by James Baldwin

Genghis Khan controls an army and a vast empire, but in this story he can't control either his thirst or his anger.

Genghis Khan was a great king and warrior.

He led his army into China and Persia, and he conquered many lands. In every country, men told about his daring deeds, and they said that since Alexander the Great there had been no king like him.

One morning when he was home from the wars, he rode out into the woods to have a day's sport. Many of his friends were with him. They rode out gayly, carrying their bows and arrows. Behind them came the servants with the hounds.

It was a merry hunting party. The woods rang with their shouts and laughter. They expected to carry much game home in the evening.

On the king's wrist sat his favorite hawk, for in those days hawks were trained to hunt. At a word from their masters they would fly high up into the air, and look around for prey. If they chanced to see a deer or a rabbit, they would swoop down upon it swift as any arrow.

All day long Genghis Khan and his huntsmen rode through the woods. But they did not find as much game as they expected.

Toward evening they started for home. The king had often ridden through the woods, and he knew all the paths. So while the rest of the party took the nearest way, he went by a longer road through a valley between two mountains.

The day had been warm, and the king was very thirsty. His pet hawk had left his wrist and flown away. It would be sure to find its way home.

The king rode slowly along. He had once seen a spring of clear water near this pathway. If he could only find it now! But the hot days of summer had dried up all the mountain brooks.

At last, to his joy, he saw some water trickling down over the edge of a rock. He knew that there was a spring farther up. In the wet season, a swift stream of water always poured down here; but now it came only one drop at a time.

The king leaped from his horse. He took a little silver cup from his hunting bag. He held it so as to catch the slowly falling drops.

It took a long time to fill the cup; and the king was so thirsty that he could hardly wait. At last it was nearly full. He put the cup to his lips, and was about to drink.

All at once there was a whirring sound in the air, and the cup was knocked from his hands. The water was all spilled upon the ground.

The king looked up to see who had done this thing. It was his pet hawk.

The hawk flew back and forth a few times, and then alighted among the rocks by the spring.

The king picked up the cup, and again held it to catch the trickling drops.

This time he did not wait so long. When the cup was half full, he lifted it toward his mouth. But before it had touched his lips, the hawk swooped down again and knocked it from his hands.

And now the king began to grow angry. He tried again, and for the third time the hawk kept him from drinking.

The king was now very angry indeed.

"How do you dare to act so?" he cried. "If I had you in my hands, I would wring your neck!"

Then he filled the cup again. But before he tried to drink, he drew his sword.

"Now, Sir Hawk," he said, "this is the last time."

He had hardly spoken before the hawk swooped down and knocked the cup from his hand. But the king was looking for this. With a quick sweep of the sword he struck the bird as it passed.

The next moment the poor hawk lay bleeding and dying at its master's feet.

"That is what you get for your pains," said Genghis Khan.

But when he looked for his cup, he found that it had fallen between two rocks, where he could not reach it.

"At any rate, I will have a drink from that spring," he said to himself.

With that he began to climb the steep bank to the place from which the water trickled. It was hard work, and the higher he climbed, the thirstier he became.

At last he reached the place. There indeed was a pool of water; but what was that lying in the pool, and almost filling it? It was a huge, dead snake of the most poisonous kind.

The king stopped. He forgot his thirst. He thought only of the poor dead bird lying on the ground below him.

"The hawk saved my life!" he cried, "and how did I repay him? He was my best friend, and I have killed him."

He clambered down the bank. He took the bird up gently, and laid it in his hunting bag. Then he mounted his horse and rode swiftly home. He said to himself,

"I have learned a sad lesson today, and that is, never to do anything in anger."

23

Shiloh

Phyllis Reynolds Naylor

Abused by his owner, Shiloh, a young beagle, runs away and is taken in by Marty Preston's family. When the owner demands that the dog be returned, Marty is close to despair. Then he strikes a bargain with the owner, Judd Travers. He will work for Judd until he has earned enough to buy Shiloh. But will Judd keep his end of the bargain? In the scene that follows, Marty displays remarkable self-control in the face of Judd's taunts and treachery.

Monday afternoon at three o'clock, I'm waiting on Judd's porch when he pulls up. All his dogs is chained out to the side of the house, and they get barkin' like crazy. I don't try to get near 'em, 'cause a chained dog can be mean. I've already restacked Judd's woodpile, but he wants me to do it again, put the big pieces here, the little ones there. He is looking mean and grumpy, like maybe he's disgusted with himself for lettin' me have that dog so easy.

When I finish the woodpile, Judd hands me the hoe. "You see that garden?"

I nod.

"You see that corn? I want the dirt chopped up so fine I can sift it through my fingers," he tells me.

Now I see what he's getting at. He's going to make it so there's no way I can please him. I'll put in my twenty hours and he'll tell me my work wasn't no good, he wants his dog back.

I hoe till I got blisters on both hands, sweat pouring down my back. Wish I could do my work in the early morning before the sun's so fierce. But I don't complain. I take off my T-shirt finally, wrap it around my head to keep the sweat out of my eyes, and I keep on. Shoulders so red I know they'll hurt worse'n anything the next morning, and they do.

Next afternoon, Judd sets me to scrubbing down the sides of his trailer and his porch, shining up the windows, raking the yard. He sits on a folding chair in the shade, drinking a cold beer. Don't offer me nothing, even water. I hate him more than the devil. My mouth so dry it feels like fur.

Third day, though, he puts out a quart jar of water for me when I go to pick his beans. I bend over them rows so long, dropping the beans into a bucket, I think I'm going to be bent for life. When I'm through, Judd sort of motions me to the porch, like I can sit there if I want while I drink my water.

I almost fall onto that porch, glad to be in the shade.

"Looks like you got yourself some blisters," he says.

"I'm okay," I tell him, and take another long drink.

"How's Shiloh?" he asks. First time he's called the dog by that name.

"He's doing fine. Still got a limp, but he eats good."

Judd lifts his beer to his lips. "Would have been a good hunting dog if I could just have kept him home," he says. "The other dogs never run off."

I think about that awhile. "Well," I say finally, "each one is different."

"That's the truth. Kick one and he just goes under the porch for an hour. Kick another, he goes off and don't come back."

I'm trying my best to think what to say to that. Like how come he has to kick them at all? Then I figure nobody likes to be preached at, no matter how much he needs it, least of all Judd Travers, who is thirty years old if he's a day.

"Some dogs, it just makes 'em mean when you kick 'em," I say finally. "Other dogs, it makes 'em scared. Shiloh got scared."

"Never beat my dogs with a stick," Judd goes on. "Never did that in my life."

I don't say anything right away. Finally, though, I ask, "How *your* dogs doing?"

"Rarin' to go out rabbit hunting," Judd says. We look over at his three dogs, all pullin' at their chains and snarlin' at each other. "That biggest dog, now," Judd goes on. "He's the loudest squaller I got. I can tell from his racket whether he's following a fresh track or an old one, if he's runnin' a ditch, swimmin', or treed a coon."

"That's pretty good," I say.

"Littlest one, he's nothin' but a trashy dog—he'll run down most anything 'cept what I'm after. Hope the others'll learn him something. And the middle dog, well, she gives a lot of mouth, too. Even barks at dead trees." The dogs were fighting now, and Judd throws his Pabst can at 'em. "You-all shut up!" he yells. "Hush up!"

The can hits the biggest dog, and they all scatter.

"Don't much like bein' chained," Judd says.

"Guess nobody would," I tell him.

I put in ten hours that week, meaning I make up twenty of the dollars I owe him; got one more week to go. When I leave of an afternoon for Judd's, Shiloh goes with me just so far, then he gets to whining and turns back. I'm glad he won't go on with me. Don't want him anywhere near Judd Travers.

Monday of the second week it seem like Judd's out to break my back or my spirit or both. This time he's got me splittin' wood. I got to roll a big old piece of locust wood over to the stump in his side yard, drive a wedge in it, then hit the wedge with a sledgehammer, again and again till the wood falls apart in pieces to fit his wood stove. Then another log and another.

I can hardly get the sledgehammer up over my head, and when I bring it down, my arms is so wobbly my aim ain't true. Almost drop the hammer. This ain't a job for me, and if Dad saw what Judd was makin' me do, he'd tell him it wasn't safe.

But Judd's out to teach me a lesson, and I'm out to teach him one. So I keep at it. Know it takes me twice as long as Judd to split that wood, but I don't stop. And all the while, Judd sits on his porch, drinking his beer, watching me sweat. Sure does his heart good, I can tell.

Then he says somethin' that almost stops my heart cold. Laughs and says, "Boy, you sure are puttin' in a whole lot of work for nothin'."

I rest my back a moment, wipe one arm across my face. "Shiloh's somethin'," I tell him.

"You think you're goin' to get my dog just 'cause you got some handwritin' on a piece of paper?" Judd laughs and drinks some more. "Why, that paper's not good for anything but to blow your nose on. Didn't have a witness."

I look at Judd. "What you mean?"

"You don't even know what's legal and what's not, do you? Well, you show a judge a paper without a witness's signature, he'll laugh you right out of the courthouse. Got to have somebody sign that he saw you strike a bargain." Judd laughs some more. "And nobody here but my dogs."

I feel sick inside, like I could maybe throw up. Can't think of what to do or say, so I just lift the sledgehammer again, go on splittin' the wood.

Judd laughs even harder. "What are you, boy? Some kind of fool?" And when I don't answer, he says, "What you breakin' your back for?"

"I want that dog," I tell him, and raise the sledgehammer again.

That night when I'm sittin' out on the porch with Ma and Dad, Shiloh in my lap, I check it out. "What's a witness?" I say.

"Somebody who knows the Lord Jesus and don't mind tellin' about it," says Ma.

"No, the other kind."

"Somebody who sees something happen and signs that it's true," Dad says. "What you got in mind now, Marty?"

"You make a bargain with somebody, you got to have a witness?" I ask, not answering.

"If you want it done right and legal, I suppose you do."

I can't bear to have Dad know I was so stupid I made an agreement with Judd Travers without a witness.

"What you thinking on?" Dad asks again, hunching up his shoulders while Ma rubs his back.

"Just thinking how you sell something, is all. Land and stuff."

Dad looks at me quick. "You're not trying to sell off some of my land for that dog, are you?"

"No," I tell him, glad I got him off track. But I sure am worried. Every trace of that deer's gone now. Don't know what Judd done with the meat—rented him a meat locker somewhere, maybe. But there's no bones around, no hide. I report him now, I can't prove a thing.

Next day Judd Travers calls me dumb. Sees me waiting for him on his steps and says I must have a head as thick as a coconut; didn't he already tell me that the paper wasn't worth nothing?

I just look straight through him. "You and me made a bargain," I say, "and I aim to keep my part of it. What you want me to do today?"

Judd just points to the sledgehammer again and doubles over laughin', like it's the biggest joke he ever played on somebody in his life. I can feel the sweat trickle down my back and I ain't even started yet.

Four o'clock comes, and I finally finished all that wood, but Judd pretends he's asleep. Got his head laid back, mouth half open, but I know it's just another way he's got to trick me. Wants me to sneak on home; then he'll say I never kept to my part of the bargain. So I go in his shed, put the sledgehammer back, take out the sickle, and go tackle the weeds down by his mailbox. Work on them weeds a whole hour, and when five o'clock comes, I start back toward the shed. See him watching me. I walk over.

"Sickle's gettin' dull, Judd. You got a whetstone around, I could sharpen it for you."

He studies me a good long while. "In the shed," he says.

I go get it, sit out on a stump, running the whetstone over the blade.

"Past five o'clock," says Judd.

"I know," I say.

"I ain't going to pay you one cent more," he says.

"It's okay," I tell him. Never saw a look on a man's face like I see on his. Pure puzzlement is what it is.

Thing I decide on when I head for Judd's again the next day is that I got no choice. All I can do is stick to my side of the deal and see what happens. All in the world I can do. If I quit now, he'll come for Shiloh, and we're right back where we started. I don't want to make him mad. No use having a winner and loser, or the bad feelings would just go on. Don't want to have to worry about Shiloh when he's running loose and I'm in school. Don't want to feel that Judd's so sore at me he'll think up any excuse at all to run his truck over my dog.

Only sign in this world we're making progress is the water Judd puts out for me. This day it even has ice in it, and Judd don't say one more word about a witness. In fact, when I'm through working and sit down on his porch to finish the water, Judd talks a little more than usual. Only bond we got between us is dogs, but at least that's somethin'.

I decide to say something nice to Judd. Tell him how good-looking his dogs are. Givin' a compliment to Judd Travers is like filling a balloon with air. You can actually see his chest swell up.

"Forty, thirty, and forty-five," he says, when I tell about his dogs.

"Those are their names now?"

"What I paid for 'em," he says.

"If they had a little more meat on their bones, I figure they'd be the best-lookin' hounds in Tyler County," I tell him.

Judd sits there, turnin' his beer around in his hands, and says, "Maybe could use a bit more fat."

I nurse my water along a little, too. "When'd you first get interested in hunting?" I ask him. "Your pa take you out when you was little?"

Judd spits. Didn't know a man could drink beer and chew tobacco at the same time, but Judd does. "Once or twice," he says. "Only nice thing about my dad I remember."

It's the first time in my life I ever felt anything like sorry for Judd Travers. If you weighed it on a postal scale, would hardly move the needle at all, but I suppose there was a fraction of an ounce of sorry for him somewhere inside me. When I thought on all the things I'd done with my own dad and how Judd could only remember hunting, well, that was pretty pitiful for a lifetime.

Thursday, when I get there, Judd's meanness has got the best of him again, because I can see he's running out of work for me to do, just giving me work to make me sweat. Dig a ditch to dump his garbage in, he says. Hoe that cornfield again, scrub that porch, weed that bean patch. But close on to five o'clock, he seems to realize that I'm only going to be there one more time. I'd worked real hard that day. Did anything he asked and done it better than he asked me to.

"Well, one more day," Judd says when I sit down at last with my water and him with his beer. "What you going to do with that dog once he's yours?"

"Just play," I tell him. "Love him."

We sit there side by side while the clouds change places, puff out, the wind blowin' 'em this way and that. I'm wondering how things would have turned out if it hadn't been for that deer. If I'd just knocked on Judd's front door two weeks ago and told him I wasn't giving Shiloh up, what would have happened then?

To tell the truth, I think Ma's right. Judd would have sold him to me by and by because of Shiloh's limp. Judd's the kind that don't like that in a dog, same as he don't want a dent or a scratch of any kind on his pickup truck. Makes him look bad, he thinks. His truck's got to be perfect, to make up for all the ways Judd's not.

The last day I work for Judd, he inspects every job I do, finds fault with the least little thing. Keeps pesterin' me, makin' me hang around, do my work over. When it's time to go, I say, "Well, I guess that's it then."

Judd don't answer. Just stands in the doorway of his trailer looking at me, and then I get the feeling he's going to tell me I can take that paper he signed and use it for kindling. Tell me I can call the game warden if I want, there's not a trace of that deer left. The two weeks of work I put in for him was just long enough for rain to wash away the blood, for the field grass to spring back up again where the deer was shot.

He still don't say anything, though, so I start off for home, chest tight.

"Just a minute," says Judd.

I stop. He goes back inside the trailer, me waiting there in the yard. What am I going to say, he tries that? What am I going to do?

And then Judd's back in the doorway again, and he's got something in his hand. Comes down the steps halfway.

"Here," he says, and it's a dog's collar—an old collar, but better than the one Shiloh's got now. "Might be a little big, but he'll grow into it."

I look at Judd and take the collar. I don't know how we done it, but somehow we learned to get along.

"Thanks a lot," I tell him.

"You got yourself a dog," he says, and goes inside again, don't even look back.

I get home that evening, and Ma's baked a chocolate layer cake to celebrate—a real cake, too, not no Betty Crocker.

After dinner, Ma and Dad on the porch, the four of us rolls around on the grass together—Dara Lynn, Becky, Shiloh, and me. Becky tries to give Shiloh her butterfly kiss, but he don't hold still long enough to feel her eyelashes bat against him, just got to lick everywhere on her face.

And long after Becky and Dara Lynn goes inside, I lay out there on my back in the grass, not caring about the dew, Shiloh against me crosswise, his paws on my chest.

I look at the dark closing in, sky getting more and more purple, and I'm thinking how nothing is as simple as you guess—not right or wrong, not Judd Travers, not even me or this dog I got here. But the good part is I saved Shiloh and opened my eyes some. Now that ain't bad for eleven.

24

The Apprentice

Dorothy Canfield

Peg hasn't made a habit of disciplining herself, and she's also neglected to discipline her dog, Rollie. As a result of a bad scare, Peg acquires a better understanding of the need for rules and decides to take her responsibilities more seriously.

The day had been one of the unbearable ones, when every sound had set her teeth on edge like chalk creaking on a blackboard, when every word her father or mother said to her or did not say to her seemed an intentional injustice. And of course it would happen, as the fitting end to such a day, that just as the sun went down back of the mountain and the long twilight began, she noticed that Rollie was not around.

Tense with exasperation at what her mother would say, she began to call him in a carefully casual tone—she would simply explode if Mother got going: "Here, Rollie! He-ere, boy! Want to go for a walk, Rollie?" Whistling to him cheerfully, her heart full of wrath at the way the world treated her, she made the rounds of his haunts: the corner of the woodshed, where he liked to curl up on the wool of Father's discarded old sweater;

the hay barn, the cow barn, the sunny spot on the side porch. No Rollie.

Perhaps he had sneaked upstairs to lie on her bed, where he was not supposed to go—not that *she* would have minded! That rule was a part of Mother's fussiness, part, too, of Mother's bossiness. It was *her* bed, wasn't it? But was she allowed the say-so about it? Not on your life. They *said* she could have things the way she wanted in her own room, now she was in her teens, but—Her heart burned at unfairness as she took the stairs stormily, two steps at a time, her pigtails flopping up and down on her back. If Rollie was there, she was just going to let him stay there, and Mother could say what she wanted to.

But he was not there. The bedspread and pillow were crumpled, but that was where she had flung herself down to cry that afternoon. Every nerve in her had been twanging discordantly, but she couldn't cry. She could only lie there, her hands doubled up hard, furious that she had nothing to cry about. Not really. She was too big to cry just over Father's having said to her, severely, "I told you if I let you take the chess set, you were to put it away when you got through with it. One of the pawns was on the floor of our bedroom this morning. I stepped on it. If I'd had my shoes on, I'd have broken it."

Well, he *had* told her that. And he hadn't said she mustn't ever take the set again. No, the instant she thought about that, she knew she couldn't cry about it. She could be, and was, in a rage about the way Father kept on talking long after she'd got his point: "It's not that I care so much about the chess set. It's because if you don't learn how to take care of things, you yourself will suffer for it. You'll forget or neglect something that will be really important for *you*. We *have* to try to teach you to be responsible for what you've said you'll take care of. If we—" on and on.

She stood there, dry-eyed, by the bed that Rollie had not crumpled and thought, *I hope Mother sees the spread and says something about Rollie—I just hope she does.*

She heard her mother coming down the hall, and hastily shut her door. She had a right to shut the door to her own room, hadn't she? She had *some* rights, she supposed, even if she was only thirteen and the youngest child. If her mother opened it to say, "What are you doing in here that you don't want me to see?" she'd say—she'd just say—

But her mother did not open the door. Her feet went steadily on along the hall, and then, carefully, slowly, down the stairs. She probably had an armful of winter things she was bringing down from the attic. She was probably thinking that a tall, thirteen-year-old daughter was big enough to help with a chore like that. But she wouldn't *say* anything. She would just get out that insulting look of a grownup silently putting up with a crazy, unreasonable kid. She had worn that expression all day; it was too much to be endured.

Up in her bedroom behind her closed door the thirteen-year-old stamped her foot in a gust of uncontrollable rage, none the less savage and heartshaking because it was mysterious to her.

But she had not located Rollie. She would be cut into little pieces before she would let her father and mother know she had lost sight of him, forgotten about him. They would not scold her, she knew. They would do worse; they would look at her. And in their silence she would hear, droning on reproachfully, what they had said when she had been begging to keep for her own the sweet, woolly collie puppy in her arms.

How warm he had felt! Astonishing how warm and alive a puppy was compared with a doll! She had never liked her dolls much after she had held Rollie, feeling him warm against her breast, warm and wriggling, bursting with life, reaching up to lick her face. He had loved her from that first instant. As he felt her arms around him, his liquid, beautiful eyes had melted in trusting sweetness. And they did now, whenever he looked at her. Her dog was the only creature in the world who *really* loved her, she thought passionately.

And back then, at the very minute when, as a darling baby dog, he was beginning to love her, her father and mother were saying, so cold, so reasonable—gosh, how she *hated* reasonableness!—"Now, Peg, remember that, living where we do, with sheep on the farms around us, it is a serious responsibility to have a collie dog. If you keep him, you've got to be the one to take care of him. You'll have to be the one to train him to stay at home. We're too busy with you children to start bringing up a puppy, too."

Rollie, nestling in her arms, let one hind leg drop awkwardly. It must be uncomfortable. She looked down at him tenderly, tucked his leg up under him, and gave him a hug. He laughed up in her face—he really did laugh, his mouth stretched wide in a cheerful grin. Now he was snug in a warm little ball.

Her parents were saying, "If you want him, you can have him. But you must be responsible for him. If he gets to running sheep, he'll just have to be shot, you know that."

They had not said, aloud, "Like the Wilsons' collie." They never mentioned that awfulness—her racing unsuspectingly down across the fields just at the horrible moment when Mr. Wilson shot his collie, caught in the very act of killing sheep. They probably thought that if they never spoke about it, she would forget it—*forget* the crack of that rifle, and the collapse of the great beautiful dog! Forget the red, red blood spurting from the hole in his head. She hadn't forgotten. She never would. She knew as well as they did how important it was to train a collie puppy about sheep. They didn't have to rub it in like that. They always rubbed everything in. She had told them, fervently, indignantly, that of *course* she would take care of him, be responsible for him, teach him to stay at home. Of course. Of course. *She* understood!

And now, when he was six months old, tall, rangy, powerful, standing up far above her knee, nearly to her waist, she didn't know where he was. But of course he must be somewhere around. He always was. She composed her face to look natural and went downstairs to search the house. He was probably asleep somewhere. She looked every room over carefully. Her mother was nowhere visible. It was safe to call him again, to give the special piercing whistle which always brought him racing to her, the white-feathered plume of his tail waving in elation that she wanted him.

But he did not answer. She stood still on the front porch to think.

Could he have gone up to their special place in the edge of the field where the three young pines, their branches growing close to the ground, made a triangular, walled-in space, completely hidden from the world? Sometimes he went up there with her, and when she lay down on the dried grass to dream he, too, lay down quietly, his head on his paws, his beautiful eyes fixed adoringly on her. He entered into her every mood. If she wanted to be quiet, all right, he did too. It didn't seem as though he would have gone alone there. Still—She loped up the steep slope of the field rather fast, beginning to be anxious.

No, he was not there. She stood irresolutely in the roofless, green-walled triangular hide-out, wondering what to do next.

Then, before she knew what thought had come into her mind, its emotional impact knocked her down. At least her knees crumpled under her. The Wilsons had, last Wednesday, brought their sheep down from the far upper pasture to the home farm! They were—she herself had seen them on her way to school, and like an idiot had not thought of Rollie—on the river meadow.

She was off like a racer at the crack of the starting pistol, her long, strong legs stretched in great leaps, her pigtails flying. She took the short cut, regardless of the brambles. Their thorn-spiked, wiry stems tore at her flesh, but she did not care. She welcomed the pain. It was something she was doing for Rollie, for her Rollie.

She was in the pine woods now, rushing down the steep, stony path, tripping over roots, half falling, catching herself just in time, not slackening her speed. She burst out on the open knoll above the river meadow, calling wildly, "Rollie, here, Rollie, here, boy! Here! Here!" She tried to whistle, but she was crying too hard to pucker her lips.

There was nobody to see or hear her. Twilight was falling over the bare, grassy knoll. The sunless evening wind slid down the mountain like an invisible river, engulfing her in cold. Her teeth began to chatter. "Here, Rollie, here, boy, here!" She strained her eyes to look down into the meadow to see if the sheep were there. She could not be sure. She stopped calling him as she would a dog, and called out his name despairingly as if he were her child, "Rollie! Oh, *Rollie,* where are you?"

The tears ran down her cheeks in streams. She sobbed loudly, terribly; she did not try to control herself, since there was no one to hear. "Hou! Hou! Hou!" she sobbed, her face contorted grotesquely. "Oh, Rollie! Rollie! Rollie!" She had wanted something to cry about. Oh, how terribly now she had something to cry about.

She saw him as clearly as if he were there beside her, his muzzle and gaping mouth all smeared with the betraying blood (like the Wilsons' collie). "But he didn't *know* it was wrong!" she screamed like a wild creature. "Nobody *told* him it was wrong. It was my fault. I should have taken better care of him. I will now. I will!"

But no matter how she screamed, she could not make herself heard. In the cold gathering darkness, she saw him stand, poor, guiltless victim of his ignorance, who should have been protected from his own nature, his beautiful soft eyes looking at her with love, his splendid plumed tail waving gently. "It was my fault. I promised I would bring him up. I should have *made* him stay at home. I was responsible for him. It was my fault."

But she could not make his executioners hear her. The shot rang out. Rollie sank down, his beautiful liquid eyes glazed, the blood spurting from the hole in his head—like the Wilsons' collie. She gave a wild shriek, long, soul-satisfying, frantic. It was the scream at sudden, unendurable tragedy of a mature, full-blooded woman. It drained dry the girl of thirteen. She came to herself. She was standing on the knoll, trembling and quaking with cold, the darkness closing in on her.

Her breath had given out. For once in her life she had wept all the tears there were in her body. Her hands were so stiff with cold she could scarcely close them. How her nose was running! Simply streaming down her upper lip. And she had no handkerchief. She lifted her skirt, fumbled for her slip, stooped, blew her nose on it, wiped her eyes, drew a long quavering breath—and heard something! Far off in the distance, a faint sound, like a dog's muffled bark.

She whirled on her heels and bent her head to listen. The sound did not come from the meadow below the knoll. It came from back of her, from the Wilsons' maple grove higher up. She held her breath. Yes, it came from there. She began to run again, but now she was not sobbing. She was silent, absorbed in her effort to cover ground. If she could only live to get there, to see if it really were Rollie. She ran steadily till she came to the fence, and went over this in a great plunge. Her skirt caught on a nail. She impatiently pulled at it, not hearing or not heeding the long sibilant tear as it came loose. She was in the dusky maple woods, stumbling over the rocks as she ran. As she tore on up the slope, she knew it was Rollie's bark.

She stopped short and leaned weakly against a tree, sick with the breathlessness of her straining lungs, sick in the reaction of relief, sick with anger at Rollie, who had been here having a wonderful time while she had been dying, just dying in terror about him.

For she could now not only hear that it was Rollie's bark; she could hear, in the dog language she knew as well as he, what he was saying in those excited yips; that he had run a woodchuck into a hole in the tumbled stone wall, that he almost had him, that the intoxicating wild-animal smell was as close to him—almost—as if he had his jaws on his quarry. Yip! Woof! Yip! Yip!

The wild, joyful quality of the dog talk enraged the girl. She was trembling in exhaustion, in indignation. So that was where he had been, when she was killing herself trying to take care of him. Plenty near enough to hear her calling and whistling to him, if he had paid attention. Just so set on having his foolish good time, he never thought to listen for her call.

She stooped to pick up a stout stick. She would teach him! It was time he had something to make him remember to listen. She started forward.

But she stopped, stood thinking. One of the things to remember about collies—everybody knew that—was their sensitiveness. A collie who had been beaten was never "right" again. His spirit was broken. "Anything but a broken-spirited collie," the farmers often said. They were no good after that.

She threw down her stick. Anyhow, she thought, he was too young to know, really, that he had done wrong. He was still only a puppy. Like all puppies, he got perfectly crazy over wild-animal smells. Probably he really and truly hadn't heard her calling and whistling.

All the same, all the same—she stared intently into the twilight—he couldn't be let to grow up just as he wanted to. She would have to make him understand that he mustn't go off this way by himself. He must be trained to know how to do what a good dog does—not because *she* wanted him to, but for his own sake.

She walked on now, steady, purposeful, gathering her inner strength together, Olympian in her understanding of the full meaning of the event.

When he heard his own special young god approaching, he turned delightedly and ran to meet her, panting, his tongue hanging out. His eyes shone. He jumped up on her in an ecstasy of welcome and licked her face.

But she pushed him away. Her face and voice were grave. "No, Rollie, *no!*" she said severely. "You're *bad.* You know you're not to go off in the woods without me! You are—a—*bad—dog.*"

He was horrified. Stricken into misery. He stood facing her, frozen, the gladness going out of his eyes, the erect waving plume of his tail slowly lowered to slinking guilty dejection.

"I know you were all wrapped up in that woodchuck. But that's no excuse. You *could* have heard me calling you, whistling for you, if you'd paid attention," she went on. "You've got to learn, and I've got to teach you."

With a shudder of misery he lay down, his tail stretched out limp on the ground, his head flat on his paws, his ears drooping—ears ringing with doomsday awfulness of the voice he so loved and revered. He must have been utterly wicked. He trembled and turned his head away from her august look of blame, groveling in remorse for whatever mysterious sin he had committed.

She sat down by him, as miserable as he. "I don't *want* to scold you. But I have to! I have to bring you up right, or you'll get shot, Rollie. You *mustn't* go away from the house without me, do you hear, *never!*"

Catching, with his sharp ears yearning for her approval, a faint overtone of relenting affection in her voice, he lifted his eyes to her, humbly, soft in imploring fondness.

"Oh, Rollie!" she said, stooping low over him. "I *do* love you. I do. But I *have* to bring you up. I'm responsible for you, don't you see?"

He did not see. Hearing sternness or something else he did not recognize in the beloved voice, he shut his eyes tight in sorrow, and made a little whimpering lament in his throat.

She had never heard him cry before. It was too much. She sat down by him and drew his head to her, rocking him in her arms, soothing him with inarticulate small murmurs.

He leaped in her arms and wriggled happily as he had when he was a baby; he reached up to lick her face as he had then. But he was no baby now. He was half as big as she, a great, warm, pulsing, living armful of love. She clasped him closely. Her heart was brimming full, but calmed, quiet. The blood flowed in equable gentleness all over her body. She was deliciously warm. Her nose was still running a little. She sniffed and wiped it on her sleeve.

It was almost dark now. "We'll be late to supper, Rollie," she said responsibly. Pushing him gently off, she stood up. "Home, Rollie, home!"

Here was a command he could understand. At once he trotted along the path toward home. His plumed tail, held high, waved cheerfully. His short dog memory had dropped into oblivion the suffering just back of him.

Her human memory was longer. His prancing gait was as carefree as a young child's. Plodding heavily like a serious adult she trod behind him. Her very shoulders seemed bowed by what she had lived through. She felt, she thought, like an old, old woman of thirty. But it was all right now. She knew she had made an impression on him.

When they came out into the open pasture, Rollie ran back to get her to play with him. He leaped around her in circles, barking in cheerful yawps, jumping up on her, inviting her to run a race with him, to throw him a stick, to come alive.

His high spirits were ridiculous. But infectious. She gave one little leap to match his. Rollie pretended that this was a threat to him, planted his forepaws low, and barked loudly at her, laughing between yips. He was so funny, she thought, when he grinned that way. She laughed back and gave another mock-threatening leap at him. Radiant that his sky was once more clear, he sprang high on his spring-steel muscles in an explosion of happiness, and bounded in circles around her.

Following him, not noting in the dusk where she was going, she felt the grassy slope drop steeply. Oh, yes, she knew where she was. They had come to the rolling-down hill just back of the house.

All the kids rolled down there, even the little ones, because it was soft grass without a stone. She had rolled down that slope a million times—years and years ago, when she was a kid herself. It was fun. She remembered well the whirling dizziness of the descent, all the world turning over and over crazily. And the delicious giddy staggering when you first stood up, the earth still spinning under your feet.

"All right, Rollie, let's go," she cried, and flung herself down in the rolling position, her arms straight up over her head.

Rollie had never seen this skylarking before. It threw him into almost hysterical amusement. He capered around the rapidly rolling figure, half scared, mystified, enchanted.

His wild frolicsome barking might have come from her own throat, so accurately did it sound the way she felt—crazy, foolish, like a little kid no more than five years old, the age she had been when she had last rolled down that hill.

At the bottom she sprang up, on muscles as steel-strong as Rollie's. She staggered a little, and laughed aloud.

The living-room windows were just before them. How yellow lighted windows looked when you were in the darkness going home. How nice and yellow. Maybe Mother had waffles for supper. She was a swell cook, Mother was, and she certainly gave her family all the breaks, when it came to meals.

"Home, Rollie, home!" She burst open the door to the living room. "Hi, Mom, what you got for supper?"

From the kitchen her mother announced coolly, "I hate to break the news to you, but it's waffles."

"Oh, *Mom!*" she shouted in ecstasy.

Her mother could not see her. She did not need to. "For goodness' sakes, go and wash," she called.

In the long mirror across the room she saw herself, her hair hanging wild, her long bare legs scratched, her broadly smiling face dirt-streaked, her torn skirt dangling, her dog laughing up at her. Gosh, was it a relief to feel your own age, just exactly thirteen years old!

Honesty

The word "true" comes from the Old English word for "tree." Like a tree, there is something solid and rooted about the truth. People who are truthful are reliable; they stand by their word. They can be counted on, and we can put our trust in them.

To get a better idea of the importance of honesty, think of true and false as being like traffic lights that signal "stop" and "go." When the light turns green, we have confidence that we can drive safely through an intersection. But suppose the lights were unreliable. Suppose they had been programmed to change at random. Suppose the lights showed green on four sides at once. Driving on city streets would become an unpleasant and dangerous activity.

Just as we count on traffic lights to be "truthful," we also count every day on the honesty of people we know and people we don't know. We count on elevator inspectors and food inspectors not to take bribes to overlook problems. We count on manufacturers to be honest in reporting defects and possible hazards in their products. We count on airline mechanics to do an honest day's work. The honesty of many people in many places combines to make life safer and more pleasant.

It's often said that honesty is the best policy. When we lie we usually end up hurting ourselves, as Cousin Charley finds out in the story that follows. Those who get into the habit of lying often lose their reputations and sometimes even their friends. But honesty is not always rewarded, and dishonesty is not always punished. As we see in *A Dog of Flanders*, Nello gains nothing from his act of honesty. And, as we know from current history, lying politicians sometimes get away with their lies, and businessmen sometimes profit from dishonest practices.

There has to be a better reason to tell the truth than our own self-interest. And there is. It's this: although lying may not always hurt us, we can be sure that someone else will be harmed. Spreading a false rumor might not hurt us, but it can ruin another's reputation. Dishonest politicians may not suffer personally, but their lies erode our confidence in all our leaders and institutions. When adults lie and get away with it, children begin to think that it's alright for them to lie as well, and in the process their character is damaged.

We often hear it said that we should love truth for its own sake. But truth shouldn't be thought of as only an abstract principle. When we understand how much we all depend on truthfulness, we can see that practicing honesty not only strengthens our own character, but also strengthens the bonds of trust that hold families and communities together.

25

Little House in the Big Woods

Laura Ingalls Wilder

Pa Ingalls has come to help Uncle Henry with harvesting. They need Cousin Charley's help or they might lose the crop of oats. Not only does Charley not help, he interrupts the men's work by "crying wolf."

Pa and Uncle Henry were working very hard, because the air was so heavy and hot and still that they expected rain. The oats were ripe, and if they were not cut and in the shock before rain came, the crop would be lost. Then Uncle Henry's horses would be hungry all winter.

At noon Pa and Uncle Henry came to the house in a great hurry, and swallowed their dinner as quickly as they could. Uncle Henry said that Charley must help them that afternoon.

Laura looked at Pa, when Uncle Henry said that. At home, Pa had said to Ma that Uncle Henry and Aunt Polly spoiled Charley. When Pa was eleven years old, he had done a good day's work every day in the fields, driving a team. But Charley did hardly any work at all.

Now Uncle Henry said that Charley must come to the field. He could save them a great deal of time. He could go to the spring for water, and he could fetch them the water-jug when they needed a drink. He could fetch the whetstone when the blades needed sharpening.

All the children looked at Charley. Charley did not want to go to the field. He wanted to stay in the yard and play. But, of course, he did not say so.

Pa and Uncle Henry did not rest at all. They ate in a hurry and went right back to work, and Charley went with them.

Now Mary was oldest, and she wanted to play a quiet, lady-like play. So in the afternoon the cousins made a playhouse in the yard. The stumps were chairs and tables and stoves, and leaves were dishes, and sticks were the children.

On the way home that night, Laura and Mary heard Pa tell Ma what happened in the field.

Instead of helping Pa and Uncle Henry, Charley was making all the trouble he could. He got in their way so they couldn't swing the cradles. He hid the whetstone, so they had to hunt for it when the blades needed sharpening. He didn't bring the water-jug till Uncle Henry shouted at him three or four times, and then he was sullen.

After that he followed them around, talking and asking questions. They were working too hard to pay any attention to him, so they told him to go away and not bother them.

But they dropped their cradles and ran to him across the field when they heard him scream. The woods were all around the field, and there were snakes in the oats.

When they got to Charley, there was nothing wrong, and he laughed at them. He said:

"I fooled you that time!"

Pa said if he had been Uncle Henry, he would have tanned that boy's hide for him, right then and there. But Uncle Henry did not do it.

So they took a drink of water and went back to work.

Three times Charley screamed, and they ran to him as fast as they could, and he laughed at them. He thought it was a good joke. And still, Uncle Henry did not tan his hide.

Then a fourth time he screamed, louder than ever. Pa and Uncle Henry looked at him, and he was jumping up and down, screaming. They saw nothing wrong with him and they had been fooled so many times that they went on with their work.

Charley kept on screaming, louder and shriller. Pa did not say anything, but Uncle Henry said, "Let him scream." So they went on working and let him scream.

He kept on jumping up and down, screaming. He did not stop. At last Uncle Henry said:

"Maybe something really is wrong." They laid down their cradles and went across the field to him. And all that time Charley had been jumping up and down on a yellow jackets' nest! The yellow jackets lived in a nest in the ground and Charley stepped on it by mistake. Then all the little bees in their bright yellow jackets came swarming out with their red-hot stings, and they hurt Charley so that he couldn't get away.

He was jumping up and down and hundreds of bees were stinging him all over. They were stinging his face and his hands and his neck and his nose, they were crawling up his pants' legs and stinging and crawling down the back of his neck and stinging. The more he jumped and screamed the harder they stung.

Pa and Uncle Henry took him by the arms and ran him away from the yellow jackets' nest. They undressed him, and his clothes were full of yellow jackets and their stings were swelling up all over him. They killed the bees that were stinging him and they shook the bees out of his clothes and then they dressed him again and sent him to the house.

Laura and Mary and the cousins were playing quietly in the yard, when they heard a loud, blubbering cry. Charley came bawling into the yard and his face was so swollen that the tears could hardly squeeze out of his eyes.

His hands were puffed up, and his neck was puffed out, and his cheeks were big, hard puffs. His fingers stood out stiff and swollen. There were little, hard, white dents all over his puffed-out face and neck.

Laura and Mary and the cousins stood and looked at him.

Ma and Aunt Polly came running out of the house and asked him what was the matter. Charley blubbered and bawled. Ma said it was yellow jackets. She ran to the garden and got a big pan of earth, while Aunt Polly took Charley into the house and undressed him.

They made a big panful of mud, and plastered him all over with it. They rolled him up in an old sheet and put him to bed. His eyes were swollen shut and his nose was a funny shape. Ma and Aunt Polly covered his whole face with mud and tied the mud on with cloths. Only the end of his nose and his mouth showed.

Aunt Polly steeped some herbs, to give him for his fever. Laura and Mary and the cousins stood around for some time, looking at him.

It was dark that night when Pa and Uncle Henry came from the field. All the oats were in the shock, and now the rain could come and it would not do any harm.

Pa could not stay to supper; he had to get home and do the milking. The cows were already waiting, at home, and when cows are not milked on time they do not give so much milk. He hitched up quickly and they all got into the wagon.

Pa was very tired and his hands ached so that he could not drive very well, but the horses knew the way home. Ma sat beside him with Baby Carrie, and Laura and Mary sat on the board behind them. Then they heard Pa tell about what Charley had done.

Laura and Mary were horrified. They were often naughty, themselves, but they had never imagined that anyone could be as naughty as Charley had been. He hadn't worked to help save the oats. He hadn't minded his father quickly when his father spoke to him. He had bothered Pa and Uncle Henry when they were hard at work.

Then Pa told about the yellow jackets' nest, and he said,

"It served the little liar right."

After she was in the trundle bed that night, Laura lay and listened to the rain drumming on the roof and streaming from the eaves, and she thought about what Pa had said.

She thought about what the yellow jackets had done to Charley. She thought it served Charley right, too. It served him right because he had been so monstrously naughty. And the bees had a right to sting him, when he jumped on their home.

But she didn't understand why Pa had called him a little liar. She didn't understand how Charley could be a liar, when he had not said a word.

26

A Dog of Flanders

Ouida
(Marie Louise de la Ramée)

Young Nello and his cart dog, Patrasche, have worked for years delivering milk to the town of Antwerp. But when Baas Cogez, the miller, turns against them, they soon find themselves without money, food, or shelter.

The snow was falling fast: a keen hurricane blew from the north: it was bitter as death on the plains. It took them long to traverse the familiar path, and the bells were sounding four of the clock as they approached the hamlet. Suddenly Patrasche paused, arrested by a scent in the snow, scratched, whined, and drew out with his teeth a small case of brown leather. He held it up to Nello in the darkness. Where they were there stood a little Calvary, and a lamp burned dully under the Cross: the boy mechanically turned the case to the light: on it was the name of Baas Cogez, and within it were notes for two thousand francs.

The sight roused the lad a little from his stupor. He thrust it in his shirt, stroked Patrasche, and drew him onward. The dog looked up wistfully into his face. Nello made straight for the mill house, and went to the house door and struck on its panels. The miller's wife opened it weeping, with little Alois clinging close to her. "It is thee, thou poor lad?" she said kindly, through her tears. "Get thee gone ere the Baas see thee. We are in sore trouble to-night. He is out seeking for a power of money that he has let fall riding homeward, and in this snow he will never find it; and God knows it will go nigh to ruin us. It is Heaven's own judgment for the things we have done to thee."

Nello put the note case in her hand and called Patrasche within the house. "Patrasche found the money to-night," he said quickly. "Tell Baas Cogez so; I think he will not deny the dog shelter and food in his old age. Keep him from pursuing me, and I pray you be good to him."

Ere either woman or dog knew what he meant he had stooped and kissed Patrasche: then closed the door hurriedly, and disappeared in the gloom of the fast-falling night.

The woman and the child stood speechless with joy and fear: Patrasche vainly spent the fury of his anguish against the iron-bound oak of the barred house door. They did not dare unbar the door and let him forth: they tried all they could to comfort him. They brought him sweet cakes and juicy meats; they tempted him with the best they had; they tried to lure him to abide by the warmth of the hearth; but it was of no avail. Patrasche refused to be comforted or to stir from the barred portal.

It was six o'clock when from an opposite entrance the miller at last came, jaded and broken, into his wife's presence. "It is lost forever," he said, with an ashen cheek and a quiver in his stern voice. "We have looked with lanterns everywhere; it is gone—the little maiden's portion and all!"

His wife put the money into his hand, and told him how it had come to her. The strong man sank trembling into a seat and covered his face, ashamed and almost afraid. "I have been cruel to the lad," he muttered at length: "I deserved not to have good at his hands."

Little Alois, taking courage, crept close to her father and nestled against him her fair curly head. "Nello may come here again, father?" she whispered. "He may come to-morrow as he used to do?"

The miller pressed her in his arms: his hard, sunburnt face was very pale, and his mouth trembled. "Surely, surely," he answered his child. "He shall bide here on Christmas Day, and any other day he will. God helping me, I will make amends to the boy—I will make amends."

Little Alois kissed him in gratitude and joy, then slid from his knees and ran to where the dog kept watch by the door. "And to-night I may feast Patrasche?" she cried in a child's thoughtless glee.

Her father bent his head gravely: "Ay, ay! let the dog have the best;" for the stern old man was moved and shaken to his heart's depths.

It was Christmas Eve, and the mill house was filled with oak logs and squares of turf, with cream and honey, with meat and bread, and the rafters were hung with wreaths of evergreen, and the Calvary and the cuckoo clock looked out from a mass of holly. There were little paper lanterns, too, for Alois, and toys of various fashions and sweetmeats in bright-pictured papers. There were light and warmth and abundance everywhere, and the child would fain have made the dog a guest honored and feasted.

But Patrasche would neither lie in the warmth nor share in the cheer. Famished he was and very cold, but without Nello he would partake neither of comfort nor food. Against all temptation he was proof and close against the door he leaned always, watching only for a means of escape.

"He wants the lad," said Baas Cogez. "Good dog! good dog! I will go over to the lad the first thing at day-dawn." For no one but Patrasche knew that Nello had left the hut, and no one but Patrasche divined that Nello had gone to face starvation and misery alone.

27

Gun Shy

Edward Fenton

Practicing honesty means more than not telling lies. In this story, Joel's Uncle Seymour could choose to remain silent; instead, he reveals an important truth at just the right moment.

Every day the mornings in the country turned chillier. The sycamore outside the kitchen window was soon bright yellow, and the trees all down the lane made a high arch of burning colors. When Joel stepped out of the house his breathing made little cold clouds of white vapor in front of his face.

This morning was early. Muggsy hadn't even finished his cereal yet. The Duchess ran ahead of him sniffing the air excitedly. With a sudden bound she dashed off into the meadow. Joel watched her weaving through the tall, dry grass, her nose to the ground one moment and the next minute springing up like a jackrabbit, her black ears flying.

Then, suddenly, there was a rustling noise and a mass of feathers rose from the clump of grass ahead over their heads. It glistened across the autumn landscape. Then it was winging out of sight.

The Duchess, now standing stiff in the middle of the field like a dog painted on a calendar picture, was looking after it too. When the bird could no longer be seen, she galumphed back to Joel's side.

Henry came toward them from the barn. Joel noticed at once that he had on his old leather hunting jacket, with the celluloid window on the back of it for his hunting license. Pushed back on his head was a red cap with a visor.

"Hi, Henry," Joel said. "Are you going out today?"

"It's the first day of huntin'," Henry asserted. "Ain't missed it in years. Don't reckon I'll miss it today. Got my license, got my gun all oiled back there in th' barn. Ought to be a good day."

"There are lots of birds around this year," Joel said. "The Duchess just flushed one a minute ago. It was a beauty! It went over that way." He pointed toward the Rocky Pasture.

Henry nodded. "I seen it," he said. "As a matter of fact," he went on, "I was thinkin' of takin' the Duchess along. Ain't never tried her out in the field as yet. Might's well see if she's any good or not."

"I'll bet she'll be better than any other dog you ever took hunting," Joel said stoutly. "Won't you, Duch?"

The Duchess, however, was much too busy pursuing a flea near the base of her tail to do anything in reply to Joel's question.

The porch door slammed just then.

"Well, here's ol' Muggsy, the great trapper!" Henry called out, swinging him up on his shoulder. Anthony had on a scarlet hunter's cap like Henry's. He looked very proud of it.

"You bet!" Muggsy began. "I'm the best hunter for miles," he announced with no attempt at modesty. "I can catch lions, 'n' bears, 'n', well, anything, 'cause I'm—"

"Oh, come on," Joel said impatiently. "I've got to get you to school. The bus'll be here soon."

They started down the lane together. Joel called back over his shoulder, "Have a good day, Henry. You and the Duchess!"

"Sure," Henry called back. "We'll make out fine together. So long!"

Johnny Nesbitt was in the bus when Joel and Muggsy clambered in. They all sat together, looking out the window. From time to time they could see men, sometimes singly, sometimes in groups, walking down the road. All of them carried guns and had their hunting licenses pinned to their jackets where everyone could see them, and they all wore bright red caps so that other hunters would not mistake them for game as they moved through the woods. Most of them had dogs following along after them.

"Rusty's a good hunter," Johnny Nesbitt said. "He can smell a rabbit a mile away."

"Henry's taking the Duchess out with him," Joel told him in reply. "She's a real hunting dog. I'll bet when I get home Henry'll have so many pheasants he won't hardly be able to carry them all!"

That day school seemed to drag on without end. All through the classes Joel's attention wandered off from his books or the blackboard to the windows. The trees outside blazed against the clear November sky. From time to time he could hear in the distance the sharp crack, crack of a rifle or the high, excited barking of a dog. All his thoughts were with Henry and the Duchess.

The Duchess, so far, had not done anything to demonstrate her true caliber. She hadn't rescued anyone yet, or had a chance to prove herself a heroine. But this time, he knew, she would show her true colors!

The school bus going home seemed to take all afternoon. Why did the driver always have to stop forever, and why did it always take the other kids such a long time to get off? At last it came to a halt with a squeaking of brakes beside the blue letter box marked "Evans."

Joel looked for the Duchess. Usually she knew when it was time for the bus to return, and she sat in the middle of the lane waiting for him. But she wasn't there now. "She's probably still out with Henry," Joel thought, although it did seem odd that Henry would be out hunting all day, and it was now nearly milking time.

He ran up the lane to the house. Muggsy had to puff like a locomotive to keep up with him.

No, the Duchess wasn't anywhere around. And there was Henry, going out to the barn.

"Henry, Henry!" Joel cried. "Where is she?"

Henry set down the pails he was carrying.

"Dunno, Joey," he replied slowly.

"Well, didn't you go out hunting and all?"

Henry nodded. "Sure we went out," he said. "She was fine too. Got a good nose on her. In fact she was all right until I raised my gun and fired."

Joel was breathless. "And then what happened?"

"First thing I know there wasn't no Duchess there. She ran off faster'n I could see her go. Looked all over for her. Looked for hours, but I never did find her. Had to come back 'count of it being milking time." Henry put his big hand on Joel's shoulder. "I'm sorry, kid," he said. "I wouldn't have taken her if I'd of known. She's what they call *gun*-shy. She's scared of shootin'."

"But—but where's she now? We've got to find her!" Joel blinked hard.

"No way of tellin'," Henry said, shaking his head. "She's probably hidin' somewheres right now. She won't come back for a while. The woods are full of gunfire."

Supper was dismal. Joel could hardly swallow, and after every few choking mouthfuls he ran out to the porch to whistle. "She might be out there now," he explained.

Mama looked up at the ceiling. "Boys and dogs!" she sighed. "They're the bane of my life!"

But when Joel came back she looked up hopefully. When he shook his head she sighed again, only it was a different kind of sigh.

Muggsy suddenly announced: "Hey, Joey, I got a idea!"

"Can't you *ever* leave me alone, ever?" Joel demanded. "I'm thinking."

"Well, I been thinking too," Muggsy persisted. "I been thinking about how I found her. I betcha you ain't looked under the bridge!"

Joel looked up in amazement. "I never thought of that!" he exclaimed. The next moment he had dashed out of the dining room.

"Put on your jacket!" Mama called, but the front door had already slammed behind him. "Oh, no, you don't, Anthony!" she said firmly as Muggsy began to squirm off his chair. "You're staying right here."

Joel ran headlong into Henry, who had been out in the barn. "I'm goin'—down to—the bridge," he panted. "To see—if—she's there."

Henry went along with him. They whistled for her at every other step, but there was no Duchess to come dashing up to them in response. They went down the lane together. Joel clenched his fists until his finger-nails dug into his palms.

But under the bridge there was nothing: just the creek trickling in the dark and the stones shining with wetness when the flashlight went on. Joel had never felt so miserable. "Perhaps she got shot, Henry."

"Dunno," Henry said. He shrugged his shoulders and switched off his flashlight. "Come on kid, better get back. It's cold out here without your sweater. Your ma won't like it. And it won't bring Her Highness back, just standing here and shivering."

They climbed up to the road again and began trudging back to the house.

Suddenly Joel stopped. "Listen!" he whispered.

They stopped. There was a faint pattering sound. It grew louder as they waited.

"Sure it's her!" Joel cried.

And it was indeed the Duchess. She came toward them at a tired trot. Joel ran forward and put his arms around her. He could feel the burs sticking to her coat. She was trembling.

Joel looked up at Henry. "Henry, remember when we first found her? Do you think she might have run off that time the same way? I mean—"

Henry shook his head. "Dunno," he said. "Cain't never tell. Could be."

"But—but that means she's no good for hunting, doesn't it?" Joel thought of Johnny Nesbitt's Rusty, and of how he himself had boasted of the Duchess. He swallowed hard. "But I don't care, Henry," he said, running his hands through the shivering dog's coat. "She needs us more than ever now, and there are worse things than being afraid of guns, aren't there, Henry? Aren't there?"

"Sure," Henry said thoughtfully, "sure. Lots worse things."

Joel stroked the Duchess. "See, Duch," he told her, "it's all right now. You're home again." He felt as though something inside him was choking him. But he was happy that he had found her again.

"Come on, Henry," he said. "Let's run back. It's cold out tonight."

One Saturday afternoon Joel Evans and Johnny Nesbitt lay spread out, faces downward, upon a nest of dry leaves. Noisily they munched on a couple of frostbitten apples from the basketful which they had gathered for Johnny's mother. Juice dribbled icily down Joel's chin. "I like 'em best this way," he announced indistinctly.

In the deep grass, not far away, waited their four legged shadows: Johnny's airedale Rusty and the Duchess. Both were panting gently. From time to time one of them stirred, making a dry rattling sound among the crisp leaves.

It was almost evening. The air was getting keen. The faces of the boys were raw from the wind. Their eyes shone. Their ears and the tips of their noses tingled.

It had been an exhausting Saturday, and all four of them were tired. Not that they had, any of them, much to show for it. Sure enough, there was the basket of apples for Mrs. Nesbitt. It had been fun climbing the trees and shaking them down, while the dogs barked furiously at the rain of fruit which thudded and plummeted to the hard ground. And there was a pleasant aching in their arms and legs from all the fields they had scrambled across, the brooks they had jumped over (one of Joel's socks was wet from the time he had missed), the gullies and ravines they had explored all through the sharp, sun-shot day.

For the dogs there were the thousands of exciting smells to remember and the miles of countless mysterious tracks which they had pursued, yipping frantically. Knowingly, they rolled their brown eyes at their masters.

Joel turned his head and stared at the darkening sky. "Gosh, Johnny, it's getting late. I'd better think of making tracks before Mama sends out a posse." He stretched lazily, then rolled back on the ground, folding his arms behind his head.

"My mother'll be worrying too," Johnny said. "It's funny; she knows I'm all right. Nothing ever happens to me. But she always worries just the same. She ought to be used to me by now!"

"I know," Joel agreed. "They ought to relax more, but they never do. I guess that's the way they are. You just can't change them."

They both lay there, wondering why mothers worried the way they did. But neither of them stirred an inch to get up and start home.

The Duchess pulled herself out of her bed of leaves, stretched luxuriously, yawned with a great creaking of her jaws, and looked at Rusty to see what he was doing. He was engrossed in the serious business of licking a forepaw. The Duchess turned her back to him and moseyed over to where Joel lay.

Joel scratched her chin. "How's the girl?" he demanded. "How's Her Highness?" In reply, she licked his face until he had to raise himself, laughing, to a sitting position.

Johnny got up then, too. They both sat among the dead leaves of the past summer and wondered where the day had gone to.

"It's been one super day," Joel said. He looked around him, at the dark trees against the setting sun. Below them—it seemed far, far below, although he knew it was only a few minutes' run—snuggled the Nesbitt farmhouse. The lights were already on. The windows glowed yellow and smoke twisted from the chimney. He picked another apple out of the basket and bit into it.

It was a good apple, firm and juicy. Joel looked at Johnny and winked; Johnny winked back. Then Joel looked at the Duchess. She had her head slightly to one side and her brown eyes were regarding him with all the trust and faith in the world. Suddenly Joel felt an overwhelming contentment sweep over him. It didn't matter about her being gun-shy, about anything. It was just perfect sitting there with her and Johnny as the sun was setting, and eating an apple. It was a moment he wanted to make last forever. "Stop, clock," he wanted to shout. "Just leave your hands where they are for a while."

Finally he said, and it seemed to him as though his voice came out strangely quiet and small, "I don't know any other place I'd rather be than right here now. Do you, Johnny?"

"Sure," Johnny said. "Lots of places. Top of the Empire State Building in New York. Or flying over Shangri-la in my own B-29. The *'Johnny N'* I'd call it, and I'd have the name painted right on her, big. That's the life!" Johnny's eyes began to glisten with excitement.

"Or I'd like to be in a foxhole at the front with a little old machine gun cradled in my arms. Rattatatattat! I'd show that enemy a thing or two or three. They could shoot and shoot at me all they liked. They'd only miss. I wouldn't even hear it! Then me and Rusty—he'd be my Specially Trained Combat Dog—we'd jump out of that foxhole and give them the rush. Just the two of us; we'd take them all prisoners." Johnny clicked his tongue. "That's where I'd like to be. Not stuck out here where it's the same thing all the time, no excitement."

"And what's more," he added, in a confidential tone, "as soon as I'm old enough to do it, I'm gonna join up. And Rusty's coming right with me. I'll bet they could use a smart dog like him in the Army. He's so tough I bet he could easy get into the Marines!"

Joel was scratching the Duchess slowly behind the ear. He didn't say anything.

"Hey, Joey," Johnny went on—he grew more and more excited as the idea became clearer—"you could come too. How'd you like that? And take the Duchess!" He looked eagerly at Joel. "What do you think of that?"

The look on Joel's face stopped Johnny short. "Oh, gee, Joey, I forgot about the Duchess. I mean, about her bein'—"

Joel jumped to his feet. "Oh, that's all right, Johnny. We sort of had other plans anyway." He tried to sound offhand. "Anyway, we have to start trekking home now. I guess it's pretty late."

"Sure," Johnny said. "Sure. And my mother will give it to me good if I don't get those apples home to her!"

Johnny and Rusty walked Joel and the Duchess as far as the glen in silence.

"So long, Johnny," Joel called as he turned off. "See you Monday."

"So long," Johnny called back.

The faint trail across the glen was the shortest way home and Joel wanted to get there before dark. The sun was pretty low already.

The Duchess was off after some scent in a clump of bushes. Her nose was to the ground and her white plume of a tail cut through the twilight. Joel whistled to her. She paid no attention to his call.

Joel's mellow mood of happiness and contentment had completely vanished. In its place he was seized by an unreasoning rage.

He whistled again. She was utterly useless, he thought furiously. A gun-shy bird dog. Everybody laughed at her. And now she wouldn't even obey him when he whistled!

"Come here, you!" He shouted harshly.

She bolted out of the bushes and came toward him. Through the growing twilight he could see how uncertain and surprised she was. Already he felt a faint twinge of shame for having spoken to her as he had. But the senseless anger still boiled inside him.

"You come straight off, the next time I call you," he said gruffly.

Then he struck off across the glen toward home. He stopped at one place long enough to cut a maple switch. As he went on, he slashed viciously now and again at the dark trunks of the trees he passed. The Duchess followed faithfully at his heel. He could hear her pattering evenly behind him but he did not turn his head once or stop to speak to her.

By the time Joel reached home, darkness had already fallen. All the lights of the house were on. From the outside, everything had a warm and friendly look.

"We'll catch it for being late," Joel muttered to the Duchess. Resignedly, he made his way to the back door.

Alma was flying about in the kitchen like a demented banshee. She paused long enough to glance up when Joel came in. "Oh, there you are!" she exclaimed. To Joel's surprise, her voice wasn't at all scolding. "Hurry on upstairs and put on your good pants and a clean shirt," she said. "Dinner'll be on soon. You don't want to be late for it."

"I thought I was late already," he said. Then he noticed that she was wearing her best apron, the one with the white ruffles starched as stiff as cardboard.

"Zowie!" he cried. "What's up? Lord Mayor invite himself for dinner?"

"Never you mind," Alma replied. She pushed him to the door and waved him up the staircase. "I've got work to do. You'll find out what's up soon enough when you come down again."

Joel scratched his head and started up the stairs. Halfway up he had a sudden idea. "It's not Ellen home for the weekend, is it, Alma?" he called hopefully down the stairwell.

"It is not," Alma called back. "And don't forget to comb your hair and take that scrubbing brush to your nails," she added. "I'll go tell your ma you'll be right down."

While Joel changed his clothes and washed, the Duchess pattered after him from his bedroom to the bathroom and back again. He could hear, faintly, voices floating up from the living room. He wondered what was happening. At first he decided that Mr. and Mrs. Grant had come to dinner. But then Alma wouldn't have put on her best apron just for them. Maybe it was an important business friend of Papa's.

"Dr. Watson, I am compelled to admit that I am completely baffled this time," Joel said, frowning into the mirror. Then, after a brief tussle between his cowlick and his brush (the cowlick won), he switched off the light and went downstairs to the living room.

He saw Mama first. She had on a long dress and her heavy silver Indian bracelets. She was saying something which he couldn't hear and she smiled as she spoke. She looked different from the way she did every day. Joel had forgotten how young and pretty his mother could look. Papa stood behind her, beaming.

Mama turned her head and saw Joel. "And here's Joey!" she announced. Laughing gaily, she pulled him into the room.

Then, suddenly, Joel realized why Alma was wearing her number-one starched apron and why Mama had on her long dress and such a radiant look and why even Papa was smiling openly. Leaning against the mantelpiece, his back to the fire, stood a tall, grinning young man in the khaki uniform of a lieutenant.

"Uncle Seymour!"

The grin widened. "Hi, Joey!"

It was a long time since Joel had seen his uncle. That had been before Uncle Seymour had gone overseas. Joel ran forward. He wanted to rush up and throw his arms around his uncle. But when he came up to him, Joel suddenly stiffened self-consciously and held out his hand instead.

Gravely they shook hands.

Muggsy, who had been quiet and awed, suddenly came to life. "Look, Joey," he cried. "He's got a gold bar on his shoulder. That means he's an officer now. And lookit all the medals he won." Muggsy stood on his tiptoes, running his forefinger across the row of service ribbons pinned to his uncle's tunic. "This one's for Good Conduck. This one's for—"

"Anthony!" Mama said. "Must you always handle everything you see?"

"I was only showing Joey!"

"Well, Joel can see for himself."

Joel could indeed see for himself. His uncle seemed to be taller, somehow, than last time. His face had a lean, almost tired look about it. Joel's eyes took in every detail of the uniform, with its knife-sharp creases, the gold insignia, and the row of ribbons. On one of the ribbons there were little stars. They stood for battles, Joel knew.

His uncle was smiling. "Don't pay any mind to those ribbons, Joey," he said. "They're only my brag rags. Fruit salad, we call 'em."

Joel smiled back at him. "Gosh, Uncle Seymour—I mean Lieutenant!—it's good to see you. When did you get back?"

"I hopped a plane over there only three days ago, and here I am!"

Papa began to whistle "Off we go into the wild blue yonder." He caught Uncle Seymour's eye and they both began to laugh.

"Oh, Charlie!" Mama wailed. "There you go. I don't see where that's so funny. Honestly, when you two get together, you carry on just like a couple of overgrown schoolboys."

That only made them laugh harder. "Listen to Grandma!" Uncle Seymour roared. "Relax, Ellie. You look too pretty tonight to pull that stern, serious stuff on us!"

Then Mama gave him a little push. "You!" she said, and she began to laugh too. She didn't look much older than Ellen right then! Joel and Muggsy looked on, grinning. The whole room seemed to be full of happiness and warmth and laughter.

There were candles on the dinner table. Whenever Alma came in, Uncle Seymour teased her and made her blush, but Joel decided that she really liked it, especially when he got up and made a speech.

He said in his speech that he wanted to be on record as being duly, properly, and thoroughly appreciative. Alma had outdone herself as an exponent of the culinary art and Uncle Seymour knew personally of several regiments that would have given their collective eyeteeth to have had her with them overseas.

"Aw, go on with all your talk!" said Alma. She got as red in the face as a poppy, but she loved every word of it.

They remained at table for a long time. Papa asked Uncle Seymour a great many serious questions, and Joel didn't dare interrupt. Muggsy tried to several times, but Papa's most sarcastic tone of voice managed to squelch him.

Finally Mama rose, which was the signal for them to go back to the living room. The Duchess was already there, comfortably ensconced on the rug in front of the snapping fire.

"Well, look who's here!" Uncle Seymour said. He turned to Mr. Evans. "Charlie, I thought you hated dogs. Where'd you ever pick this one up?"

"I still abominate the noisome yapping creatures," Mr. Evans answered. "This particularly ill-favored specimen happens to be a waif. It is only suffered on the premises because of some mysterious reason my children seem to have become hysterically attached to it."

"She's a beauty," Uncle Seymour said. He knelt and stroked her warm hair. She thumped her tail lazily against the floor.

"I found her," Muggsy said. "She was under the bridge and I found her!" Between them, the Evanses poured out the story of how the Duchess came to be with them.

"So!" Uncle Seymour said. He turned to Mr. Evans. "And is she a good hunter, Charlie?" he asked.

Joel swallowed hard. What would Uncle Seymour think if he found out the truth about her? It didn't matter with most people. But Uncle Seymour was different. Besides, he was a soldier.

Tensely, Joel watched his father and waited to hear what he would say.

Mr. Evans cleared his throat.

"Charlie!" Mama said warningly.

Joel didn't dare to swallow again.

"Hm," Papa said. "Well, as a matter of fact—hm—to tell the precise truth—I haven't had her out in the field myself, so—hm—I couldn't exactly testify."

Joel shot his father a grateful glance.

But they had reckoned without Muggsy. The youngest Evans had never been at a loss for words. This time was no exception.

"But Henry took her out, Uncle Seymour. And do you know what? She ran away. She's gun-shy!" He turned triumphantly to his brother. "Isn't she, Joel?"

It was Mama who broke the ensuing silence.

"Up to bed with you," she said. "This Very Minute," she added. It was her firmest tone of voice. From past experience, Muggsy knew that it was the one Mama used when she Meant Every Word She Said.

With a carefully assumed "I-don't-care" look on his face, Muggsy got up from the footstool where he had been sitting and started for the stairs. Uncle Seymour's voice, booming across the room, stopped him in his tracks.

"What I want to know is, what's so awful about being gun-shy?"

Muggsy turned and looked around at his uncle. His eyes were wary with suspicion.

"I'm gun-shy myself," said Uncle Seymour. Joel gaped incredulously at the bright ribbons awarded for valor which were pinned to his uncle's chest.

"Yes, Joey," his uncle said. "You can look at those all you like. But in spite of them I'm still gun-shy. Most of us were, although we didn't always admit it. It scared the dickens out of us when those big guns used to go off. Only there we were, and there was nothing we could do about it, so we had to be heroes."

"But—but—" Joel stammered.

"Sure, after a while we got used to it," his uncle said more quietly. "But if I'd have been able to bolt the first time, I'd have gone like a lubricated lightning streak. And practically all the other men with me would have, too."

Joel and Anthony stared at him.

Their uncle's voice lowered to a confidential whisper. "And you know, even though it's all over, I still dream about those guns sometimes." He thoughtfully shook his head. "And take it from me, chum, those are pretty bad dreams to have."

Mama broke in. "Seymour," she said, "I do think it's time they went to bed. Both of them, in fact. It's been a big night, and there's all tomorrow ahead of us."

After Joel and Muggsy had said good night and started up the stairs, the Duchess got up and cocked her head after them. Then, wagging her tail, she made her way up to bed behind Joel.

Long after Muggsy had fallen asleep Joel lay awake in the dark, staring at the ceiling. He was trying to make up his mind about what Uncle Seymour had said.

It was hard to figure out exactly. There was something funny somewhere.

Imagine admitting that you were afraid of guns and battle and all that kind of thing! Especially when you were a soldier! He would never have dreamed of admitting to Johnny Nesbitt that he had often wondered just how exciting being a real soldier would be. But Joel had always had his private doubts.

And now it was Uncle Seymour who had confirmed them! And he was no coward. He'd been through plenty, and he knew what it was like if anyone did, Joel guessed. Joel lay staring at the dark ceiling, trying to imagine what Uncle Seymour had gone through those nights when he lay in his foxhole with the guns going off all around him. The quiet room became alive with imaginary tracer bullets spitting from planes and the whine of artillery shells.

Joel's arm stole around the Duchess. She was breathing quietly in her sleep. Somehow everything had changed around. It was as though a weight which had been pressing against his chest had been miraculously lifted. He wasn't going to be ashamed of her any more for something she couldn't help.

"Well, Duch," he whispered, "I guess there are lots worse things than being gun-shy." He was sure of that now.

Faith

During the riots in Los Angeles many years ago, a man and his ten-year-old son were watching televised images of stores being burned and looted. "Would you loot if you thought you wouldn't be caught?" asked the man. "No," replied his son, "it's against the Ten Commandments." The man was pleased to hear this. He realized many adults would rather hear their children say, "No, because I *think* it's wrong," or "No, because I *feel* it's wrong." The trouble with such answers, he reasoned, is that some people might very well say, "Yes, I think it's okay to loot," or "Yes, I feel it's alright," and it would be hard to argue with them.

If personal thoughts and feelings are the only standard for judging right and wrong, then we have no right to say anything about others who feel they have the right to steal or lie or cheat. In addition, as the man knew, thoughts and feelings are always changing. What we feel is wrong today may seem permissible tomorrow. So he was glad that his son had an unchanging standard outside himself by which to judge right from wrong. He knew there would be days when his son might be strongly tempted to steal or lie—days when he would need to be guided by more than feelings.

For most people it is difficult to practice the virtues without a belief in a God who wants us to act in certain ways even when our feelings or thoughts prompt us to do wrong. For example, in *Sounder* (though not in the chapter you will read) the boy is powerfully tempted to strike out at a man who has ridiculed and injured him. Part of what keeps him from acting on his impulse is his strong faith in God's providence and justice. Rather than give in to his own feelings, he submits to a wiser source of authority.

Faith supports moral behavior in another way as well. Belief that God has a plan for us helps to make sense out of life. And without a sense that life makes sense, all the other reasons for behaving well begin to seem insufficient. Unless there is something like a point or a purpose to our lives, it's hard to see why we should try to lead good lives. Religious faith gives us a meaningful story within which the story of our own lives makes sense. Faith helps to explain life's trials and tragedies and so helps to sustain us during difficult times when we might be tempted to despair or to give in to anger or jealousy. The boy in *Sounder* has to endure poverty, the sting of prejudice, and the loss of his father. It is easy to see how without his faith he might be tempted to give up his struggle to be a good person.

This doesn't mean that we should never question God. Job does it in the Bible. And, as we see in *So Dear to My Heart,* so does young Jeremiah as he suffers through one loss after another.

Finally, faith supports family life by giving it a structure and a center, as we see in the story *Ten and a Kid*. Faith not only supplies ceremonies, traditions, and holy days, it also reminds parents of their obligations to their children, and children of their obligation to honor their parents and to love their brothers and sisters—even when they don't seem lovable. Many of the forces of modern life—careers, media influences, pressure from friends—work to pull families apart. Faith in God is one of the strongest forces for bringing families together.

28

Ten and a Kid

Sadie Rose Weilerstein

Reizel lives with her large family in a small town in Lithuania. Although they are poor, their lives are rich with games, songs, dances, and festive holidays. On Passover Eve the family leaves an empty place at the table hoping the prophet Elijah will leave a sign of his visit.

Reizel's eyes turned toward the door. This was the moment of which she had been dreaming. She knew exactly what would happen. The door would open and a stranger would enter, an old man with a flowing beard, a wanderer's staff in his hand. He would sit down at the table. The chair was waiting for him. His voice would rise with the sweetness of King David's harp. Only she, Reizel, would know that this was Elijah. Suddenly, at the close of the *seder,* he would disappear, leaving behind him . . .

Reizel could not think just what he would leave behind. In the stories it was a cone of sugar, or *matza* and wine, or a fine fowl. But, thanks to the Highest One, they already had *matza* and wine and *matza* meal and eggs, and a fowl, and goose fat, even a cone of white sugar. True, the sugar did not sparkle with the brightness of the water carrier's cone. But when you hammered it into bits and kept a bit on the tongue, it melted with a delicious sweetness. God himself had provided them with their needs, enough for the whole eight days of Passover.

Kezele's voice, high and excited, broke into Reizel's dreaming.

"Father," he was saying, "I will ask you four questions."

Reizel looked up with a start. Elijah's chair was still empty. The only guest at the table was Mume Bryna, Reb Baruch's widow, and she had been there from the beginning. All eyes were on Kezele.

"Ma-nish-ta-nah ha-lai-lah ha-zeh, wherefore is this night, *mi-kol ha-lei-los,* different from all other nights," recited Kezele, his voice rising and falling in the customary chant.

The sisters listened tensely, repeating the words under their breath. They were more relieved than Kezele when the last question had been properly asked.

"Now I will give you your answer," Father said. Again he took up the chant. *"Avodim hayeenu*—slaves were we unto Pharaoh in the land of Egypt and the Lord our God brought us forth . . ." He read, not in their everyday speech, which was Yiddish, but in Hebrew, the holy tongue.

Reizel went back to her dreaming. Elijah's chair was vacant, but he might yet come—in the second half of the *seder* when they opened the door for him. She should not have expected him so early. Did he not have homes in all the lands of the world to visit, in far Russia, and Germany, and the land beyond the Sambatyan River, and America?

Reizel's thoughts went wandering with Elijah.

The first part of the *seder* was over. They had said the proper blessings and eaten the proper foods: bitter herbs dipped in sweet *haroses;* bitter herbs between pieces of *matza;* hard-boiled eggs in salt water; delicious chicken soup with circles of fat, "golden eyes," floating on the top; *matza* meal balls that melted in the mouth.

Now Father was reciting the grace after meals.

Reizel's eyes turned to the vacant chair. Soon, soon Elijah would take his place there. His cup was already filled with wine.

"Who will open the door?" Father asked.

"I'll open it. Let me open it."

Reizel was out of her seat and at the door before Father could answer.

The night air felt soft and cool against her cheeks. Songs floated through the darkness. A full moon silvered the house tops.

"Come, Elijah, please come! I have set a chair for you," Reizel whispered. Then, fearful that she had been too bold, she added, "Maybe you are too busy to stay. Then come unseen as you always do. Only leave a sign."

Had something brushed past her in the darkness, something white and cloudlike?

"You can shut the door now. Father has finished," said Momme.

It made no difference which child opened the door on *seder* night. Momme was always close behind. Now Momme bolted the door carefully.

At the table the children were bending over Elijah's cup.

"He came," said Kezele. "I saw the wine go down."

"It only wiggled. Goldie pushed the table," Tseppele insisted.

"Hush," said Esther.

Reizel wasn't listening. Her eyes were on Elijah's chair. *The chair was vacant.* Elijah had left no sign.

"Out of my distress, I called upon the Lord," Father chanted.

The melody had a sadness in it like Reizel's own thoughts.

Suddenly the singing changed to a joyous *Halleluyah.*

"Our Passover service is over and done," Father concluded.

But the *seder* was not done. There were songs to be sung.

Who knows one?
I know One.
One is God who made Heaven and Earth.
Who knows two?

Question, answer! Question, answer! The words tripped over each other, faster and faster, joyous, eager, verse piled on verse.

Father led, the children followed—all but Kezele. Kezele had fallen asleep, his head resting in his arms on the table.

"I'll carry him to bed," said Momme.

"Not now," Esther pleaded.

She shook little brother gently.

"Wake up, Kezele. It's time for 'Had Gadya.'"

It would not do for Kezele to miss "Had Gadya," the final song, the crown of all the songs.

An only kid, one only kid
My father bought for two zuzim.
Then came a cat and ate the kid
My father bought for two zuzim.

On and on went the song. Dog bit cat, stick beat dog, fire burned stick.

The verses grew longer and longer, coming at last to a triumphant end.

"Then came the Holy One, Blessed be He, and slew Death's Angel that had slain the butcher, that had slaughtered the ox, that had drunk the water, that had quenched the fire, that had burned the stick, that had beaten the dog, that had bit the cat, that had eaten the kid, that my father bought for two zuzim—

Had Gadya
Had Gadya
One only kid!"

The children ended breathlessly, all eyes on Father.

Suddenly they heard a plaintive, shivery maa-aa-a.

Reizel turned. A kid was standing on Elijah's chair, a tiny snow-white kid.

Had Gadya!

The cat had eaten it. Dog, stick, fire, water, ox slaughterer, the very Angel of Death—all had been caught up in its misfortune. And here it was, sound and whole at their *seder* table.

How had it come about? Where had the kid come from?

"From out of doors," said Father. "Is there a shortage of goats in our town? It must have wandered in when Reizel opened the door for Elijah."

Elijah! Of all Father's words Reizel caught up this one. Of course! *Elijah* had brought the kid. He had heard her prayer and left a sign.

A commotion interrupted her thoughts. The tiny kid had jumped on the table. Its pink nose was poking at a *haggadah.* Reizel grabbed the kid in her arms, but not before it had upset a wine cup.

"It wanted to read in the *haggadah,*" said Kezele, now wide-awake.

"It wanted to *eat* the *haggadah,*" said Father.

Momme came to the kid's defense.

"Did you offer it other food?" she asked. "Who was it that said: 'Let all who are hungry come and eat'?"

Momme, too, could quote a passage when she wanted to.

The leftover greens were gathered up, and the kid coaxed to the center of the room. All the family gathered round to watch it eat.

Suddenly, with the last bite, the little kid jumped up on its hind legs and began to dance. Its ears flopped, its stubby tail wagged, its forepaws swayed.

Father took hold of Kezele's hand. Kezele grabbed Esther. Goldie, Reizel, Teppele, Tseppele, the whole family joined in the dance. Even Momme and old Mume Bryna were drawn in. Round and round the little kid they circled, singing,

Had-gad-yoh! Had-gad-yoh!
One only kid! One only kid!

Next morning Father inquired of all the neighbors. None of them had lost a kid. He had the sexton make an announcement in the synagogue. Throughout the Passover week the family kept looking for the owner. In vain! At the end of the festival they knew no more than at the beginning.

"I told you," said Reizel. "*Elijah* brought the kid. Wasn't it standing in Elijah's chair?"

"I have some questions in my mind about that," said Father, "but we will save them for Elijah to answer. It is Elijah who will answer all unanswered questions in the time to come."

So the little white kid remained with the family. They named him Had Gadya, which was soon shortened to Gadya.

"Do you know what I think, Gadya?" Reizel said, hugging him. "I think you *are* Had Gadya. I think you didn't die, but went up to heaven like Elijah. Now Elijah has brought you to us."

A sudden thought set her heart dancing. Elijah worked wonders. Maybe his kid would work wonders.

Anything might happen.

29

So Dear to My Heart

Sterling North

Since the tragic death of his mother and father, Jeremiah Kincaid has been raised by his widowed grandmother, a stern but loving woman who manages to run a backwoods farm single-handedly. Young Jeremiah is determined to enter his pet ram, Danny, in the county fair but meets with resistance from "Granny," who is fed up with the lamb's destructive antics. When Danny becomes lost in the forest, Jeremiah searches for him without success in the midst of a raging storm. Sick from exposure to the storm, and grief-stricken at the loss of his pet, Jeremiah bitterly questions the mercifulness of a God who would take away both his parents and his beloved lamb.

Rain, rain, rain," said Uncle Hiram, wiping his feet on the doormat; "never seen so much rain since Noah built the ark."

"Come in, Hiram, and set by the fire; real unseasonable weather, ain't it?" Granny drew a shawl around her thin shoulders, shivering.

"Old bones is cold bones," Hiram admitted, looking at Samantha sharply. "I been aworryin' about you, Granny."

"Don't keer about myself," the tired woman said, putting another piece of hickory on the fire. "It's that boychild I'm frettin' about. He ain't et a square meal the last three days."

"You fed him yarbs?"

"I fed him a passel of yarbs. I fed him sassyfras tea and catnip tea and sage tea. I fed him yellow dock, bitterroot, and spice bush. I doctored him with sulphur 'n' molasses and sugar 'n' kerosene, and I don't know what all."

"I reckon that should kill him or cure him," said Uncle Hiram, drawing up a settin' chair.

"It ain't yarbs he needs, Hiram."

"No," said Hiram, gazing thoughtfully into the fire. "It ain't yarbs."

"He's wastin' away for that lost lamb of hisn."

"He's a lost lamb his ownself," said Uncle Hiram sadly.

"Iffen we could only take his mind offen his troubles," said Granny, twisting the corner of her apron. "I'm at my wit's end, Hiram."

"I keep alookin' for the lamb," Hiram said. " 'Tain't much use, I'm afraid. Them sheep-killin' dogs got him by this time, most likely."

"You keep alookin' and I'll keep adoctorin', and we'll both keep aprayin'," said Granny, "and in the Lord's good time he'll see it our way."

"Didn't tell you about goin' up to Lafe Tarleton's place," Hiram said. "Guess he's tetched in the haid all right."

"Lafe run you off the place with a shotgun?"

"Nooooo. Acted real neighborly. I asked him if he'd seen a black lamb. He nodded his head like crazy. Grabbed my arm and led me over to his sheep paddock."

"Glory be," Granny cried. "Glory hallelujah. Why didn't you tell me the lamb's safe?"

"Hold your horses, Samantha. Lamb ain't safe and never was, most likely."

"Well, say yore say and spite the devil," said Granny with exasperation.

"Went over to the paddock. Couldn't see hide nor hair of ary a black lamb."

"Jumped the fence, maybe."

"Purty high fence."

"Look for footprints?"

"Lafe did. Put on quite a show. Course the rain mighta washed 'em out." Hiram lit his pipe thoughtfully and tossed the match into the fire. "It's jest possible Lafe caught the lamb, put him in the paddock for safekeeping. Then maybe that old devil-ram of hisn seen this strange young buck sheep and chased him to hell and gone out of there."

"Could be."

"'Tain't likely."

"No use gettin' the boy's hopes up," Granny said; "either way the lamb's still lost."

"Best not to tell him," Hiram agreed.

But it was a sorrowful thing to see Jeremiah lying in his bed, cheeks pale and drawn, pining for his lamb. Uncle Hiram had made him a slippery-elm whistle with a whole octave of notes. Jeremiah said, "Thank you kindly, Uncle Hiram," but did not try to blow it. Granny had made fresh doughnuts, always Jerry's favorite victual, but she could not tempt him. Sometimes he did not answer when she spoke to him, but lay rigid, staring at the rafters, his lips tight.

"Maybe you should call old Doc MacIntosh," Hiram said as he was leaving.

"Killed more folks than he ever cured," Samantha said scornfully. "What kin he do that I cain't?"

"Wal, take his pulse and temperature, for instance."

"I don't need no little glass tube to tell if Jeremiah has the fever. Any fool kin tell that by feelin' a person's forehead and seein' if his lips are cracked."

"Doc might give the boy some medicine."

"Pink pills ain't agoin' to cure lost-lamb sickness," Granny said; "only cure for that is findin' the lost lamb."

"I'll keep lookin'," Hiram promised, "but I'm losin' hope."

Daytimes were bad enough, but when the stormy nights came down upon Cat Hollow, Samantha was beside herself with worry. The lightning would flash through the loft window followed by the rumble of thunder and the wash of rain across the roof. And Granny sitting there beside Jerry's bed in lamplight was at a loss to comfort him.

"I know it's a vexin' thing, a cruel thing. But maybe he's safe somewhar in a big old hollow log."

"You reckon he ain't dead?"

"Ain't saying he is and I ain't saying he ain't. But leastways he's in the hands of the Lord. And one way or the other we ain't agoin' to question the ways of the Almighty."

"I'll question His way," the boy whispered, "iffen He lets sheep-killin' dogs get my lamb."

"Jeremiah," Granny said sharply, "how dare you blaspheme the Holy Spirit?"

"Oh, Granny. He cain't, He cain't, He cain't kill my little black buck lamb."

"Didn't say He would," Granny comforted. "I only said, 'The Lord giveth and the Lord taketh away, blessed is the name of the Lord.' "

"If He takes my lamb . . ." Jeremiah began.

He was interrupted by a terrific flash of lightning and an earth-shaking explosion of thunder.

"Hear that, Jeremiah? That's the Lord God Almighty gettin' riled. You better say yore prayers and say 'em humble."

"He can't have my lamb," Jerry whispered, glaring past his granny into the storm beyond the window, into the very face of his tormentor.

Granny felt as though she had been slapped. It was a shocking thing to hear those words from Jeremiah's lips, a frightening thing to be there under the slanting roof, storm-bound and at God's mercy. But she feared more for Jerry than for herself. Squaring her thin shoulders in the lamplight, she said:

"Jeremiah Kincaid! You ask the Lord's forgiveness."

"No," Jerry whispered.

Granny shook her head in self-condemnation.

"It ain't his fault. O Lord, it's mine," she informed the Almighty. "I've tried to be mother and father to him, feed his soul and feed his body, but I reckon I've failed."

She hoped that Jeremiah would deny her words, but he lay rigid and rebellious, hard in his heart as seasoned hickory.

"You've turned away from God," Granny said. "You've sassed yore Creator. It's one thing to blame poor Tildy for lettin' the lamb get away, or to blame yore uncle Hiram for not findin' it. But it's another thing entirely to raise up on yore hind legs and give back talk to yore Maker.

"You hear me, Jeremiah Kincaid?" (There was a note of panic in her voice which mingled with the wind crying at the eaves.) "Must the Lord smite you as he did Saul of Tarsus on the road to Jericho? Must you be blinded that you may see the light? You loved that lamb, and so I let you keep him. But lovin' a lamb more than you love God Almighty . . ."

"Love ain't wicked," Jerry said.

"No," Granny said, "love ain't wicked, unless you love yore ownself better than you love God."

"How kin I love God," Jerry asked, "when He took my mam and pap and now my lamb?"

It was a hard question to answer, and Samantha Kincaid was silent, seeking guidance. Except for the whisper of rain on the roof and the sputtering of the lamp wick, the only sound in the room was that of Jeremiah's heavy breathing. His face was hard as he stared wide-eyed at the rafters and beyond. Suddenly he began to shiver as with a chill and to ask for extra covers.

A sad thought struck Samantha as she descended to the great room to bring a cover. There, all complete and beautiful and new, lay "Cat Hollow Wedding" which was to be Jeremiah's Christmas present. But the boy might never live to see another Christmas. Better to give it now, when he needed its warmth. Snatching up the handsome coverlet, she mounted the ladder to the loft. Tenderly she spread it over him, tucking it in around the edges.

"I brung you a present, Jerry."

"Danny?" the boy said eagerly. "You found my lamb, Granny?"

"No," said Granny slowly, "jest this new Cat Hollow Wedding kiver."

"Oh, thank you kindly," the boy said. "That's a real nice present, Granny." But she could hear the disappointment in his voice, sorrowful as the unseasonable storm now raging around the cabin.

"I were savin' it for yore Christmas present."

"Onliest present I want," Jerry whispered, "is that little black buck lamb of mine."

Independent of his mind, Jeremiah's fingers began to trace the patterns of his new cover. Little by little his chill departed.

"Where's my mam and pap buried at, Granny?"

"Hush, child, I ain't finished my ballad song yet."

"Iffen I should die before I wake," Jeremiah said, using the words of the prayer he had steadfastly refused to say since the loss of his lamb, "it would be a sorry thing, not even knowing what become of my mam and pap."

"Got burned up in a stable fire," Granny said. "I were agoin' to break it to you gentle in a song ballad . . ."

"Where at?"

"Down in the bluegrass on a stormy night like this."

"What for did they go in a burnin' stable?"

"I fault yore mam for it," Granny said. "I allus figgered she sent yore pap into that flamin' barn jest to git rid of him."

"Was Mam's race horse in that barn?"

"Course that was her excuse," Granny said.

"How did my mam get burnt?"

"Never could figger it out. Now go to sleep, child. It's gettin' late."

His head was filled with questions about that other stormy night. But stronger than his curiosity about his own parents was his wonder at the ways of the Almighty.

"Is God all-merciful?"

"Yes, Jeremiah."

"Is God all-powerful?"

"Yes, Jerry."

"He cain't be both. He jest cain't."

"Blasphemin' again," Samantha mourned.

"'Cause if He's all-merciful He wouldn't burn up my mam and pap and kill my lamb."

"Maybe He couldn't do a thing about it."

"Then He ain't all-powerful," Jeremiah said fiercely. "Iffen He's all-powerful He can find my lamb right now. I dare Him!"

"It's the Lord's own mercy we ain't struck by lightnin'."

"I double-dare him!"

"Yo're a little kingbird fightin' an eagle," Granny said. "If you wasn't sick-a-bed I'd larrup you. I don't know where I've failed or what I kin do to make you see the light. Looks like it's up to you and yore Creator to thrash it out between you. Time'll come, however, when you know yo're wrong and He's right. Don't know how and don't know when. Maybe tonight in yore dreams you'll find the truth deep in yore own heart with the help of Him yo're now blasphemin'."

Granny sighed and turned toward the ladder. Slowly and wearily she went to the room below. Taking her lamp and her Bible, she went into her bedroom, closing the door behind her.

Granny Kincaid stirred restlessly in her bed. Long years of rising with the birds made it difficult for her to steal extra winks of sleep after first cock's crow. Besides, it was purely sinful to lie abed like a hussy. She prided herself that winter or summer, rain or shine, breakfast was always on the table by six in the morning.

She did not wish to wake Jeremiah if he were still sleeping, so she took special care not to bang the stove lids as she started a chip fire for frying the bacon. Heaven be praised, the storm had finally ceased and the summer morning was cool and clear; but there was no answering sunshine in her heart as she contemplated the burden of sorrow that a lost lamb and a prideful young'un can bring to a cabin in the hills.

Half an hour later she mounted the ladder to the loft to see if Jerry were awake and if she could bring him a tempting breakfast. But the bed was empty and the boy's clothes were gone from their oaken peg.

She had a moment of terror remembering how Jeremiah had been blaspheming the Lord.

“No, ’tain’t likely,” she comforted herself; “iffen Satan come to fotch him, he wouldn’t had time to put on his britches.”

But the other alternative was frightening enough. He was doubtless wandering through the woods weary and wan and half out of his mind, still searching that lost lamb of his. The creek was so flooded by the rains he might fall in and drown. She hurried to the room below, untied her apron, slapped on her slat bonnet, and was rushing out the door when she heard the sound of hoofs on the gravel. A moment later Hiram was dismounting from his tired, mud-stained horse.

“Been combing the countryside for that lamb. How’s the boy?”

“Boy’s gone, lamb’s gone, and I reckon my patience is about gone too.”

“Hmmm, hmmm,” Hiram said. “Got right up out of his sick-bed to hunt for Danny. I’ll say one thing. Him and Tildy are *that* determined.”

“Tildy?”

“She’s out ahuntin’ the lamb too. I suppose, soon as the storm let up, her maw had to say ‘Yes.’ Saw her about sunup, jest a patch of red gingham climbing the ridge. She figures she let the lamb out, and she’s agoin’ to get it back in the pen.”

“Poor forlorn little critters.” Granny sighed.

“Three lost lambs.”

“Don’t know what to do with lamb or boy,” Granny said. “I’ve tried bein’ firm and I’ve tried bein’ kind. I’ve tongue-lashed Jeremiah and I’ve cried over him. I’ve scolded and coaxed, fed him yarbs, and read him Scripture. He’s hard as granite in that young heart of hisn.”

“Can’t expect an unshod colt to pull steady as an old horse. Give him time, Samantha, give him time. And give him enough rope.”

“Said the same about my own son. Gave him too much time and too much rope . . .”

“You’re still aprayin’, I suppose?”

“Wore dents in the floorboards aside my bed.”

“Lord ain’t helpin’ much, is He?”

"He certainly ain't. I got real sharp with Him last night, same as I do with you and Jerry."

"Might as well speak up in meetin'," Hiram agreed.

"Always pride myself that I speak my mind."

"It would have pleasured me to hear it. What all did you tell the Lord, Samantha?"

"I says, 'Lord, I'm about wore out with the way yo're messin' up our lives down here in Cat Hollow. I'm gettin' old and I'm gettin' tired. You tuk my David and you tuk my Seth, and it looks like yo're afixin' to take my Jeremiah. I'm a God-fearin', hard-workin', Christian woman, and you been asmitin' me and apesterin' me till you jest about broke my old heart.'"

"Amen," said Hiram. "What else did you tell Him, Samantha?"

"I says right out, 'I ain't askin' you, Lord; I'm atellin' you. Tetch that young'un's heart. Shew him the light that he may be saved. And iffen you got a mite of mercy, find that little lost black lamb of hisn.'"

"That was tellin' Him, Samantha."

"Hiram, I ain't a heathen, back-slidin' woman, you know that. I'm stanch in the faith; I'm aclimbin' slowly up the straight and narrer toward the pearly gates. But I'm afeared that iffen God don't answer one of my prayers pretty soon I'll misdoubt He ever *does* answer prayers."

"I've misdoubted it many a year," said Uncle Hiram quietly. "Mostly prayin' is just lettin' God know how you feel about things. Lettin' him share the burden that's on your mind."

"Howsomever," Samantha said, "after gettin' up off my aching old knees, I clumb into bed and dropped right off to sleep and had real pleasant dreams for a change. I sorta figgered God had took over and decided to do the worryin' for a while."

"And then you woke up and found the boy was gone," Hiram prompted.

"It's enough to shake the faith of the twelve disciples," Samantha mourned.

Just then from far away came a small happy voice, crying, "He's safe. Jerry found him."

"That's Tildy, ain't it?" Granny asked.

"Sounds like her voice."

"He's found him, he's found him." Breathless and glowing, the small girl came racing up the lane bearing the good tidings. Now they could see Jerry and the lamb coming more slowly from the far edge of the pasture, skirting the widened creek.

"Must have been a guardian angel," Hiram said.

"We've been needin' one."

"Looks like prayer is answered now and then."

Granny Kincaid was too filled with emotion to answer. She merely glanced gratefully heavenward as girl, boy, and lamb came up the long lane.

"Don't seem much the worse for wear at this distance."

"Sorta wet and bedraggled," Granny said, "but alive and kickin'."

"You figure on takin' them to the fair, Granny?"

"I reckon. I'm that grateful to the Almighty."

Tildy opened the gate, and in another moment children and lamb were coming around the corner of the barn. They were babbling happily about getting Danny a meal of good warm mash; of combing the burs out of his wool. They were petting him and laughing over him and calling him endearing names, then scolding him lovingly for running away to the hills.

"I found him, Granny," Jerry said. "I had a dream."

"Where *did* you find him, son?"

"In a manger, like in Bethlehem," the boy said, with a strange, faraway light in his eyes. "I mean . . ."

Uncle Hiram gave Granny a swift puzzled look.

"I mean in that old cave up the creek in the Tarleton woods."

"How in the name of Glory . . . ?" Granny began.

"I told you. I had a dream. And, Uncle Hiram?"

"Yes, son."

"Kin you carve beautiful animals and wise men and angels and maybe even a baby Jesus for a crèche?"

"That's a real big job," Hiram said, "but we might try."

"Glory be," said Granny; "allus did say the Almighty answered prayer. You jest gotta know how to handle Him, that's all."

As the children hurried the lamb off to his pen, Hiram said to Samantha:

"I can pick up the tickets tomorrow. And I already got a box for your covers and a crate for the lamb—that is, if it's all right with you."

Samantha followed the children with her eyes, then heaved a long sigh of relief and resignation. "Land of Goodness, there's a sight of things to be done. We ain't got half our wearin' clothes yet."

"You reckon the boy should have a pair of store-bought britches?" Uncle Hiram asked delicately.

"Store-bought britches one day," Granny said sharply, "high-falutin notions the next. Many a young man has gone to hell 'cause his mam started him out in store-bought britches. Homespun's good enough for any Kincaid."

"No hard feelin's, Samantha. I jest thought you'd want him to look his best among all them outlanders."

"I reckon," Granny said, a dreamy look coming into her eyes. "And while we're squanderin' our cash money I might as well take off my slat bonnet and linsey-woolsey and get me a store-bought hat with a pretty on it and a black bombazine—no, maybe even a changeable silk. Lord in heaven, it's purely sinful, but I've always wanted an umbrella."

"Samantha," said Hiram, "you'll be the belle of the Pike County Fair."

"Cain't abide the thought of scornful outlanders asneerin' at our clothes. Gotta hold up our heads, don't we?"

"Tune up your fiddles," said Uncle Hiram. "Here comes the pride of Cat Hollow, dressed fit to kill."

"It's a good thing I knit me them new black mitts."

"Umm, umm," said Uncle Hiram. "What shockin' high-heeled notions. A new hat with a pretty, a changeable silk dress, black mitts, and a purely sinful umbrella."

"It's a turrible temptation," Granny said with a happy sigh.

But as though no dream could last for long in Cat Hollow, Tildy now came running from the pen, wailing as though her heart would break, her face all tear-streaked and woe-begone.

"Why, what's the matter, baby?" Uncle Hiram asked.

"We're not agoin' to the fair."

"Huh, what's that?"

"He said—he—wasn't—agoin' to the fair."

"Like to know why not?" Granny bridled.

"He jest said ''cause.'"

Uncle Hiram cocked an eyebrow and exchanged a puzzled glance with Granny. Then he pulled Tildy to him and tried to comfort her, wiping away her tears with a big, clean bandanna handkerchief.

Wonderment and gentle determination struggled for possession of Samantha's face. She started toward the pen, followed by the others. Jerry was pouring mash into the feeding trough. He looked up as they entered.

"He's got enough burs in him," Granny said, removing a cluster of burdock.

"Yes'm, but he ain't got hardly a scratch on him."

"What you want to make Tildy cry for?"

"I told her she could go to the fair—and you—and Uncle Hiram." Jerry averted his face, brushing away a large unwanted tear.

"You and Danny ain't figgerin' on goin'?"

Jerry shook his head. "Changed our mind."

Samantha Kincaid put a gentle hand under the boy's chin, turning his face upward so that she could look into his eyes.

"What for did you change your mind, Jeremiah?"

"Made a secret promise—to God."

"What kind of promise, son?"

"Promised God iffen He'd let me find my lamb, I wouldn't *take* him to the fair, and," Jerry added, his face breaking into a sunny smile, "He let me find him."

Jeremiah put his arm protectively around the lamb's neck. "Danny and I don't want no blue ribbons. We just want each other."

"Wal," said Granny, "wal, now. If this ain't a fine how-de-do."

Jerry looked questioningly at his grandmother.

"Happens I—that is," Granny faltered, "happens I made a promise too. Promised God if you *did* find yore lamb we *would* go to the fair."

Jeremiah stared with shocked and joyous disbelief. The whole situation was much too complicated and wonderful for comprehension. Slowly his face began to light with ecstasy.

"And," Granny added firmly, "since I've known God fifty-one years longer than you have, I reckon He'll be expectin' *me* to keep *my* promise."

Jeremiah threw his arms around his granny and gave her weather-beaten face a loving kiss, tasting the salt of tears upon it. Samantha straightened up quite suddenly.

"Run, fotch the currycombs, Jerry. There's a sight of burs in Danny's wool."

As Jerry and Tildy ran happily to do as they were bidden, Granny and Uncle Hiram exchanged a meaningful look. Then, turning away, Granny raised her eyes toward the bright morning sky.

"Forgive me, Lord," she said, "and thank you kindly."

30

Sounder

William H. Armstrong

A poor black sharecropper's family struggles to survive after the father is imprisoned for stealing a ham. Sounder is the family coon dog, and his courage and dedication are matched by those of his young master, who is thrust abruptly into the world of adult responsibilities. In the months and seasons that follow, the boy searches persistently among rock quarries and chain gangs for word of his father. As he searches, he is sustained by the memory of Bible stories, particularly the story of Joseph, who endures suffering and captivity before his wisdom and goodness triumph.

Now the cabin was even quieter than it had been before loneliness put its stamp on everything. Sounder rolled his one eye in lonely dreaming. The boy's mother had longer periods of just humming without drifting into soft singing. The boy helped her stretch longer clotheslines from the cabin to the cottonwood trees at the edge of the fields. In the spring the boy went to the fields to work. He was younger than the other workers. He was afraid and lonely. He heard them talking quietly about his father. He went to do yard work at the big houses where he had gathered weeds behind his father. "How old are you?" a man asked once when he was paying the boy his wages. "You're a hard worker for your age."

The boy did not remember his age. He knew he had lived a long, long time.

And the long days and months and seasons built a powerful restlessness into the boy. "Don't fret" his mother would say when he first began to talk of going to find his father. "Time's passin'. Won't be much longer now."

To the end of the county might be a far journey, and out of the county would be a far, far journey, but I'll go, the boy thought.

"Why are you so feared for me to go?" he would ask, for now he was old enough to argue with his mother. "In Bible stories everybody's always goin' on a long journey. Abraham goes on a long journey. Jacob goes into a strange land where his uncle lives, and he don't know where he lives, but he finds him easy. Joseph goes on the longest journey of all and has more troubles, but the Lord watches over him. And in Bible-story journeys, ain't no journey hopeless. Everybody finds what they suppose to find."

The state had many road camps which moved from place to place. There were also prison farms and stone quarries. Usually the boy would go searching in autumn when work in the fields was finished. One year he heard "Yes, the man you speak of was here, but I heard he was moved to the quarry in Gilmer County." One year it had been "Yes, he was in the quarry, but he was sick in the winter and was moved to the bean farm in Bartow County." More often a guard would chase him away from the gate or from standing near the high fence with the barbed wire along the top of it. And the guard would laugh and say "I don't know no names; I only know numbers. Besides, you can't visit here, you can only visit in jail." Another would sneer "You wouldn't know your old man if you saw him, he's been gone so long. You sure you know who your pa is, kid?"

The men in striped convict suits, riding in the mule-drawn wagons with big wooden frames resembling large pig crates, yelled as they rode past the watching boy, "Hey, boy, looking for your big brother? What you doing, kid, seeing how you gonna like it when you grow up?" And still the boy would look through the slats of the crate for a familiar face. He would watch men walking in line, dragging chains on their feet, to see if he could recognize his father's step as he had known it along the road, coming from the fields to the cabin. Once he listened outside the gate on a Sunday afternoon and heard a preacher telling about the Lord loosening the chains of Peter when he had been thrown into prison. Once he stood at the guardhouse door of a quarry, and some ladies dressed in warm heavy coats and boots came and sang Christmas songs.

In his wandering the boy learned that the words men use most are "Get!" "Get out!" and "Keep moving!" Sometimes he followed the roads from one town to another, but if he could, he would follow railroad tracks. On the roads there were people, and they frightened the boy. The railroads usually ran through the flat silent countryside where the boy could walk alone with his terrifying thoughts. He learned that railroad stations, post offices, courthouses, and churches were places to escape from the cold for a few hours in the late night.

His journeys in search of his father accomplished one wonderful thing. In the towns he found that people threw newspapers and magazines into trash barrels, so he could always find something with which to practice his reading. When he was tired, or when he waited at some high wire gate, hoping his father would pass in the line, he would read the big-lettered words first and then practice the small-lettered words.

In his lonely journeying, the boy had learned to tell himself the stories his mother had told him at night in the cabin. He liked the way they always ended with the right thing happening. And people in stories were never feared of anything. Sometimes he tried to put together things he had read in the newspapers he found and make new stories. But the ends never came out right, and they made him more afraid. The people he tried to put in stories from the papers always seemed like strangers. Some story people he wouldn't be afraid of if he met them on the road. He thought he liked the David and Joseph stories best of all. "Why you want 'em told over'n over?" his mother had asked so many times. Now, alone on a bed of pine needles, he remembered that he could never answer his mother. He would just wait, and if his mother wasn't sad, with her lips stretched thin, she would stop humming and tell about David the boy, or King David. If she felt good and started long enough before bedtime, he would hear about Joseph the slave-boy, Joseph in prison, Joseph the dreamer, and Joseph the Big Man in Egypt. And when she had finished all about Joseph, she would say "Ain't no earthly power can make a story end as pretty as Joseph's; 'twas the Lord."

The boy listened to the wind passing through the tops of the tall pines; he thought they moved like giant brooms sweeping the sky. The moonlight raced down through the broken spaces of swaying trees and sent bright shafts of light along the ground and over him. The voice of the wind in the pines reminded him of one of the stories his mother had told him about King David. The Lord had said to David that when he heard the wind moving in the tops of the cedar trees, he would know that the Lord was fighting on his side and he would win. When David moved his army around into the hills to attack his enemy, he heard the mighty roar of the wind moving in the tops of the trees, and he cried out to his men that the Lord was moving above them into battle.

The boy listened to the wind. He could hear the mighty roaring. He thought he heard the voice of David and the tramping of many feet. He wasn't afraid with David near. He thought he saw a lantern moving far off in the woods, and as he fell asleep he thought he heard the deep, ringing voice of Sounder rising out of his great throat, riding the mist of the lowlands.

31

Lead Not Forth, O Little Shepherd

Eric P. Kelly

The trusting faith that sheep place in their shepherd is often used as a symbol of religious faith. This story, set in the mountains of Poland, reminds us of the parable of the Good Shepherd.

On a day in early spring, Jasek had led his sheep high up among the mountains. All day they toiled upwards into the stony pastures where savory and nourishing grass grew in the spaces between rocks. Above them where trees and grass ended suddenly because of thin air, the sun shone on the rugged peaks and was reflected in that deep dark lake, the Eye of the Sea, and down the furrowed slopes swift streamlets of snow water ran in little streaks of white foam against the rocks.

It was time to go higher. Standing on a rock halfway across a huge opening in the mountains where tons of earth and stone slid down every year, the boy raised his pipe and played the age-old melody, "Lead not forth, O little shepherd." It was a lively air, sad too in places, and had in the third set of verses a distinct minor which the shepherd's pipe could reproduce best. It was the story of a shepherd boy, who, centuries ago, had led his flocks upon lands reserved for cattle, and of the ensuing feuds that had made it dangerous for the shepherd to trespass.

And as he began to play the sheep pricked up their ears and the leader moved towards the boy. Now with Jasek leading and playing, the sheep followed in single file across the cleft in the hills, stopping here and there to crop a mouthful of grass. On and on they went across the slopes until they came at length to the Black Lake amidst the clouds; higher than this there was no growth.

What were the thoughts of this fifteen-year-old boy alone all day long amidst the solitary silences of the mountains? In his tight goatskin trousers, with the colored embroideries along the seams, his wool-lined jacket and round blue hat with its border of small shells, he seemed wholly apart from a world of prosaic duties. Yet his thoughts were akin to those of the richest Warsaw lad in his academy or of the government chosen boy at Modlin. For in the winter he went to the new school in the village of Zakopane many miles below. He had completed most of the preliminary work of the school and hoped to finish the lycée which led to the University. By a certain talent for playing upon the woodwind instruments he had attracted the attention of local musicians who hoped to get him a scholarship for his musical education.

Dusk settled over the mountains. Jasek assembled the sheep again and went ahead, playing the pipe, while they followed after him down the slopes and through the ravines until there lay between him and the folds below only one steep slope thickly strewn with loose stones. Looking about before plunging down this incline, he could barely see the white fleeces through the gloom.

"Wanda-Wanda," he called.

Instantly the leader of the flock was so close that her nose touched his leg. Stooping, he caressed the woolly head. There was plenty of intelligence in that sheep's head, and much affection in her heart. In the midsummer nights when the sheep remained in the hill pastures from dusk to dawn, the boy had often slept with his head upon her soft mass of wool. When it was lonely in the peaks and the stars alone gave light, the beating heart of the leader of the flock served for comradeship. The two had had adventures in those heights and each could trust the other.

But as Jasek stood to resume his playing, Wanda wheeled around his legs and went ahead of him. Surprised, he stopped and called her, then hurried ahead to catch up to her. The next moment he nearly went sprawling. Wanda had come to a stop on the broad stone that marked the beginning of the descent into the last ravine; she stood right across the path, blocking the way entirely.

Wanda had never acted like this before. Must he tease her and push her away before he could get through and start down the descent? As his pipe had ceased its music momentarily the sheep behind him, trained to advance or stand still as he played, had come to a stop. . . .

He pushed at Wanda hard. She refused to budge. He tried to lift her feet out of the way. That didn't work either. Suddenly it dawned on him that she was blocking the path because something was wrong.

It was pitch dark now. The stars were partly clouded and the moon had not risen. All at once he saw lights far below swinging up the ravine and heard voices calling out his name.

"Hallo-hallo-hallo-" he shouted.

His father and brothers answered. He was about to step over Wanda when the words came booming up "Stay in your place. Don't move. The whole slope has fallen away."

As the three lanterns were massed together he saw what he had escaped. The whole slope, undermined by spring rains, had fallen into the crevice which the torrents had washed out, leaving a muddy, perpendicular wall almost forty feet high from the base where the path had once run up it, with boulders and jagged rocks all about.

Jasek threw himself on his knees and put his arms about the neck of the old sheep. But for her sure mountain instinct he must have plunged over the wall. And when his father and brothers came up by a roundabout path and helped him get the flock home, he did not release his hold upon the wool of her back. That night and for many nights thereafter, the sheep slept at the foot of his cot in the home on the meadow in the intervale.

Late that summer Tadeus Skarzynski, director of the Warsaw Philharmonic Orchestra, and Henryk Sulkowski, a leading actor in the Krakow Municipal Theater, were touring in the mountains with a guide from Zakopane. One misty morning they had come by automobile up to the Eye of the Sea, and with knapsacks and mountain axes were crossing slowly a stone-strewn slope beyond which rose the peak they intended to climb.

"The clouds hang too low," the guide suddenly observed. "If we got up on the height they might thicken and we would be lost."

Skarzynski was impatient. "I am not afraid of fog."

Sulkowski answered, "That is because you come from Warsaw. In Krakow we know better. Too many people have been killed in these mountains."

Skarzynski struggled with his feeling. At last, "Well, have it your own way then. I suppose we can stay in some peasant hut here and go on tomorrow. There's nothing to prevent our walking up a little way, though, is there?"

"Not so long as we keep on the path."

They went along toward the stone wall that marked the outer limit of the highest slopes.

All at once the guide stopped. "Do you hear anything?"

Sulkowski cupped his ear with his hand. "Why yes, voices—a great calling and shouting and whistling."

The guide quickened his step; "Someone in trouble!"

The mountain guides, who dress as did their remote ancestors, wear soft alpine shoes, long goatskin trousers, wool-lined jackets, round black shovel hats, and short hooded capes that fall to the waist. About their bodies they wind a coil of rope, long, and, though fine, very, very strong. Their keen mountain axes are always ready for work, either in cutting a foothold in ice or in clinging to bushes or rocks or trees.

The three men hurried along the path until they got into the sloping ground where tons of broken and almost powdered stone had collected so thickly that their feet sank in the mass almost as if they were walking in feathers. Progress was utterly impossible; their legs went up and down as if they were walking on a treadmill. Yet they were only on the bottom of the slope, which rose in a dizzy slant for several hundred feet above. One would come sliding down with an avalanche of small stone before he had attained one quarter the distance to the nearest rock showing gaunt and grim in the mist.

Suddenly they were aware of shadowy figures about them, of men and boys and some women. All were shouting and pointing toward the place where, upon a projecting rock some hundreds of feet above, yet far below the top, was a continually moving form. The guide mingled with the crowd. He was one of them; of the visitors the mountain folk took no notice.

"It is Wanda," the shepherd Jasek exclaimed. "We were crossing the height above when in the mist she went too near the edge and fell. I brought my sheep down by the other path, but I can't get to her. Can't we lower someone from the top?"

The guide, who had uncurled his rope, shook his head. The wind momentarily cleared away some of the fog, and they saw the helpless sheep clinging to the narrow rock.

"A bad place," the guide exclaimed. "Those sharp rocks above would cut a rope almost immediately. If it were a man, I'd take the chance; seeing that it's only a sheep I wouldn't risk my life nor anybody else's."

"But we must do something." The tears surged into Jasek's eyes. "It's my Wanda. Can't you lower me?"

The guide shook his head. "Impossible," he said.

"If I could only climb up from below!" But Jasek, stumbling forward through the mass of sliding stones, came tumbling back in an instant as the treacherous footing gave way.

"There is nothing to do," exclaimed his father.

"I won't leave Wanda," declared Jasek. "You say there is nothing we can do?" he asked the guide.

"Not a thing."

"Then Wanda will stay there and finally either die of hunger or else lose her balance and fall on the stones directly below?"

The guide nodded.

"Then I will try something." He had thought of the sliding gravel. "At the foot of the cliff, the points of the boulders stick out; beyond that the top of the gravel begins. It is very deep there and almost perpendicular, but the slope becomes more and more gentle. If one could leap beyond the boulders one might land in the gravel." This he thought to himself. On the other hand, striking a pile of gravel from a jump of three hundred feet might be little less fatal than striking the hard rocks. But perhaps his idea might work.

Marching out to a place where Wanda could see him occasionally as the wind swept little clear spaces in the fog, he took out his shepherd's pipe. Since he was at a distance, Wanda would, he thought, attempt to get to him as quickly as possible if she did decide to leap. If she jumped directly down, she would strike the rocks; however, she might leap far in the direction of the music, and sheep do leap far when in danger or when they feel the need of hurry.

When he had gone a little distance he put the shepherd's pipe in his mouth and began to play the song of the Little Shepherd. This was no mere signal to the sheep to follow his path. This was to be a signal to Wanda whom he loved, and he knew that he must put heart and soul into that song in order to inspire her to brave the danger of the leap. He must make every tone clear. He must play as never before. He felt as he played that this music was the greatest and most powerful in the world. . . . He remembered tales he had read in school of men of old who had done great deeds in song, one who had rescued his wife from the underworld; one who had reached heaven through the strains of a harp. All this came into his mind as he played.

Far below him two men listened, enraptured.

"Do you hear that?" ejaculated Skarzynski. "And on one of those simple reeds they call shepherd's pipes. Did you ever hear anything like it?"

"No," exclaimed the other, "I never did. Is it this setting, I wonder, this wall of rock and shadowy peaks rising above the clouds, or is it such a wonderful performance as it seems?"

"It is magic," said the first speaker. "But it is real magic. That boy loves that animal. And you have the whole story in that simple piece of music."

"It's the 'Little Shepherd,' isn't it?"

"Yes, they've played it for hundreds of years. Listen now, and follow with these words:

"Now the shepherd leads them gaily,
Though death hovers near;
Holds the pipe in nimble fingers,
Holds the pipe in nimble fingers,
Music trickles through his fingers
While the people cheer,
Oi dana, dana, oi dadana—"

"What music! There is no player of his age in my school that approaches it . . ."

"Pity it's all wasted on rocks and sheep."

"Sulkowski, I'm going to see that that boy gets a chance in the school of music in Warsaw! But see what he is doing."

Far up, the helpless Wanda was moving back and forth as much as the narrow rock allowed. From below came the familiar strains of that pipe. When it played there could be but one command—to move ahead. Yet now there was no way of moving in the regular direction. But Jasek was her master, her lord, her god—she must do what he summoned her to do.

The order was to come.

Wanda braced herself on the rock. She worked her feet about until they found firm support. He was a long way off over there, commanding her to come, and she must reach him as soon as she could. The peril that lay below was vanished; she had orders from her shepherd and she trusted him.

She leaped as far as she could out into the misty void, her forelegs down and her hind legs up, just as she had taken many a dive over the rocks that often beset her course.

A cry rose from below. The watchers would have pressed forward, but the barricade of sliding rock prevented. Still the notes of the pipe were heard.

There was a crash, and through the cloud of dust the onlookers could see the body of the sheep hurtling down the slope at terrific speed.

Wanda had cleared the rocks successfully and landed with stiffened feet in the mass of sliding debris. There were dozens of feet of this loose material below her, yet it gave way so fast, and the slope was so precipitate that, like a ski jumper, she fell and fell and fell for a long distance before there was any resistance at all. Dust and small stones got into her mouth, and into her eyes and ears and nose, yet she must perforce keep on.

When the people below realized what was coming, they set up a great shout of joy as they ran from the approaching cyclone of rock and pulverized stone. At the bottom of the slope, the cyclone burst and the rock and dust gathered suddenly in a heap; but a live sheep bleating and coughing went rolling over and over along the ground. In a moment her shepherd ran up to her, wiped away the dust, and brought water in a cup. A few minutes later she joined her flock and started grazing as if nothing had happened.

But if there were tears in the eyes of Jasek when he realized that Wanda was safe, there were still more when Skarzynski led him aside and suggested the plan of a schooling in Warsaw to perfect his playing, with a chance afterward of joining some great orchestra.

"Oj, dana, oj, dana," he sang as he danced about the cottage that night, embracing his mother and father and brothers. "I am a made man, and it was Wanda that made me." At this, the sheep, which had lain down at the end of his cot, opened her eyes and looked up at him. He could have sworn that there was a twinkle there.

Permission Acknowledgments

For permission to reprint copyrighted material, grateful acknowledgment is made to the copyright holders. Reasonable care has been taken to trace ownership and contact the proper copyright holder.

"The Storm" from THE BLACK STALLION by Walter Farley, copyright ©1941 by Walter Farley. Copyright renewed 1969 by Walter Farley. Used by permission of Random House Children's Books, a division of Random House, Inc.

"The Hermit of the Southern March" from THE HORSE AND HIS BOY by C. S. Lewis, copyright © C. S. Lewis Pte. Ltd. 1954. Extract reprinted by permission.

Excerpt from CALL IT COURAGE, reprinted with the permission of Simon & Schuster Books for Young Readers, an imprint of Simon & Schuster Children's Publishing Division, from CALL IT COURAGE by Armstrong Sperry. Copyright 1940 Macmillan Publishing Company; copyright renewed ©1968 Armstrong Sperry.

"Androcles and the Lion" retold by Louis Untermeyer. Published by arrangement with the Estate of Louis Untermeyer, Norma Anchin Untermeyer c/o Professional Publishing Service Company, Westport, CT, 06880. This permission is expressly granted by Laurence S. Untermeyer.

"The Dream." From ALL ALONE by Claire Hutchet Bishop, illustrated by Feodor Rojankovsky, copyright 1953 by

Claire Hutchet Bishop and Feodor Rojankovsky. Copyright © renewed 1981 by Claire Hutchet Bishop and Feodor Rojankovsky. Used by permission of Viking Penguin, an imprint of Penguin Putnam Books for Young Readers, a division of Penguin Putnam Inc.

A DOG ON BARKHAM STREET by Mary Stolz. Text copyright ©1997 by Mary Stolz. Used by permission of HarperCollins Publishers.

"Old Yeller." Excerpt, as submitted from OLD YELLER by Fred Gipson. Copyright ©1956 by Fred Gipson. Reprinted by permission of HarperCollins Publishers, Inc.

"The Yearling." Excerpts reprinted with the permission of Atheneum Books for Young Readers, an imprint of Simon & Schuster Children's Publishing Division, from THE YEARLING by Marjorie Kinnan Rawlings. Copyright 1938 Marjorie Kinnan Rawlings; copyright renewed ©1966 Norton Baskin.

"Zlateh the Goat" from ZLATEH THE GOAT AND OTHER STORIES by Isaac Bashevis Singer. Text copyright ©1966 by Isaac Bashevis Singer. Used by permission of HarperCollins Publishers.

"A Rare Provider." Reprinted with the permission of Simon & Schuster Books for Young Readers, an imprint of Simon & Schuster Children's Publishing Division, from MAGICAL MELONS by Carol Ryrie Brink. Copyright 1939, 1940, 1944 Macmillan Publishing Company; copyright renewed ©1967, 1968, 1972 Carol Ryrie Brink.

Excerpt from ISLAND OF THE BLUE DOLPHINS by Scott O'Dell. Copyright ©1960, renewed 1988 by Scott O'Dell. Reprinted by permission of Houghton Mifflin Co. All rights reserved.

Chapter 21, "Journey's End" from LASSIE COME-HOME by Eric Knight. Copyright ©1940 by Jere Knight, copyright renewed ©1968 by Jere Knight, Betty Noyes Knight, Winifred Knight Mewborn, and Jennie Knight Moore. First appeared as a short story in THE SATURDAY EVENING POST. Copyright ©1938 by The Curtis Publishing Company, copyright renewed ©1966 by Jere Knight, Betty Noyes Knight, Winifred Knight Mewborn, and Jennie Knight Moore. Reprinted by permission of Curtis Brown, Ltd.

"The Race" and "The Finish Line" from STONE FOX. Text copyright ©1980 by John Reynolds Gardiner. Used by permission of HarperCollins Publishers.

Excerpt from NORTH TO FREEDOM, copyright ©1963 by Gyldenal, Copenhagen, English translation by L. W. Kingsland copyright ©1965 by Harcourt, Inc. and Methuen & Co. Ltd. and renewed 1993 by Harcourt, Inc., reprinted by permission of Harcourt, Inc.

"The Dog of Pompeii" from THE DONKEY OF GOD by Louis Untermeyer. Copyright © 1999 The Estate of Louis Untermeyer. Published by arrangement with the Estate of Louis Untermeyer, Norma Anchin Untermeyer c/o Professional Publishing Service Company, Westport, CT 06880. This permission is expressly granted by Laurence S. Untermeyer.

Excerpt from LAD: A DOG by Albert Payson Terhune, copyright 1919, 1959 by E. P. Dutton, renewed 1987 by E. P. Dutton. Used by permission of Dutton, a division of Penguin Putnam Inc.

"Shiloh." Excerpt reprinted with the permission of Atheneum Books for Young Readers, an imprint of Simon & Schuster Children's Publishing Division, from SHILOH by Phyllis Reynolds Naylor. Copyright ©1991 Phyllis Reynolds Naylor.

"The Apprentice" by Dorothy Canfield Fisher. Copyright 1947 by Curtis Publishing Co., copyright renewed 1949 by Dorothy Canfield Fisher. Used by permission of Vivian S. Hixson.

Excerpt from LITTLE HOUSE IN THE BIG WOODS by Laura Ingalls Wilder. Text copyright 1932 by Laura Ingalls

Wilder; copyright renewed 1959 by Roger Lea Macbride. Used by permission of HarperCollins Publishers.

"Gun Shy" by Edward Fenton from US AND THE DUCHESS by Edward Fenton, copyright 1945, 1946, 1947 by Edward Fenton.

Excerpt from TEN AND A KID by Sadie Rose Weilerstein. Copyright 1961 by Sadie Rose Weilerstein. With permission from the Jewish Publication Society, Philadelphia.

Excerpts from SO DEAR TO MY HEART by Sterling North. Copyright 1947 by Sterling North. Used by permission of David S. North and Arielle North Olson.

"Sounder." Chapter 6 from SOUNDER by William H. Armstrong. Text copyright ©1969 by William H. Armstrong. Used by permission of HarperCollins Publishers.

William K. Kilpatrick taught education psychology for many years at Boston College and is now a frequent speaker at conferences and seminars on the topic of character education and Christian faith. In addition to his best-known book, *Why Johnny Can't Tell Right from Wrong,* Kilpatrick coauthored two projects recommending books and films that build character in children.